'Seeing that you are here, you can work for your keep! Pick up that box – the big one – and help me to shove it in the trunk.'

'Boot.'

'Trunk. And quit answering back! If anything's happened to my Broken Star, I'll have you for breakfast. It's worth a small fortune,' Elizabeth warned.

The Broken Star was still in the boot of the Citroen, but not exactly in the same pristine state as when she had loaded it.

She examined it under the Victorian street light.

She made a most unpleasant discovery.

'Blood? My God . . . !'

Gingerly she lifted one corner of the quilt. The body lay in a heap under the Broken Star. The face stared up at her with a hideous expression.

'Call the police, Max.'

Also by Lizbie Brown

Turkey Tracks
Shoo-Fly

About the author

Lizbie Brown, mother of a grown-up son and daughter, was brought up in Cornwall and now lives with her husband near Bristol. She has published numerous short stories of suspense.

Broken Star

Lizbie Brown

NEW ENGLISH LIBRARY
Hodder & Stoughton

First published in Great Britain in 1993
by Constable & Company Ltd.
First published in paperback in 1999
by Hodder and Stoughton
A division of Hodder Headline PLC
A NEL Paperback

10 9 8 7 6 5 4 3 2 1

A CIP catalogue record for this title
is available from the British Library.

ISBN 0 340 71884 6

Printed and bound in Great Britain by
Mackays of Chatham PLC, Chatham, Kent

Hodder and Stoughton
A division of Hodder Headline PLC
338 Euston Road
London NW1 3BH

1

As he emerged from the church porch into a blue October morning, Dr Charles Wetherell, seventy-nine years old and a tall, bulky old man, leaned on his stick and decided that South Harptree was, for the most part, inhabited by fools.

He made a flanking movement round the Very Reverend Lionel Silk's receiving line and marched straight down the path. That blasted accountant, Crichton, was trying to attract his attention. Wetherell pretended he'd forgotten his hearing aid – that would show the young puppy!

He cast his mind back to what Crichton had had the cheek to say to him at the last Roof Fund committee meeting. 'I'm afraid you're out of touch with modern forms of fund-raising, Dr Wetherell. We have to move with the times, you know.' Well, if moving with the times meant letting the clergy be hoodwinked by financial whiz-kids only just out of nursery school, he'd rather be old-fashioned, thank you very much.

Dr Wetherell, irritated by the creaks and aches of his arthritic bones, thought to himself, 'None of them stuck up for me – not even Julia Aitken.' But then Julia wouldn't say boo to a goose. There she was now, by the yew tree, letting the Forbes woman walk all over her, as usual.

'Have you notified the Bishop?' Rebecca Forbes' cool, astringent voice floated over the gravestones.

'I . . . think so,' Julia stammered. 'I'll . . . I'll check when I get home.'

'Do that, for heaven's sake! You know how busy he is.'

Wetherell frowned. Poor, dithery little Julia, caught once again by that female praying mantis. She looked jumpier than

5

usual. Still, most women would be a bag of nerves if they had to live with a bloody awful ham actor like Larry Aitken.

Aitken had a receiving line of his own down by the lych-gate. His voice boomed out to all and sundry:

'Splendid sermon! Most invigorating!'

You only had to listen to the chap's voice to know he was a phoney, just a jumped-up music-hall turn with delusions of grandeur. To think that the grubby little parvenu had actually been able to buy the Manor House!

Aitken boomed in the same hearty way: 'Ah, good *morning*, Dr Wetherell. I was just saying, *splendid* sermon! No need to bring the old alarm clock, eh? Plenty of laughs to keep one awake.'

'Laughs?' Wetherell gave Aitken his petrifying stare.

'Sweetens the holy pill, don't you think? Lionel's promised to lend me his joke book if I run out for the next series.'

Lionel indeed! Wetherell snorted inwardly. His stare moved to Aitken's spanking new Norfolk jacket, his brown, shiny brogues. He imagined some television commentator describing the outfit. *And now, to complete the country look, here is Larry in a Norfolk jacket – the mark of the true gentleman. Guaranteed to make villagers touch their forelocks when the Squire passes by.*

He remembered the tweed jacket his own father used to wear. Shabby, with worn-out elbow patches . . . had a peaty tang to it.

'Will this fine spell last, do you think?' Aitken was still beaming like a lighthouse. It would take major surgery, probably, to wipe the smirk off the silly devil's face.

It was a wild, sunny day. Blue sky, blowing branches. 'Shouldn't think so,' Wetherell said dismissively. 'Bound to rain.'

He enjoyed contradicting the fellow, did it with relish at every committee meeting. For hadn't it been Aitken's idea that the Eadfrith Gospel, a priceless eighth-century manuscript belonging to St Swithin's, should be hauled off on an exhibition tour of America to raise funds for the roof restoration? His gift of the gab, his actorish ways that had talked the committee into voting for the scheme? Of course, Silk, gullible as ever, had been taken in by him. But then, the Very Reverend Lionel always had been a bit otherworldy; reading the *Church Times*, slopping over his

6

lady wife and consulting the Lord every morning about how best to augment the church finances. 'I have prayed on this matter' – wasn't that what he'd bleated in that damned quavery voice of his at the crucial meeting where the vote had been taken? 'I have prayed on this matter and it seems to me that Eadfrith would have been *with* us in this venture . . .'

The first tour, in April, had been a roaring success, to Wetherell's discomfiture, netting a profit of more than £80,000, but then came the follow-up tour of Australia this summer . . . Quite a different story! Not that anyone *wanted* St Swithin's to lose money – far from it – but Wetherell couldn't help feeling elated, as the only member who had voted against the Gospel being toted round like some vulgar peep-show, to find that one of Aitken's big ideas seemed, at last, to have come unstuck.

'Shall we see you at the meeting on Wednesday?' Aitken enquired.

'Why?' Wetherell glared at him. 'Hoping I'll stay away or something?'

'Not likely! Nothing I like more than a good ripe old barney, Doc!'

Wetherell shuddered. That voice! Plummy and thrown from the diaphragm so as to reach the furthest corners of the churchyard and impress the masses. But Wetherell had a little surprise planned for Aitken and his cronies at the committee meeting on Wednesday. Yes, indeed!

His mind went back to the pow-wow he'd caught them having in the Barley Wagon the other night. Aitken, Crichton and Forbes . . . He'd dropped in purely by chance to book early for the Not So Young Club Christmas dinner. Wouldn't have spotted them at all if Arnold, the landlord, hadn't let on. 'They be up to something or other,' he'd said, pointing backwards over his shoulder in the direction of the snug bar. 'Reckon you'd better nip in there, Doc, and get an earful.'

At what point had they realized he was there? When Larry jumped round and said, 'Why, look who's here . . . Dr Wetherell! How about a snifter? What can I get you?'

He'd refused, of course. Wasn't going to be seen hobnobbing with that little bunch. But he had the feeling that Aitken was afraid of him.

7

Mark my words, he thought, I'll clean the floor with them before we're finished.

2

Larry Aitken was admiring himself in the baroque mirror at the bottom of the eighteenth-century staircase. One hand smoothed his crisp, chestnut hair (roots touched up once a month by Paul-Jean of Kensington) . . . The lovat grey double-breasted suit was immaculate. But for once he had more on his mind than his appearance.

He was scared out of his wits that Rebecca Forbes might, accidentally on purpose, let it out to one of her cronies in the village that he'd been stupid enough to get her between the sheets . . . Not that it was the first time Larry had been unfaithful to Julia, and he didn't think for one minute that it would be the last. It was just that he'd always been careful, until now, to keep his image of family man *extraordinaire* reasonably intact. Not to foul the ground near the nest, so to speak.

It had been stupid of him, he now realized, to give into temptation. Rebecca had a vicious tongue, he was finding out to his cost. The savagery that had erupted from her when he'd told her that he wanted out!

'I'll get you for this!'

'Becca . . .'

'Don't call me that!' She had sat on the bed, chain-smoking, and picking at the red varnish on her nails. 'Don't you *ever* dare call me that again, do you hear?'

'Listen – be a sensible girl. You know it can't go on.'

'Don't you patronize me, you . . . you . . . pathetic little jerk! You can't shake me off that easily. I won't be dumped! I'll . . .'

'You'll what?'

A vengeful smile had crossed her face. 'I'll make sure Julia knows. You wouldn't like that, would you?'

She was bluffing, of course. He'd met it with counter-bluff.

'And Bob? You're going to thrown yourself on his mercy, are you?'

'Are you saying you'd tell Bob?'

'Fire with fire, my darling. Try informing Julia. Then you'd find out . . .'

'You pig!' She picked up the heavy glass ashtray from the bedside table.

'Bob's pretty indulgent, moneywise, I'd say, wouldn't you? With the old credit cards and the monthly allowance. Do you think he still would be if he found out what you'd been up to?' He'd managed to laugh. 'I can't see you, somehow, living on the dole.'

That was when the ashtray had come flying at his head. It had shaken him somewhat. Yes, he'd have to be much more careful in future, when the old libido got out of hand. Keep his . . . recreational activities safely in London, he thought, filching a carnation from the jug on the table and wedging it into his buttonhole.

He certainly didn't want Bob finding out. That would bugger up a lot of things.

Emily and Julia were having another little spat as he crossed the hall to his oak-panelled study. 'Listen,' Emily was saying, 'I'm nineteen years old. I don't *have* to report every little movement to you, surely to God?'

'Not every little movement, no.' Julia's voice sounded deliberately patient. 'But I do expect to be told where you're spending the night when you don't come home.'

'Look – I don't always *know* where I'll be crashing out! And you surely don't want me driving home late at night when I've had a few too many?'

'No. But it wouldn't hurt you to pick up the phone and . . .'

Larry went into the study and closed the door behind him. He had no intention of getting involved in *that* little argument. Emily had always had a mind of her own. My little rebel, he sometimes called her. She'd grow out of it . . . Drama students were allowed to be somewhat – dramatic, he told himself, picking up his keys from the desk.

'You've had no breakfast again!' a voice chided behind him.

Brenda Macmillan, his secretary, was in her Scottish aunt mood. Larry turned the famous aquamarine gaze to full power.

'Got to watch the old figure, Mac,' he sighed. 'Now you wouldn't want me looking less than my beautiful best?'

'You should have some coffee, at least.'

'Stop chivvying me, woman. You're much too gorgeous to act as my nanny.'

As usual, she flushed a deep shade of pink. 'Och, get away with you! Get off to your meeting.'

And so at twenty-five minutes past nine, he eased the Jaguar down the drive past the Old Schoolhouse towards the great wrought-iron gates. Geoffrey Le Grice was emerging from the Lodge, dressed for one of his long, mooching walks. Aitken lifted a hand, but Le Grice declined to return the greeting. Bloody snob! Who the hell did he think he was? He'd bought the Le Grices out lock, stock and barrel, hadn't he? Yet for some reason they could still – after all this time – make him feel like the kitchen boy with a snotty nose.

Larry put his foot down hard on the accelerator and roared off down the hill. Past the Barley Wagon, the telephone box, the handful of ducks waddling out of the pond. Oh, well, no good brooding about the Le Grices, he reasoned. He had bigger things on his mind. Like the letter he'd received in the post that morning. Anonymous, of course, like all the others . . . Mentally he reread it:

Enjoying yourself, you bastard? Well, make the most of it. You won't be there long. I'll make sure of that. You've got a nasty shock coming, Larry, old son!

There was always a certain amount of hate mail when you were top of the tree in the business – from cranks who had nothing better to do and from obsessive loonies – but these felt different. Somehow nastier than usual. And definitely more persistent.

The valley that lay in front of him was still and morning quiet. Down there, where the green slopes fell away on all sides, row after row of elegant Georgian terraces lay bathed in amber sunlight. But for once the view was wasted on him.

He thought to himself: And then there are the phone calls. It's no good. Some time soon, I shall have to do something about it . . .

*

10

Julia Aitken, letting her irritation subside after the argument with Emily, took her coffee through into Brenda's office. She put the cup down on the desk and rifled through the files for one of the exhibition programmes.

The Eadfrith Gospel was to be on show for the last time at the Old Schoolhouse the following afternoon, before being returned to its normal resting place, a vault in the bank. Julia was not really looking forward to all the fuss that this entailed. The mere thought of it gave her a twinge of panic somewhere in her stomach. She remembered how closely they'd had to keep watch over the priceless volume when travelling from airport to airport in the States and Australia. How the Gospel had to be accompanied at all times by two people whenever they changed planes. Goodness, those insurance stipulations!

The Eadfrith! Would she ever forget the wrangling and the in-fighting about who should be chosen to go on the tours? Not to mention the hassle about the budget for accommodation and travel. It would be a blessing when the whole wretched business was over and finished with. Then perhaps they could get back to some sort of normality.

Brenda was on her knees in the corner, searching frantically through the bottom drawer. 'Lost something?' Julia asked.

'The folder with the minutes of the last meeting. I know I put them in here. Where on earth can it have gone?'

'Try the other side.' Julia knew what the trouble was. Brenda was still in a flutter from her morning chat with Larry. Julia sighed. Sometimes she wished that her husband had less charm and more sense. He knew that the gangling Brenda was loony about him, that she wasn't fit for work for ages after his morning briefing, but he still couldn't stop himself chatting her up.

Julia had spells when she grew madly jealous of the effect Larry had on other women, but she always gritted her teeth and tried not to show it.

She took herself out through the french windows to the knot garden. Strolled down across the lawns towards the orchard, where there was a heady green smell of herbs and greenness. Rosemary, thyme, juniper and savory . . .

She thought to herself: I love this place. It's the only thing that endures. I shall stay here until they carry me out in my coffin.

11

3

Larry parked the Jag in the yard behind Wood's Hotel and switched off the Mozart which had been blasting at full power. The last movement of the Jupiter . . . Bath was a city that made you truly appreciate the finer things in life, he told himself, with a little flare of self-indulgent pride in his own achievements.

He left his worries outside, for the moment, and sailed through the swing doors into the eminently proper English atmosphere of Wood's as if he hadn't a care in the world. Gerald Fortescue, who ran the place, was engrossed in some figures at the reception desk that had been fitted into an archway next to the dining-room.

A trifle . . . sniffy, Gerald had been in the early days. Yes, somewhat reluctant to put himself on first name terms with a game-show host. But he'd soon come down off his high horse when he found how much business Larry could put his way. For all the top names appearing at the Theatre Royal now stayed at Wood's – on Mr Aitken's personal recommendation, they let it be known.

So the old stiff-neck had been forced to unbend. He had even offered them the use of the small conference room on the first floor for committee meetings, free of charge, until such time as the leaking roof of the St Swithin's hall had been mended.

Larry said in his most jovial voice, 'Good to see someone working, Gerald! How's the death watch beetle this fine morning?'

The beetle joke had been running ever since one of the guests had complained about hearing a strange tapping noise at the back of the panelling.

'Morning, Larry.' Fortescue looked up. 'Got them cornered, I think. Forgot it was your day.'

'As long as you don't forget a good supply of your very fine coffee, my friend! Going to need it this morning, if I'm not mistaken.'

The stairs creaked with age as he took them two at a time. It wasn't until he turned the corner by the sign pointing to the Gainsborough suite that he spotted Wetherell lying in wait for him, armed to the teeth with his clipboard and his silver ballpoint.

Oh, God . . . he thought.

Wetherell was a stubborn old so-and-so when he was on the war-path. They'd offered the old sod a trip to Oz back in the summer to try and shut him up, but he'd curtly turned them down.

Well, it was too late to back away. *Smile, Larry. Butter him up!*

'Dr Wetherell!' he said heartily. 'Just the man I wanted . . .'

Thank God for his stage training. He'd need every ounce of it this morning if he wanted to survive.

Larry wasn't the only one who was cursing Dr Wetherell. Rushing into Wood's twenty-five minutes later, Brenda Macmillan decided that it was all that old fool's doing that she'd lost the minutes.

Yes, Wetherell's fault. It was because he'd been abusive on the phone to her yesterday that she'd put the folder in such a daft place – underneath the cushion in the window recess, of all places.

She never lost things normally. She prided herself on a place for everything. Yes, it must have been his phone call that made her do it.

She remembered every word of it. 'I wasn't born yesterday,' he had bellowed into the receiver. 'I know Aitken's there and I want to speak to him. I won't have some blasted little stenographer telling me lies!'

As if she'd bother to lie to the old fool. Well, unless Larry wanted her to, that is. In fact, she *had* told a few whoppers for him in her time, but she didn't have a conscience about it . . . not for one moment.

'You're late,' a voice said behind her.

She jumped and spun round, but it was only the barman-cum-coffee-waiter who had a joke with her every time she passed through.

'That four-poster of yours too comfortable, then?' he asked.

'I keep telling you – I don't have a four-poster!'

13

Larry and Julia had one, though. A massive great thing with peach and pink drapes. Brenda wondered what, if anything, went on in it these days . . . Nothing very much, she fancied. I mean, he couldn't possibly have married the wishy-washy Julia for her sex appeal. Not in a million years.

'I couldn't find the minutes,' she told the barman with her schoolgirl's laugh. .

'Never mind,' he said in her ear as he went by. 'You're safe enough with Larry. *He'll* never fire a pretty face.'

'He might fire *me*, though.' She was blushing as she went on up the staircase. She knew that the compliment was only empty flattery. Her face would never launch any ships. Sink them, more like . . . But she was grateful for the fact that the barman (she still didn't know his name) was very good-looking. Reddish-brown hair and bedroom eyes . . .

But that was enough of that, thank you very much, Brenda. Naughty little thoughts only led to trouble, as she had once or twice learned to her cost.

She knew that the employees at Wood's gossiped about Larry liking the ladies. Brenda never reacted to it, though. It didn't pay to gossip, in her special position. See all, hear all, keep your whishties to yourself, her mother used to say back home in Glasgow.

Brenda knew for a fact that Larry was . . . well, a bit of a one sometimes. And that was an understatement. But then, he could get away with it, couldn't he? And in his profession, well . . . you half expected it.

She still went scarlet every time she looked at that so-called Aborigine love carving he'd brought her back from Australia. Really, it was the crudest thing she'd ever seen in her life. Almost pornographic. And what he'd written on the card that went with it – well, best forgotten, she told herself.

Brenda Macmillan thought to herself: But afterwards, he produced my real present – the most beautiful silk shirt. Must have cost a fortune. Really, he's the most generous man!

She loped along the corridor into the conference room.

14

4

Brenda Macmillan, waiting not so patiently at the counter of the Bath and Wessex Building Society on Thursday morning, wondered if it was herself or the girl clerk who was a bit dim.

'Sorry,' the girl said. 'This one's going to be a bit difficult.' Her eyes kept roving around the counter. 'Now where did I put it?'

The phone rang sharply behind her and she jumped.

'Why should it be difficult?' Brenda asked crisply.

'Oh . . . the computer's out.' The girl seemed abstracted. She kept looking at her watch. Brenda knew the type. Couldn't wait to get out of there to meet some callow youth.

Sharply, Brenda said, 'You've got a ledger book, haven't you?'

'What? Oh, yes.' The girl groped for a pen. She had pale green eyes peering at you from behind granny glasses. A flowered top and a jaw like a sad horse . . .

'Well, then, you can enter it by hand for now. What's the problem?'

Paying a cheque into the St Swithin's Roof Account was the simplest of matters, surely? Yet somehow the girl always seemed to make a complete mess of it. Last week, she'd lost her official stamp and gone looking for it, vainly, all over the back office.

'No real problem. It's just that I've got to . . .' Absently, the girl picked up the cheque and started to search for something in the drawer behind her. But the drawer seemed to be jammed and no amount of ramming at it made it any better. 'Look – I'll have to take it to Mr Ransome . . .' she mumbled. And disappeared without warning through a door at the back.

'Well, really!'

Brenda shook her head in disbelief. If there was one thing she couldn't abide, it was incompetence and muddle. She'd always had, as she would say with that barking little laugh of hers, a passion for order.

She remembered Larry telling her once at some party she had organized (his fiftieth birthday, if she wasn't mistaken) that he was surprised she didn't make all the guests stand in lines like dominoes to keep the place tidy. Well, he could joke about it, but let's face it, she thought, the occasion would have been a complete shambles if it had been left to *Julia's* powers of organization.

How handsome Larry had looked that night! How charismatic . . . as if a light glowed from inside him. No wonder there had been hundreds of guests (half the parish, it seemed) still dancing out there in the marquee at four in the morning . . .

Her thoughts returned to the present as Bob Forbes himself emerged from his office. With a glance at the queue, he said, 'One of those mornings, is it? Where's our Miss Stewart?'

'You might well ask,' Brenda replied with an edge to her voice.

He understood what she meant at once. 'Abandoned ship again, has she? Gill, be a good girl and fetch me a coffee. I'll see to these customers.'

'All I wanted was to pay in the Roof Fund cheque!' Brenda complained. 'It would seem a simple enough matter, but she's gone off with it somewhere.'

'Our Miss Stewart has her off-days,' Bob said. He leaned forward for a private word. 'Wetherell excelled himself yesterday, don't you think? Suggesting that Larry was using the Eadfrith as publicity to further his career!'

'Somebody ought to shut him up,' Brenda commented briefly.

'Chap's gone ga-ga, if you ask me. Threatening the fraud squad!' Bob Forbes winked. 'As if any funds could go astray while *your* eagle eye was on them!' He added quickly, 'Still, we'll get it sorted tonight at the sub-committee meeting. Prefer a smaller group myself – especially if Wetherell's excluded. Seven o'clock, wasn't it?'

Brenda nodded.

'Of course there were *some* discrepancies in the Oz tour receipts, but it's only to be expected.' He imparted the fact as if it were a casual piece of information. 'David wasn't there to keep them up to the mark. Pity, really. He could have monitored what my dear wife was spending . . .'

His lips parted in a grin. He was grossly overweight, Brenda

16

thought. She couldn't bear men who wore rumpled suits and who had a five o'clock shadow at eleven in the morning.

'Anyway,' Forbes went on, 'if the receipts were down in Ozzieland, it was because they just weren't interested in a mouldy old Pommie manuscript. The Yanks lap up anything to do with the history of the old country – and they're a religious lot! But all they want to do in Sydney is bum around on the beach. I mean, hardly anyone *came* to the exhibition!'

'Er . . . the cheque . . .?' Brenda suggested, with a lift of the eyebrow.

Forbes? He was as bad as the dopey girls he employed! And she didn't want to stand here gossiping all day. She had things to see to.

5

In the drawing-room at the Manor, Brenda Macmillan was getting on Larry's nerves. She was whistling through her teeth and kept fussing about arrangements for the meeting. It was a quarter to seven in the evening.

'For God's sake, Mac – will you get out from under my feet for five minutes?' he said irritably.

She said, 'I'm only trying to help. And the minute I disappear upstairs, you'll be yelling for me. I know you will!'

It was a still evening, warmish for the time of the year. The long windows remained open to the scents of the garden, where Julia could be seen pottering round in the dusk with a trowel in her hand.

One by one, the others arrived. David Crichton, in a crisp, striped shirt, apologized that he'd have to leave early as he had another appointment at eight thirty.

'Be finished well before then,' Larry told him. 'Please God . . .'

'At least the good doctor won't be here to put a spanner in the works,' Crichton said with a grin.

'One of these days I'll sue him for libel,' Larry grunted. 'Trouble is, he'd enjoy it too much.'

The Very Reverend and Mrs Silk came in together, arm in arm. Charmingly old-fashioned, both of them, and still vaguely in love after forty years together. Eleanor Silk had brought along a letter from the *Church Times*. 'I saved it to use at Bible class,' she said. 'But it has rather a good joke about Elijah's financial affairs. I thought you'd all appreciate it.'

Bob Forbes was late and cursing because he'd left a vital file at home.

'I reminded you only this morning,' his wife said in that hard, expensive voice of hers. 'You never listen.'

'Never have in twenty years,' he told her. 'Bit late to start now, my darling!'

'A drink, anybody?' Larry said.

'I will,' Rebecca said succinctly. 'A gin and tonic and make it a stiff one.'

Forbes said, 'Just a beer for me, old chap.'

'It's a bit early,' Crichton said as he accepted a stiff whisky, 'but under the circumstances . . .' What circumstances exactly he didn't elucidate. Momentarily his gaze met Rebecca's, then transferred itself to the open windows and the dusky garden.

The meeting was called to order. The Reverend Silk apologized profusely for having to take up more of their extremely valuable time. 'But I'm sure that if we can discuss things in a temperate manner for once . . .'

Rebecca Forbes said, 'I can't see what all the fuss is about! I mean, even if the figures don't balance, we've still raised thousands.'

Crichton fished a gleaming Parker pen from his breast pocket. 'Nevertheless . . .' he said. 'All money has to be accounted for. It can't just disappear.'

Forbes laughed. He said, 'You're on a sticky wicket trying to get *that* little principle into my wife's beautiful head.'

Rebecca gave him a hard glare. She sat on the plump sofa opposite Crichton with her legs crossed, so that their long, shapely length was displayed to the best advantage.

'I agree with David,' Aitken said smoothly. 'It's church money, not our own. We raised it for St Swithin's.' His aquamarine gaze touched them all in turn. 'Every penny must be accounted for, no matter how awkward it gets.'

There was a short, difficult silence.

'What exactly do you mean by "awkward"?' Eleanor Silk enquired. She was a heavy woman in her hand-knitted lavender jumper, and when she grew warm, as she appeared to be now, her pale cheeks turned a blotchy red. Her thin lips were primmed as she added, 'You're surely not suggesting that anyone here would . . .'

'Misappropriate funds?' Larry said. 'I'm not saying that for one minute, but you must see that, to refute the suggestion, we have to be ruthlesly honest with each other.'

A pause.

Larry said, 'I'll start the ball rolling, if you like. The sound track that I made for the Sydney exhibition to tell the punters about the Eadfrith . . . Well, the chap that did the tapes for us – friend of mine in London – gave me a chit, but it went astray somewhere. I can get another, of course, but as he's in the States at the moment, it might take time.'

A fragrant little wind blew in from the garden.

'Then there was the art consultant – for the programme covers,' he went on at great speed. 'He didn't put his bill in straight away and when it did come, I found he was charging a hell of a lot more than he'd quoted me. So there's a discrepancy there between the estimated and the real cost.'

No one seemed to want to comment, so he moved on to the next point.

'Lionel, I think you wanted to mention your sister-in-law . . .'

The Very Reverend Lionel seemed startled. He stuttered slightly as he said, 'Y . . . yes. As you are no doubt aware, my wife's sister travelled with us to Sydney. Miss Priscilla Hughes. I wish to emphasize at this stage her position as Assistant Keeper in the department of Manuscripts at the London Library . . . so there was no question of free-loading. None at all! She helped to defray *some* of the cost of her air fare and worked *jolly* hard while she was over there, giving talks on the Anglo-Saxon scriptorium to a largely uncomprehending public.'

'Like the surfer who wanted to know if the interlaced bird motifs meant they were mating . . .' Eleanor Silk shuddered.

'They're all sex mad down there,' Rebecca commented. Her gaze lingered on Larry for just one second, then she asked coolly, 'So how much of your sister-in-law's air fare *did* we actually contribute to? I think we should know.'

19

'Now look here – ' Eleanor said.

'No need to get uptight about it, Eleanor. We all do it, you know.'

'Do what?'

'Take freebies if we can get them.'

'My sister did *not* take a . . . a . . . freebie, as you put it!'

'But she wasn't exactly with the official party, was she? I mean, no one informed the committee . . .'

'Ladies . . . ladies!' Larry intervened.

'Look, can we cut the backbiting?' Crichton said. 'I've brought balance sheets so that you can all take a look at the figures.'

He distributed the sheets. A heavy silence fell.

'We can't have lost *this* much!' Lionel Silk said. His mouth had literally fallen open.

Aitken adjusted his spectacles. Forbes cleared his throat. The clock continued to tick in the corner.

The shocked silence would, perhaps, have continued, had not Crichton's attention been drawn by some movement that caught his eye as he sat gazing out through the french windows. 'Oh, God . . .!' he said. 'Not tonight. Please, no!'

A heavy, jowled figure was coming across the lawn. Wetherell in full battle formation.

He was breathing heavily as he came in through the french windows. 'I demand to know why you wouldn't vote on my proposal to get an outside audit!' he bellowed. 'And I want to know *now* – do you hear?'

Skirting her employer, Brenda Macmillan tried to head the old man off. 'It wasn't on the agenda,' she said. 'Perhaps next time . . .'

'Next time? Give them time to cook the books and hide the evidence? You must be joking! I'm not abiding by that damned rigged meeting yesterday. And I'm not going to be conned by any little cabal!'

'For God's sake, give him a drink, Larry,' Forbes muttered. 'Calm the old war horse down.'

Wetherell turned on Forbes. 'I'll have you know I'm proud to be thought of as an old war horse! I won an *MC* in the war! Tank regiment!'

Larry poured a stiff Highland Park from the decanter.

'I won't be bribed!' Wetherell spluttered. 'You can put that thought right out of your heads.'

Taking the whisky from Aitken, Forbes Said, 'Get that down you, you silly old fool. Best Highland Park.'

For a second, it seemed that Wetherell would knock the glass out of his hand – but then he took it and drank it off at a gulp.

When he spoke again, his voice was blurred. 'I'm not going anywhere, you understand . . . Not until I get some answers.'

He was wheezing a little from the strength of the whisky. He swayed slightly. Then started to cough, with a violence that frightened them.

Had it gone down the wrong way? His face turned purple as he choked. He gasped for breath – then went crashing down in the doorway, the glass falling from his hand.

6

For Elizabeth Blair, who liked to dip into the pages of the *Bath Chronicle* during the quiet patch before tea, the headline DOCTOR POISON DRAMA. LARRY AITKEN QUESTIONED made fascinating reading. Her shop in Pierrepont Mews had browsing customers, but it wasn't rush-hour busy. Rays of sun dropped softly through the patchwork quilts in the window and Caroline was rattling cups in the small kitchen at the rear.

Elizabeth was a sucker for a juicy story.

At first, she read, *it was thought that Dr Wetherell, aged 79, founder of the South Harptree Red Cross unit, had suffered a heart attack. But further investigation revealed that his death was the result of a fatal combination of drugs and alcohol. Mr Aitken, 57, who has raised thousands of pounds for local charities, said after being released from Manvers Street police station, where he had been questioned for several hours: 'I am shattered by this tragedy. The pathologist's report claims that the glass of Highland Park I handed Wetherell was laced with amphetamines, but I have no idea how such a substance got into the decanter. He had a heart condition and apparently had been warned not to take alcohol, but I had no way of knowing that.' Mr Aitken fears that an intruder got into the Manor while the grounds were open for*

the Eadfrith exhibition on Thursday afternoon and maliciously tamp-
ered with the whisky. 'You get all sorts of nuts after you when you're
at the top of the tree,' he confided, revealing that he has recently
received a number of threatening phone calls.

'Interesting,' Elizabeth murmured, adjusting her half-moon
spectacles. Aitken's face, grinning hugely, peered up at her
from the middle column alongside the article. The blurred
photograph depicted a man with carefully styled hair and a
faint whiff of vanity.

There was a hint of exhilaration in her green eyes as she
slipped the newspaper back under the shelf and took a pincushion from the blue-rinsed customer who had materialized at
the counter. Of course she knew you shouldn't enjoy other
people's calamities . . . but if you had spent forty years of your
life in Turkey Creek, Virginia – a mere speck on the map in
mountain country hard by Roanoke, where nothing ever happened except the wind blew and the trees grew and the sky
turned from deep blue by day to chrome blue by night . . .

Well, forget politeness! You positively *relished* little items like
the doped whisky in Mr Aitken's cut crystal decanter.

'That's £2.95, thank you so much.'

Turkey Creek, Virginia . . . God's own country, Jim used to
call it. A place where you could stand on your own back
doorstep and pot yourself a wild turkey from up in the woods
any time you needed a Thanksgiving dinner. The thing was,
Elizabeth thought, popping the pincushion into one of her
distinctive, cherry-coloured bags, there were other things in life
besides turkey dinners.

In Bath, England anyway . . .

She handed the bag to blue-rinse. 'There we are. Drop in
again soon,' she said, wondering where the hell Caroline had
gotten to with the Earl Grey. In the mews the crowd was
thinning by the minute. It had been a good season, she
reflected. *That* would be something to report back home to Jim
Junior. She tried to guess whether it would please her son or
not and decided that very probably he would be torn in half.
The business side of his nature would hug itself, but the rest of
him would hate to approve of anything that kept her here in
England longer than necessary.

For Jim Junior had been horrified when she announced her

plans. And a little bewildered. 'Why the hell do you want to go and live in England?' he'd asked.

'Because I'm hooked on the place,' she'd told him.

'So what are you going to live on?'

'I'm going to buy a little shop and sell patchwork quilts. Ship them over from the States.'

'It rains every day in England,' he'd said.

'Not when I was there,' she told him. 'It was beautiful. Mellow and warm and like something out of a picture book.'

'Well, it'll rain if you go back,' Jim said. 'I'll give her three months at the most,' she'd heard him tell Ed, her second boy.

Looking back, it was ironic that it had been Jim Junior who had set the whole thing in hand in the first place. He had hated seeing her grief after Jim's death. Why not take a vacation, he'd said. You always wanted to go to Europe. Stay a month or so . . . Trace all those darned ancestors you're always going on about! Of course, he wasn't to know what an effect the visit would have on her.

Bath! There had been something about it that captured her from the beginning. She had returned to Turkey Creek after that first trip, but she never forgot the colour of the Bath stone, golden in the morning sun, squash-coloured when wet, a mixture of pale dust and honey in afternoon heat . . . She never stopped telling people about the flowers in the streets, about the river and the broad pavements and all those Georgian terraces.

It would probably have been more prudent to broach the subject with the kids *before* buying the shop instead of the other way round, but she was extremely bull-headed – always had been – and didn't want any of them talking her out of it. Just once in her life, she was going to please herself and to hell with the consequences!

Anyway, Jim would have approved of Martha Washington, a doll's house of a shop with a Georgian bay window, wedged between The Music Box and Death by Chocolate in Pierrepont Mews. Real neat, he'd have called it.

You had to have something to do, after all. And she'd have gone stir crazy sitting round in a rocking chair on the porch on a quiet day in Turkey Creek . . .

Caroline's yuppyish little voice interrupted her reverie. 'Tea up! I'm afraid I've been a bit reckless, Mrs Blair. I bought buns.'

Caroline looked like a duchess forced to go slumming. Her black hair was cut into a fine bob and her eyes were as grave and grey and candid as a boy's. 'Butter or not?' she asked now as she parked the papier-mâché tray on the corner of the counter.

The eternal quandary . . . Yet Bath buns were nothing without a good dollop of butter. Oh hang the diet, Elizabeth thought – but before she had time to say so, her face changed. 'Would you believe it?' she said. 'Look who's here. How the devil does he know?'

Too late to remove the tray and hide it in the kitchen. Max was already coming down the narrow, corkscrew staircase from his office on the first floor.

'Fetch another cup,' she told Caroline with mock weariness.

When she took over the premises, Elizabeth had been rather impressed by the slim sign outside in the shared hallway: MAX SHEPARD. PRIVATE DETECTIVE. Well, well, she had thought, expecting Holmes or Watson.

But then she'd met Max . . .

'Must have smelled the kettle,' he said now, coming through the door and gazing at the tray on the counter. 'Hey . . . buns! Somebody's birthday?'

'Caroline bought them,' Elizabeth said, gazing him out. He was worth gazing at, she had to admit. Twenty-six years old, blue, downward-slanting eyes, thick, brown hair . . .'So how's business?' she asked.

'Great. Terrific.' He ignored her 'oh yeah' look and took the cup that Caroline had just brought in. 'For me? Thanks, Caroline. Shall I be mother?'

'Did you ring the bank manager?' Elizabeth asked.

'Not yet. Thought he might be busy.' He dropped into the wing chair, poured milk into the cups, then said, 'Friday's their rush day. Thought I may as well leave it till Monday, when he's got a minute to himself.'

Elizabeth shook her head. 'You're hopeless! It won't be any easier on Monday, you know.'

'But if I rang today and he won't extend my overdraft, I'll be miserable all weekend. I'd rather be miserable on a Monday, wouldn't you?'

Max had a part-time relationship with money. He was always behind with the rent and the new business rate was going to cripple him, but his constant ruckus with his bank manager amused her. And he had this skewed sense of humour and Elizabeth liked her men whip-crackingly sharp . . . In short, she found him an entertaining companion.

'Ah, well, you're not in it for the money, I suppose.'

'I'm in it for the dames,' he said in his best Sam Spade voice.

Elizabeth could well believe it. Max had a problem with women: he liked them.

'I'm starving,' he said plaintively. 'Didn't have time for lunch.'

Elizabeth sighed. 'Go on,' she said. 'Help yourself. I'm on a diet.'

He said, 'You are, aren't you?' And took a huge bite out of one of the buns.

'That's a new jacket, isn't it? I thought you were broke?'

He glanced down at the loose weave of the jacket with its natty buttons. 'Got it in the sale,' he said. 'Price slashed by a third.'

'Mmm.' Elizabeth sounded far from convinced.

'Listen, this is down-town Bath, not Coal Row.' Max came from Manchester and his first job had been with a detective agency in a less than salubrious part of that city. 'Better class of clientele. I've got to impress them.'

'Uh-huh?'

'I mean, it's the same for you, really.'

'What's the same for me?'

'Well, we're both outsiders . . . Aliens, so to speak, in polite Bath society. They won't accept us, you know, unless we look upmarket and watch our manners.'

'My manners are perfectly sound!' Elizabeth told him. 'I'll have you know I was a Lightfoot before my marriage.'

'A Lightfoot?'

'One of the Virginia Lightfoots, of old colonial stock.'

'And now you're Elizabeth Blair?'

'Yes.'

'But you call yourself Martha Washington. Clear as mud.'

'Everybody understands Martha Washington,' she told him. 'It's a kind of shorthand, I guess.'

'I guess.' He echoed her Virginian accent. 'Elizabeth Lightfoot . . . With a name like that, *you* should be the Private Eye!'

And I could probably do a better job, she thought, fixing him with her calm, grey-green gaze. But she wouldn't say so. After all, Max had his feelings.

He munched away at the bun for a moment or two and then, almost casually, said, 'Seen the front page of the *Chronicle*?'

'The Aitken thing? I was reading it before you came down.'

'I bet you're glad you bought a cottage in South Harptree,' he said grinning. Then, casually, 'Actually, I had a call from Aitken on Thursday morning. Before this latest happened. He wanted me to find out who's got it in for him.'

'Aren't the police dealing with it?'

'Yes. But he didn't seem to have much faith in them. Thinks they're pretty useless, by the sound of things.'

Elizabeth took off her spectacles and gazed at him quizzically. 'So . . . Aitken rings you in the morning and by supper time he's got a corpse on his hands? Great going, Max. You really helped the guy.'

'Give us a chance!' said Max. 'I haven't been near the place yet.' He said, 'Should be worth a bob or two, though.'

Elizabeth said, 'We're talking megabucks, are we?'

'With any luck. I'm going up there tomorrow.'

'You're too busy right now, I presume?' Elizabeth said drily. His elegant, size ten desert boots rested on her desk as he gazed out at the scenery – mostly female – passing by outside.

'No. *He's* too busy.' He finished off the bun and leaned back in the chair and gazed at her. 'Actually, I had this feeling there was something a bit fishy about it . . .'

'Fishy?'

'Mmn. I got the impression there were things he didn't want the police to know about. He sounded a bit furtive, I thought.' The chair swivelled round. His feet came off the desk. 'Tell me,' he said. 'What do they call you back home in Turkey Creek? I was thinking to myself yesterday, I bet they call you Betsy.'

'They call me Elizabeth.' She sipped her tea. 'I had them in the shop one day, you know. The Aitkens – Did I tell you? *He* was a bit . . . overpowering. Loud, I was going to say.'

Max grinned as he took the remains of his tea in one gulp. 'That's rich, coming from a Yank,' he said.

She ignored the dig. 'All he wanted to do was talk about himself.' She'd got the impression of a big theatrical fish in a small pond. 'But *she* was quite sweet. We had a good chat about the museum in Roanoke. They went there, on their church tour, apparently.'

A customer was approaching with a quilt book in her hand.

Elizabeth, said, 'OK, Max, so you've been fed and watered. Haven't you got a home to go to?'

'Say what you mean, why don't you?' He unfolded himself from the chair and had a good stretch. 'So long, Caroline. The bun was delicious.'

'Oh . . . right,' said Caroline.

Once he had gone, Elizabeth could give the customer her full attention. 'That book's got a whole bunch of designs,' she said cheerfully. 'One hundred and seventy-five in a hundred pages. Should keep you out of mischief for a while.'

7

The following morning, Max downed two cups of instant coffee in his basement flat in Edward Street and, after a profound study of the sports section in the *Independent*, banged the door behind him. He took the steps up to the street two at a time and set off to see what kind of a mood Phoebe was in.

Phoebe was his cannibalized old wreck of a car. He kept her in a lock-up garage behind the rugby ground. This morning, she appeared to have developed a chest infection. As he eased her up into the architectural splendours of Great Pulteney Street, she coughed now and again as if her lungs were about to give out.

'Keep death off the road,' Elizabeth said every time she set eyes on Phoebe. But Max couldn't afford to change her – for a month or two, at least.

He went over in his mind all that had appeared in the papers about the Aitken case. The *Sun*'s headline had been HOW LARRY

27

PASSED THE POISON. The *Mirror* had led with DOC TURNED RED AND DROPPED, but reports in joined-up writing on the inner pages seemed to imply that, although Aitken and his family had been questioned intensively, Wetherell's death was still being treated as accidental.

The *Mirror* was clear in its diagnosis. *Your average chap in good health wouldn't cop too much harm from a whisky/amphetamines cocktail. But combine it with the drugs an old man had been taking for his heart condition . . . and there you have a recipe for disaster!*

In the *Express* Larry was quoted as saying: 'The old so-and-so had been making a bloody nuisance of himself with his constant complaints about the church accounts – but it's ridiculous to suggest that I'd poison him in my own drawing-room in front of the Rector and half the committee!'

Alfred Monroe, of 6, The Green, a widower and a member of the Parochial Church Council, had apparently said: 'Dr Charles often got stroppy with folks. Them bikers especially. You want to watch yourself when you tangle with riff-raff like that. They used to push stuff – I won't mention what – through his letter box and I myself heard one of them threaten to do for him . . .'

Bikers getting into the Manor to wipe out Wetherell? Max somehow couldn't see a posse of Hell's Angels, all leathers and tattoos, wandering unnoticed among the Harris tweeds and the floral frocks of the Eadfrith devotees.

Aitken had given him instructions on how to find the house. Through the village, turn left at the crossroads and follow the lane up to the wrought-iron gates at the top of the hill. As it turned out, he couldn't have missed the Manor entrance. It was well and truly under siege by the press.

Oh, well, he supposed it was all good publicity . . .

Assuming his most urgent, house-detective and man-of-the-world expression, Max gave a blast on the horn. Rattled Phoebe through the flashbulbs with immense aplomb.

The house was, quite frankly, impressive. All those windows and the long, green shadows under the beech trees . . . As he climbed out, the gravel crunched satisfyingly under his feet and the garden even had a little temple.

He reached out the brand-new file he'd acquired to impress Aitken and was turning towards the pillared arch of the main door and the bell pull when he heard the sound of quick footsteps. The girl who came round the side of the house was a small, shiny blonde in shiny green, mermaidy tights that made her legs even more shapely.

'Are you supposed to be here?' she demanded curtly. 'This is private property, you know. The press stop at the gates.'

'I'm not press,' Max told her. 'I've an appointment with Mr Aitken at ten o'clock.'

'You're the detective?' She seemed to find it hard to believe. Her aquamarine gaze moved from his Fair Isle cardigan to the scuff mark on the right-hand toe of his suede shoes.

'Max Shepard. That's me.'

'Good God! We were expecting someone . . . well . . .'

'More conventional?' Max asked hopefully.

'Older.' The girl, looking quite tiny and exotic, stood a yard away and stared at him.

Max was stumped for a moment: then he said 'You're . . .?', knowing that she'd be bound to introduce herself.

'Emily Aitken.' Still she stood there.

'I should have known.' Max felt his throat dry at her lushness.

'Why should you?'

'You look like him.'

'Do I?'

'The eyes,' Max said, feeling himself drowning in them.

'Look – are you sure you're a detective?' she demanded. 'Only you don't look like one. And if you're trying to wheedle a story out of me for some crappy paper.'

'I'm not! Honestly.' He fished into the depths of a pocket. 'Here's my card.'

She took it, studied it suspiciously, then handed it back. 'OK. I just had to be sure. You'd never believe what those sharks out there get up to. One of them was throwing things at my window last night to attract my attention. I told him that even if I'd seen anything, I wouldn't tell the bloody newspapers.'

'You . . . weren't here then, when the old fellow copped it?' Max for some reason found himself mixing Bogart laconic and yuppy-speak.

'No. I was at a seminar in Bristol.'

'So what time did you get home?'

'Oh . . . it was the small hours actually,' she said. She

29

unleashed a stunning smile that practically did for him on the spot. 'I had a dinner date.'

'So you didn't know anything about it?'

'No.' She laughed. 'I was quite sorry to have missed all the excitement actually. Not that it was much fun for anyone, the old guy dropping down like that.'

'Tell me – did anyone else get a shot' (good work, Max) 'of the doped whisky?'

She leaned back against Phoebe and thought about it. 'Apparently not. Daddy doesn't drink because of his ulcer. The Rector's tipple was always a glass of Madeira. David Crichton had a whisky poured for him, but the doc crashed out before he could touch it. And then . . .' She made a gruesome face. 'Well, of course, he decided not to.'

'What about the building society manager? Bob Forbes?'

She put up a hand to lift her hair from the nape of her neck, stretching very delicately as she did so. 'He asked for a beer, I believe. It wasn't like him, Daddy said. He usually goes for the malt, but he said he'd got to drive into town later so better not. The ladies had coffee. Brenda made it.'

'Did the police find any fingerprints on the glasses or the decanter?'

'No.' There was a throaty chuckle now as she said, 'Brenda got into trouble about that. While all the hoo-ha was going on about getting an ambulance, she washed everything up – even emptied and polished the decanter. She says she always cleans things when she gets nervous. It's true actually. She cleans things non-stop. I think it's a fetish. Anything else?'

Suddenly, uncharacteristically, Max couldn't think of a thing. Emily was blonde, beautiful, laid back, sexy. She was doing his head in. He stood there grinning at her like a lemon. 'Not for the moment,' he said weakly.

She stretched both her arms in front of her and sighed. 'Oh, well . . . Better brave the gates, I suppose.' But she didn't sound unduly worried by the wolf pack down there.

In fact, Max couldn't imagine anything much fazing such a gorgeous creature. 'And I'd better brave your father,' he said.

She laughed. 'Don't worry about him. He's a pussy-cat.'

No, you're the pussy-cat, Max thought. Green-eyed, beautiful

. . . I wonder, would you purr or spit if I asked you out for a drink?

He didn't have the nerve to find out – for the moment. But . . . next time, he told himself, he might just risk it.

8

The door was opened by a becardiganed secretary with a thick Scottish accent, who said that Mr Aitken was expecting him and he was to wait in the drawing-room.

There were shaggy plants in the wide hall and black and white Dutch tiles. A lurid flower painting – all lavender petals and pink splodges – hung over the staircase.

The drawing-room still had a lot of the pretty, original plasterwork, but the furniture was gilt Louis-Quatorze stuff, splendid to the point of being faintly tacky. And as for the soft furnishings . . . Well, pretension reigns, Max thought. Swags, chintz, drapes, tassels! Only the huge television set was free of frilly encumbrances.

The secretary waved him to a brocade-covered chair. 'I'll tell Mr Aitken you're here. He's in his study, I think.' With a finicky movement, she nipped up a trace of gravel that had come from Max's shoe and dropped it into the waste-paper basket, which had a hinged lid.

She must have seen him staring at it. 'I cannot *stand* looking at a messy pile of rubbish,' she explained with a half-embarrassed laugh.

Brenda Macmillan. A bit peculiar, Emily Aitken had said. Well, yes, Max thought.

She went off to fetch Aitken. He came into the room minutes later and shook Max's hand. 'Good of you to come!' he said. He was dressed with killing elegance in a pale Italian cardigan. But the well-known face of stage and screen showed signs of strain, Max thought. There were pleats under the famous blue eyes and his hair needed a respray.

In fact, at close quarters, he looked a touch seedy.

'I gather you've had more . . . trouble since you rang me?' Max began, treading carefully.

'You can say that again!'

Max said, 'Dr Wetherell was hassling you, I believe, about the Roof Fund accounts?'

'Among other things. The chap was a bit potty, quite frankly. Senile decay, I shouldn't wonder.'

Max hesitated. 'This hate campaign . . .' he said. 'What are the chances that it might have been Wetherell?'

Aitken shook his head. 'Not his style. Anyway, it wasn't his voice on the phone. And if he'd tampered with the whisky, he was hardly likely to take a glass and drink it . . .'

Max was forced to agree.

'No. It was somebody else. Somebody pretty vicious and determined – but having said that, it wouldn't have been hard to get into the place. There were swarms of people in the grounds. And the house was empty for a large part of the day.'

'Was it locked?'

'No. We were in and out, you see. And the Schoolhouse is only a hundred yards down the drive.'

Max said, 'I'd like to make a note of your exact movements, if you don't mind. Where you all were and when . . .'

Aitken clapped a hand to his forehead. 'Right – now let me see. I was here for the first half of the morning, then I went over to meet some bigwigs at the exhibition. Brenda went down to the post office early, but after that she was in and out – between her office and the Schoolhouse, I mean. Julia pottered down to the studio for an hour, then came back and got a light lunch. Emily was in Bristol.' He moved across the heavy green carpet and took a cheroot from an antique box.

'And in the afternoon?'

'We spent the whole of the afternoon at the Schoolhouse and in the garden . . . circulating. We came back here and collapsed – sorry . . . unfortunate choice of word – we came back for tea at five when the exhibition closed.'

Max said, 'So do you have any idea who's got it in for you?'

'If I had, I wouldn't be employing you, dear boy.'

'But you must have some suspicions,' Max persisted. 'Old enemies. Someone with a grudge against you?'

32

Aitken said sardonically, 'Where do you want me to start? In this business people take pot shots at you all the time.'

'Pot shots?'

'Oh, not literally. I mean they resent your success. Once you're up there, the first thing they like to do is knock you down.'

'But I'd imagine it was something more personal than the tall poppy thing, Mr Aitken, if they'll go to this length. So – let's start with the last twelve months. Any quarrels or disagreements? Anything local in the village?'

Aitken laughed and reached for the lighter. 'Well, I suppose we could start with the Le Grices. You can't get more personal than that.'

'The Le Grices?'

'Geoffrey and Laura. They used to own this place, but now they live in the Lodge just inside the gates.'

Max got out his notebook. 'You think they resent you that much?'

Aitken hesitated. 'God knows. It's common knowledge that they think I'm not quite *comme il faut*. That my profession is, shall we say, slightly vulgar.'

'And do you mind that?'

'I won't pretend I wasn't upset by their attitude – at first. Any changes I make here they regard as cheap and nasty. Oh, they don't say it to my face. They don't open their mouths to me if they can possibly help it. But they make their views known all right. Whispers go round the village. He's done this. He's done that. Isn't it dreadful?'

'Does their attitude surprise you?' Max asked.

Larry shrugged. 'Not really. I've got enough filthy lucre to indulge in – ' he waved a hand around the room – 'shall we say, a certain style. And people get jealous. You have to get used to that fact and ignore it.'

'So you think the Le Grices are likely candidates?'

'Frankly, yes. They're as resentful as hell.' He paused. 'But as I said to my wife only the other day, they didn't do so badly out of me. They made their killing. A bloody fortune I paid them for this place and it's still sitting in their bank account, presumably. Can't think why they don't go off and live it up in the Bahamas or somewhere, rather than sitting round here with bloody long faces.'

Max drew a pile of coins on his notepad and waited.

'Oh, it's obvious they don't think I'm fit to be guardian of this sacred pile, but . . .' Aitken shrugged. 'I'm used to it, old boy. I get it all the time from the fancy critics in the newspapers! "Oh, God, not him again!" they complain. "Isn't he over-exposed and over-paid?" But they like me!' he said with triumph, jerking a hand in the direction of the village. '*They* enjoy my shows, even if the bloody snobs don't.'

Max said, 'So you're friendly with the villagers, on the whole?'

'No doubt about it! *They're* on my side,' Aitken laughed. '*They* know which side their bread's buttered. Some of the cottages were in a hell of a state, you know, when I took over.'

'You own cottages in the village?'

'Comes with the Manor, old son. Bit of a responsibility, you know.' Larry puffed himself up a bit, then said, 'Without bathrooms even, some of those cottages were, when I took over. Still in the bloody eighteenth century! Geoffrey high-and-mighty Le Grice didn't give them decent plumbing, did he? It was muggins here.'

Max looked suitably impressed. He said, 'So you think the Le Grices should go on my list?'

'I suppose so.' He gave Max a quick, sideways glance. 'But I'm still not sure they're capable of . . .'

'Doping the whisky?'

'I wasn't thinking of that, oddly enough.' Larry ground out his cheroot into a large, cut glass ashtray. Then reached for a new one. 'No, what I was going to say was . . . well, somebody poisoned my dog, Hamlet. And they're dog lovers, both of them, the Le Grices. I don't think they could cold-bloodedly poison one, no matter what their grievance. But they do know their way round this place pretty well . . . I can't deny it. They'd know when to slip in and how.'

'Anyone else?' Max asked.

Aitken rolled the new cheroot in his fingers, struck a match and attempted to light it. 'Well, I suppose I'd better come clean about my relationship with a certain lady who came on the Australian leg of the Eadfrith tour. My very *brief* relationship, I might add . . .' There was an odd note of braggadocio in his laugh. 'But her name would have to come next on the list of those who might, shall we say, have it in for me.'

'And her name is . . .'

'Rebecca Forbes.' Aitken had now got the cheroot going and attempted a defensive gesture as he waved it around in front of him. 'Oh, I'll admit I was a bit of a fool – but she'd been playing up to me for ages. You know how it is . . .'

Nudge-nudge, wink-wink. 'These things happen,' Max said with a deadpan face.

'It happened when we were in Sydney. I'd had too much – '

'I thought you didn't drink,' Max said quickly.

'I don't, dear boy.' Was that a flash of alarm in his eyes? Had he made a tiny, but revealing slip? Smoothly, Larry went on, 'I'd had too much hospitality, I was about to say. The trouble with the Aussies is that they're too damned friendly – we'd been out fraternizing all day and I developed this bloody awful headache. Rebecca came to our hotel room later with these magic pills that she said would cure it . . .'

'Was your wife with you on the tour?' Max asked carefully.

'Yes, but she'd gone to the opera with some friends. Anyway, the pills did work, as it happened, and Rebecca ordered some supper from room service and . . . well, one thing led to another.'

Max assumed his most innocent, blue-eyed gaze. I bet it did, he thought.

'She wouldn't leave me alone. Several nights after that we . . . shall we say . . . indulged.' His gaze met Max's then slithered away again as he attempted to find a note of jovial *bonhomie*. 'I should have stuck to one of those ruddy Aussie Sheilas, don't you think? Not so much come-back. Better looking, too. Of course when we got back home, I told her it couldn't go on . . .'

'And Mrs Forbes was difficult about it?'

'As mad as hell. But I couldn't help that.'

'Did she come near the Manor on the day the doctor died?'

'She was here that morning, actually. Determined to have a row with me. But I showed her the door.'

There was a pause. Then, 'Anyone else call that morning?' Max asked.

'Lionel Silk. He called with the *Church Times*.'

'Was he here in the drawing-room?'

'Certainly.'

'Alone?'

'Yes, as a matter of fact. Julia was upstairs when he arrived, she told me. She was in the bath, so he had to sit around and wait for a while.' Larry laughed. 'You don't actually suspect the good Reverend?'

'Just checking. Would Silk harbour any grudges against you, do you think?'

'I owed him for a couple of parish magazines, but I hardly think that's enough to make him send hate mail.'

'Does your wife have any ideas about who's persecuting you?'

'Julia doesn't have ideas. She just does the flowers. And her painting.'

'And the charity work . . . You both do a lot of that, I hear?'

'I like taking the time to do charity work. It gives me a flip.' He glanced at Max briefly. 'And before you ask, I paid for my own bloody return fare to the States and to Sydney.'

Who's asking? Max thought. Sounds like someone might have a guilty conscience . . .

'I wasn't going to have anyone suggesting I was taking a free ride. I can afford it. Some of the others couldn't, so theirs came out of the fund. Quite right, too. Horses for courses.'

Was it genuine, Max wondered, the love of philanthropy, or a load of old hogwash? But then he probably did get a kick out of being seen to do good works. Or was that unfair?

'Anyone else who might have a grudge against you?' Max asked.

Aitken hesitated. He walked over to the window, then came back. 'Only one name,' he said at last.

'Which is?'

He looked first confidential, then edgy, then indecisive. 'There was someone called Tabernay – a spot of trouble I was involved in years ago in Oxford, when I was in rep.'

'What kind of trouble?'

'I'd rather not say at this stage, if you don't mind. Not until all other lines of enquiry are eliminated.'

He threw the second cheroot on the fire.

Reached for another.

'It's probably got nothing to do with it anyway,' he said hurriedly. 'Let's leave it there for the moment, shall we?'

So what kind of skeleton did Larry have in his cupboard that was threatening to fall out? Max would have liked to insist on more detail, but Aitken had made it clear that the interview was over. 'I'd like to take a look round the ground floor if I may . . .'

'Help yourself,' Aitken told him. 'Brenda will show you out when you're ready. I'm afraid I have another appointment.'

As they emerged into the hall, the secretary, Brenda Macmillan, was positioned outside the door, almost as if she'd been standing there eavesdropping. Her gaze met his for a second, then she jerked away.

How old was she? Thirty? Forty? Impossible to tell, but she looked like a woman who was a walking bag of nerves.

Traffic was jammed up all the way down to the centre. Max switched off the ignition because Phoebe's temperature gauge needle was on the red.

A life-style package, he thought idly. That's what Larry bought when he acquired the Manor . . . Guaranteed to up the image of an immensely vain TV star.

And then with a swift change of mood, he thought: But there was something else as well. A vulnerability hidden deep underneath. Really, all in all, he was a bit pathetic.

9

It was out of sheer curiosity that Elizabeth decided to attend Charles Wetherell's funeral. Well, everybody else in the village would be there, she reasoned. Why should I be the only one to miss the excitement?

She had left Caroline in charge of Martha Washington for the afternoon. 'Just field any orders that come in,' she'd said. 'I'll deal with them tomorrow.'

'Oh – right,' Caroline said.

Sometimes Elizabeth wondered if the child's vocabulary was confined to those two words.

Max had shut up shop for the afternoon and come too. Well, he might learn something, he told her. In other words, she wasn't the only one whose nose stuck out five miles in front of her face!

They fought their way through the scrummage of photographers and villagers round the lych-gate. It was a golden afternoon, crisped around the edges. Tacked directly below the churchyard wall was the square stone Rectory. There were odd cottages that had mullioned windows and barley sugar chimneys, but South Harptree was an eighteenth-century village, for the most part, plain and pleasant, built of stone from Ralph Allen's quarries a few miles away.

Inside the church, the organ played muted Beethoven. The pews were packed with the cream of South Harptree society – gentlemen farmers, Hunt Ball types and retired gentry. Aitken, elegantly attired in dark suit and black tie and spray-on hairstyle, came in last and took the middle seat in the second row.

Elizabeth watched as he gave a deep nod of greeting – an exquisitely tuned gesture of social flattery – to the Very Reverend Silk, as he passed with the choir procession.

'Bit of a show-off,' Max muttered, 'don't you think?'

'A kind of walking advertisement for himself,' Elizabeth agreed.

'Tell you something . . .'

'What's that?'

'He wears a fortune on his back.'

He's not the only one, Elizabeth thought, as she noted Emily Aitken's short and leggy suit.

'How about *that*, then?' Max said, his blue eyes on stalks, as big as saucers.

'Hmm,' murmured Elizabeth.

'Hmm what?'

'Hmm . . . I can see why you should get the hots for her.'

'Betsy! We're in church!'

It made her smile to see his discomfort. 'I guess the Lord knows all about the hots, Max. In my book, anyway.'

'You think so?' He was still gawking at Emily. 'She stayed talking to me for ages the other morning.'

38

Following his gaze, she said, 'Forget it, Max.'

Max switched his attention to the stained glass window. 'She looks like that angel in the top panel, don't you think?'

Some angel, Elizabeth thought, with a rear like that.

'You don't think I'd stand a chance? Is that it?'

As though on cue, Emily Aitken turned and gazed at Max and then faced front again like a good little girl. A pretty little girl from Bedales, Elizabeth thought, who may or may not be as innocent as she looks . . . 'I wouldn't bet on it,' she told him.

'I reckon I could murder for her,' he said.

'She'd be fine in bed. But irritating with the cornflakes.'

'You're a hard woman, Betsy.'

'I know,' she said. Then, 'That's a swell tie you're wearing.'

'You like it?' Proudly he touched its rather splendid (if suitably muted) blue Picasso print.

'I do.' Pity about the pizza stain, she thought.

A gust of chilly wind hit them as they came out of church an hour later. Huge sycamore leaves were dropping from the trees and the air had turned sharper. While the burial went on in a quiet spot behind the tower, Elizabeth found herself reflecting how random, how chancy a business life . . . or death . . . was.

Lingering on the edge of the crowd, she thought: Wetherell takes a glass of whisky from a neighbour and snuffs himself out. I come to England on vacation and decide on the spur of the moment to make my home here. Terrifying, really . . .

The only thing you could predict was that nothing was predictable.

The interment rites over, the crowd began to shift and disperse. 'Not a bad send-off!' A voice from behind her cut a swathe through the mourners. 'Never seen so many in church. Faces here that haven't seen the inside of St Swithin's in twenty years.'

Dorothy Marchant was a stout old party with thin, white hair and a pre-war accent. She owned the cottage whose garden adjoined Elizabeth's. Now as the wind caught at her black straw hat with the felt band, she said, 'Not sure what Charles would have said to the choice of bearers!' The small band in dark suits, their task over, were coming back over the grass, still in close formation. 'No family left to do the honours, so they had to fall

39

back on the Roof Fund committee . . . Only last week he was tearing strips off them all!'

Elizabeth watched them break formation as they reached the path.

'Who's the dark young man?' she asked.

'Crichton. Accountant.'

'And the fat guy? The one with the paunch and the middle-aged slouch?'

'Forbes. Building society manager. That's his wife in the big hat, talking to Crichton.'

'The blonde?'

'Probably out of a bottle, but that's her.'

The Forbes woman. The one that Aitken had dumped, according to Max. Artful and knowing-looking, Elizabeth decided, taking a long look at the lady's poppy-coloured lipstick and nails to match. 'Aitken's on the committee, isn't he?' she asked her companion.

'Yes, but he didn't offer his services on this occasion.' The black bombazine blouse that Dottie had dug out from some Victorian cupboard rustled ferociously every time she moved. 'I imagine he'd think himself too august for such a task.'

Or scared stiff of making tomorrow's front page pictured with the coffin, Elizabeth thought, watching Aitken make his way out through the crowd, turning like a homing satellite dish to fix his gaze and his voice on the pretty girl reporter who'd just thrust a microphone in front of him . . .

'This must be a very difficult day for you, Mr Aitken?'

'Not the easiest, my dear . . .'

He treated the camera lens almost like a mirror. But Elizabeth noticed that there were tiny beads of sweat on his temple as he gave the girl his special smile. So there *was* genuine emotion of some kind wrapped up in all that false sincerity.

The circus moved off down to the lych-gate. One of the reporters tripped backwards over a sunken gravestone. Julia Aitken threw him a distressed look and escaped into the back seat of the Jaguar.

'She insisted the flowers for church came from the Manor garden.' Dottie fingered the silk chiffon scarf wrapped round and round her throat.

'From what I gather,' Elizabeth said, 'the good doctor had it in for her husband.'

'Hatreds boil up inside villages. Always have. Always will do.'

'Did you know Wetherell well?' asked Elizabeth.

'Known him for years. There have been Wetherells in the village for centuries. But no more, I fear.' Dottie shook her head. 'He was the last of them. Never married. No children – that we know of, anyway. Sad, I suppose.'

'Yes, I knew Charles,' she said again as they walked home together in the sharp, autumn sunshine. 'In fact, the three of us – Charlie and Julia Aitken and myself – fought a few battles together last year.'

'Battles?'

'See that?' Dottie was pointing at a spot in front of them with her stick.

'I can't see anything,' Elizabeth told her.

'Exactly. It's not there.'

'What's not there?' Was the woman mad?

'The bus shelter. We got it removed, the three of us. Took a lot of lobbying, but we did it.'

'Really?' For the life of her, Elizabeth couldn't see why they should think it an achievement to remove a bus shelter.

'It had become a collecting place for all the local misfits at night. Motor bicycles, skinheads, idiot children intent on baiting the poor ducks. Well, it's no use grousing on about something – whingeing, I believe they call it – unless you're going to do something about it. So the three of us got together and we got rid of it. Concerted campaign. Letters to the papers, a petition, lobbied the parish council . . .'

No matter that you get wet while you wait for the bus, Elizabeth thought drily.

'No buses now anyway,' said Dottie, seemingly reading her thoughts. 'Only two a day. Wasn't worth the trouble it caused. It's a funny thing,' she went on as they passed the shop window, filled today with fresh bread rolls and cakes, 'but Julia was the only person I ever knew who could actually coax the old devil out of his rages.' She pointed to a tall Queen Anne house on the edge of the Green. 'That's where he lived.'

'What will happen to the house now?' Elizabeth asked.

'Couldn't tell you. There's a distant cousin somewhere, I believe. Suppose it'll pass to him. You'd better come in and have a spot of tea. Soon have the kettle on . . .'

The world shot back a few decades at Dottie's tea table. Or rather at the wooden trolley that she heaved towards the hearth, where a neglected log fire sizzled in the grate. A framed photograph of Winston Churchill was hung on the wall. 'Mother's hero,' Dottie told Elizabeth to the clink of cups.

There were fresh cream strawberry tarts that would not help the waistline, but Dottie had evidently given up on all that. She parked her teeth in a tart and said, 'Charles was at Winchester. Oxford scholar. He spent a lot of his life abroad – mostly in India. Of course, he could be stuffy sometimes. And he was bossy. I can't deny that. A difficult old devil, inclined to feud – but he did a lot for St Swithin's in his time . . .'

'Who else did he fight with?' Elizabeth asked.

'He had a spat with Lionel Silk once about the state of the Wetherell family plot. Maintained that it was disgracefully overgrown and that Silk had let the Church Commissioners sell part of it off to a local farmer. Of course, Lionel's rather liberal, you know – a bit wet, between you and me! He didn't want the church to stand still . . . and Charles hated change of any kind.' She shook her head as she said, 'But then he hated a lot of things of late. Car radios, hippies, dogs fouling the village street . . . He threatened to shoot them if he caught them at it.'

'It's sad he had to go in this way,' Elizabeth said.

'Well, he always said he wanted to drop dead one day. No nonsense about being ill first. So he had his way in the end. There's something to be said for that, wouldn't you say?'

More tea was poured and the subject came round to Aitken and the Manor. 'Rumour has it,' Dottie confided, 'that he's spent at least two million renovating the place.'

'That's a great deal of money,' Elizabeth said. 'How much do you suppose he has left?'

'Well . . . I wouldn't expect him to be struck dumb with horror every time a bill came in. But then I shouldn't be surprised if he has less than people think . . .'

'They seem to do a great deal for charity.'

'I'll grant you that. They're always opening the house up for this fund-raising event or that. Of course, they love showing off what they've done to the place, I've no doubt, but at least it's all in a good cause.'

'So a good many villagers would have been familiar with the inside layout of the Manor? With the ground-floor rooms, at least?'

'Oh, hordes of them, my dear! They held ghost walks there last year, in aid of the Parish Hall appeal.'

'Ghost walks?'

'Don't tell me you haven't heard about the Manor ghost?'

'Actually, I haven't.'

'One of the seventeenth-century Le Grices who committed suicide over some girl or other. Sir Roland . . . or was it Sir Roger?' Dottie said. 'Mind you, no one ever thought of harnessing him up to raise money before. Sign of the times, I suppose.' She reached for a piece of fruit cake, dropped it on her plate, and suddenly swiped at the air, like a woman being attacked. 'There they are again! Those funny little flies . . . mosquito-like creatures. Pass me that spray, would you? They come in through the back scullery and I *can't* get rid of them! Not that I use the scullery any more, but that's not the point. I had the man in and he put down a bucket of stuff to smoke them out, but it didn't work. They're coming from the other side of His Nibs' wall, you know . . .'

'His Nibs?'

'Aitken. I'm planning to pay him a visit to find out what he's doing over there to attract the bugs.' And then, ka-boom, she was on to the next subject. 'Which way do you vote? Democrat or Republican?'

Back in her own cottage half an hour later, Elizabeth dropped her coat on the small sofa by the window. Now at last she could kick off her shoes and relax!

She had never lived in such close confinement in all her life. The gabled cottage was about the length of a stretch limo . . . She had first seen it in summer. Cream roses round the door and that sweep of green down over the hills to Bath. There had been then, as now, a mown smell . . . a good fresh-air smell hanging over the valley.

She crossed, as she did every evening, to admire the incomparable view from the window. Then put on the TV. Damn it, she'd missed the news! She was flicking round the channels and about to switch off again when suddenly, disconcertingly, Larry Aitken's face appeared on the screen.

It was one of those early evening game shows that he hosted. Grinning hugely, hair utterly coiffed, he stood there with his arm round some woman's plump shoulders, calling her 'darling' . . . Elizabeth gave a grimace. It made you cringe.

And yet, he wasn't bad for his age, she supposed – if you liked that kind of over-handsome man with bedroom eyes. She thought back to what Max had told her about Aitken's affair with Rebecca Forbes. Yes, he looked the type for casual brutality in sexual relationships. You could see it in the hard but sensual mouth. The knowing gaze . . .

She switched off the set and went into the kitchen.

Thought absently, as she put coffee into the filter of the machine, how odd it was that you found yourself alternately enthralled and appalled by the man.

10

On Tuesday evening, Max had suggested to Elizabeth that they should go for a bevvy at her favourite pub, the Old Green Bush just around the corner from Pierrepont Mews. Elizabeth had jumped at the chance.

Squares and crescents were emptying of tourists. Only the starlings were left screeching in flocks on the Guildhall roof.

It was pleasantly warm in the pub. She still couldn't get over how tiny the place was. How many mad people crammed themselves in there, wedged against the Dr Oliver panelling to mull over the day's work – or to forget it.

Elizabeth said, 'So what did you make of Aitken?'

'I think he's scared witless,' Max told her.

'Did he say so?'

'No. Quite the opposite. He's trying to bluff and swagger his way through it.'

'He'd probably need to.' She said, deadpan, 'Did he offer you a whisky?'

'Oh, very droll.'

'Sorry. One shouldn't joke about what happened to the poor old doc. Did you see all that junk they dug up in the papers today?' There had been several newly invented versions of the relationship between Aitken and Wetherell of the 'Dope and booze in posh country hide-away' sort. 'It's the absolute pits!'

'He's a bit of a gas-bag, I gather.'

'What about the secretary?'

'In and out. She went to the post office earlyish. After that . . . in and out to help with the exhibition. Oh, she went off to town for an hour in the afternoon.'

'And was the house empty after the Reverend had gone off to the exhibition?'

'For a short time while Julia was down at the studio. Larry came back for lunch and brought David Crichton with him. Julia got soup out of the freezer, made sandwiches for them, but decided to leave them to discuss whatever it was Crichton had come for and take herself off down to the studio for another hour. If we're talking about a stranger getting in and doping the whisky, I reckon the best time would have been between two o'clock, when the Aitkens were at the exhibition, and three thirty, when Brenda arrived back from town.'

'Took her time, didn't she?'

'It was officially her afternoon off. She went to see a friend, she said. The crowds visiting the exhibition were at their thickest after lunch apparently. Easy camouflage for the odd soul to slip in by the back way or through a side door.'

'So half the village could have got in there, when you look at it logically.' Elizabeth looked thoughtful. 'You were saying something about Larry giving you a list of suspects. Who comes top, in your estimation?'

'I suppose the Le Grices, Geoffrey and Laura. Larry doesn't think they're capable of it, but I'm not so sure. You do get the feeling they were disappointed Aitken wasn't charged with murder.'

'Like vultures hovering . . .'

'But then, as Larry said, he was hardly likely to bump him off in his own drawing-room in front of the Rector and half the committee.'

'No matter how much Wetherell was hassling him . . . I think

45

I'd agree with you, Max. Unless, of course, the letters and the phone calls were an elaborate hoax – unless Aitken set the whole thing up so that he could kill Wetherell and blame the phantom caller.'

'This isn't *Murder, She Wrote*,' Max told her. 'It's South Harptree . . . So for the time being we'll go along with Larry's theory that an intruder got in some time during the Eadfrith Open Day. By the way, he says he'd opened a new bottle of whisky and decanted it that morning before he went across to the exhibition.'

'That limits the time-scale somewhat. So tell me what they were all doing that day.'

Max consulted his notebook. 'Well, Emily went out at eight twenty-five in the morning. She had to get to Bristol for a nine o'clock lecture.'

'Fat chance,' said Elizabeth. 'Have you seen the traffic on the Bristol road at that hour of the day?'

'Well, she left at eight twenty-five, whether she got there on time or not. And Larry was in the house until about eleven, when he went over to the Old Schoolhouse. The Reverend Silk arrived at ten minutes to eleven and stayed for a coffee with Julia. He left at about half-eleven.'

'Long time to spend chatting, wasn't it, on such a busy day?' Elizabeth paused. 'Funny you should mention the Le Grices.' She pulled a guide to the Manor from her handbag and proceeded to open it.

'What's this?' Max said.

'I've been doing some homework for you. They were selling them at the village store in aid of the Roof Fund. 50p. Foreword by Larry himself – plus a lovely photo. A pound for the signed ones.'

'This is the cheapo version,' Max said, examining it.

'They'd run out of the other – luckily.' She put on her spectacles and proceeded to read from the guide. '*In 1068, Guillaume Le Grice, Duc de Rossillon, sailed for England from Normandy. He obained a grant of land on the outskirts of the Roman city of Bath, comprising the area now known as Warren Woods, which he intended to use for hunting and on which to build himself "a faire manor".*'

'I was good at history at school,' said Max.

There was a slight, quick lift of Elizabeth's eyebrow before she read on. *'Most of the original house was destroyed at the Reformation. In 1602, Philip Le Grice ordered the rebuilding of the mansion in goodly stone. A portion of land on the south side (described as the rise west of the church) was later chosen as the site for a folly.'*

'When was the Lodge built?' Max asked.

'1810. Pretty-pretty mock Gothic. Why?'

'I was thinking. It's a bit of a come-down for Geoffrey and Laura Le Grice.'

'One hell of a come-down.'

'Must be pretty galling to be reduced to living in the Lodge of your ancestral home . . .'

'Devastating, I should think. Is that why you've got them at the top of your list?'

'There's bad blood between them and Larry. They know the Manor intimately. And the Lodge is the perfect place from which to watch the Aitkens' comings and goings.'

'So you think they watched until the coast was clear, then slipped in to tinker with the whisky?'

'They resented Larry being there, didn't they? They had motive, knowledge and means. Yes, I think I might have a little chat with them tomorrow . . .' There was a brief silence while he gazed into his glass. Then he said, 'You know, Larry still likes to think of himself as Jack the Lad, in spite of his squire's ways.'

'Jack the Lad who married a don's daughter . . .'

'Yes. Odd, that.'

'Oh, I don't know. I've come across stranger matches.'

'She seems such a pale shadow,' Max said. 'Can't see how she attracted him in the first place. Do you think she had money?'

'Sexist statement . . .' Elizabeth told him. 'I don't know if she had money, but she definitely had class. That would interest Larry, the social climber . . . be quite a feather in his cap. Actually, I think she's rather lovely in a pale English way. I can imagine old Larry, twenty or so years back, making a play for her, bringing out that engaging smile that he uses to his advantage. I can imagine her falling for it, too. Cupid's a funny little fellow, Max . . .'

'Oh, hilarious,' said Max in a hollow voice.

47

After a minute, still conversationally, she said, 'Do I gather he may have played the odd trick on you now and again?'

'There have been times,' said Max, 'when I'd have murdered the little bugger if I could have got my hands round his neck.'

'You're such a romantic, Max.'

'As it happens, I am.'

Another minute passed, then she said, 'So what brought you down to Bath in the first place?'

'Women,' he said in a sepulchral tone.

'Women? Plural?'

'Plural.'

'I knew you had style, Max – but *plural* . . .?' She was thoroughly intrigued.

'A mother and three sisters,' he finally explained.

'*Three* sisters?' She started to laugh. 'Henpecked, were you?'

'You can say that again!'

'Did they spoil you? I *bet* they did!' This was wonderful. Elizabeth suddenly felt very enlightened. Major secrets were being unlocked with regard to Max's psyche.

'They drove me mad. Do this, Max! Do that, Max! Marry her, Max. Don't tie yourself down, Max . . .'

'Marry her?' She wondered for one moment if she had misheard. 'You almost got married?'

'Close shave,' he said. He sat there shredding a paper napkin and consuming peanuts.

'So what happened?'

'I'd rather not talk about it.' Then he said, 'Oh, sod it, she found somebody else, that's all. So I got the hell out of it.' He was sombrely philosophical. 'And here I am two years later with another bossy female on my back.'

'Poor you.' Elizabeth was dying to ask more, but decided that the expression on his face called for extreme caution. 'Did you run your own agency up in Manchester?' she asked.

'No. I worked for one . . . for an old mate of my dad's. I helped him out.

'And learned some of the tricks . . .'

'A few.' He found a grin. 'But not enough. And doesn't it show?'

'Bath . . . Odd place to run a detective agency,' Elizabeth

said. 'Ed McBain meets Jane Austen . . .' But on second thoughts she deemed it an *interesting* combination.

'I've read Ed McBain,' Max volunteered.

'I'll lend you *Northanger Abbey*,' Elizabeth told him. 'You'll enjoy it.' Then, 'Actually, I've been doing some detective work myself today,' she told him. 'Continuing my research on Robert Lightfoot at the library.'

'Who's Robert Lightfoot?'

'Robert Henry Lightfoot, who left the village of Little Gurney in Somerset for Virginia in 1744.'

'Oh, God!' Max rolled his eyes. 'Don't tell me! You're tracing your family tree . . .'

'What's wrong with that?'

'Yanks!' he said. 'They all do it.'

'I'll have you know I'm proud to be one of the Virginia Lightfoots!'

'The Virginia Lightfoots . . .? My dear!'

'Stop laughing at me, you little schmuck. Robert Henry Lightfoot was one hell of a guy. He became a substantial property holder in York County and ran an ordinary that was patronized by the gentry.'

'An ordinary?'

'A tavern to you.'

'Oh, a pub! Probably a good bloke then.'

'Right. He built the place himself.' She quoted from memory. '*A large, two-storey brick dwelling house with four rooms on a floor, lying in Orchard Street near to the market.*' She said, 'It had a steep gabled roof, and a decorative front fence showing the Chinese influence. It's still standing – a fine old place. My brother lives there now.'

'Fascinating!' Max gave a great yawn.

She ignored this pitiful attempt at irony. 'Old Robert *was* a very interesting character . . . He eventually brought his mother, Elizabeth Lightfoot, over to Virginia, too. Deeded her a strip of land and an annuity of £40 and a servant to look after her, *in consideration of the natural love and affection which he hath for her.*'

'Gee, Betsy, that's real sob stuff!'

'Isn't it? What I'm really trying to find out is why he left England.'

'Probably the black sheep,' Max said. 'Got some girl in the pudding club.'

'You may well be right.' Her mind came back to the point where the conversation had started. 'Larry's list of suspects . . . Who else is on it?'

'Some hazy character in Oxford that he doesn't want to expand on as yet. Then there's Rebecca Forbes.'

'Larry's very glossy bit on the side,' Elizabeth said. 'Well, I can imagine her wanting something more exciting than her husband. Old Fatso looked about as exciting as a lard can.'

'Betsy – ' Max didn't seem to have been listening – 'would you like to do me a very big favour?'

'Such as?' Elizabeth immediately looked suspicious.

'Nip up to the Forbes residence one afternoon and have a girlie talk with Rebecca for me. Only I've got to see this woman whose boyfriend got her pregnant. She calls him the Eel.'

'The Eel?'

'Slippery . . .' he explained. 'He's done a disappearing act and she wants me to track him down to get maintenance. Anyway, you'd be better than me at winkling things out of the Forbes woman.'

'A girlie talk? You mean you want me to be your unpaid assistant for the afternoon?'

'I wouldn't put it quite like that.'

'Wouldn't you?' She wondered why exactly he was ducking out of the assignment. 'What are you afraid of?'

'Nothing.'

'Are you sure?'

'I told you. I've got to see this woman.' But his eyes wouldn't meet hers. He busied himself fiddling with the cruet set.

'Max Shepard, you're scared of her!' A laugh like a nutmeg grater rose in her throat. 'What happened? Go on – you might as well tell me.'

'She just came on a bit strong when I chatted to her after the funeral, that's all.'

'Came on a bit *strong*?' It was wrong to tease him so relentlessly, but Elizabeth was enjoying herself.

'Like a bloody female piranha.' His ears were actually beginning to turn scarlet. 'I thought she was going to eat me . . .'

'Oh, Max . . .'

'Stop laughing.'

'I thought you were a man about town.'

'I am,' he said weakly. 'But she's . . . something else.'

Elizabeth said, 'So you don't fancy being alone with her in her suburban villa?'

'You'd do a better job.'

'Really?' She made an attempt at reluctance. The trouble was, Max knew she couldn't resist such an assignment.

'So will you do it?'

'I'll think about it. I'll tell you one thing, Max.'

'What's that?'

'When I came to South Harptree, I thought, what a peaceful place! Nothing going on except a few ducks paddling round.'

'You've changed your mind?'

'I sure have. It's all happening, but behind closed doors. There's one hell of a lot of secret sin . . .'

11

It was a minute past ten in the morning as Max pulled into the grass verge by the Manor Lodge. He'd had a picture of it in his head since his last visit, a sort of dim photograph of trim, latticed windows with Gothic arches.

But this morning he found it a bit drab-looking and neglected. Rain clouds were gathering and the golden rod was running wild all up one side of the garden.

He decided to take a look round the layout of the Manor grounds before calling on the Le Grices. By the look of the sky, it would be tipping down in ten minutes and if he had to go poking about in the great outdoors, he preferred not to get his new Italian flannels specked with mud.

He slipped over the wooden stile into the Manor woods. The pleasantly laid out spread of beech trees felt creepy this morning. It had something to do with the light – or rather, the lack of light, as the approaching storm gathered down there along the coast . . . coming in from the west, as usual, from Lundy and Exmoor and the flatter approaches of the Bristol Channel.

Max wasn't prone to nerves. But he did feel slightly bothered by all that high silence up there where the tall branches met the grey of the sky. The only sound for miles and miles was the soft swishing of air above his head as the wind passed through the trees.

A five-minute hike to the north took him to the far end of Warren Wood and the high stone wall that marked the limit of the Manor grounds. Turn right before the ruins of an old stone quarry and you came to the folly, perched up on top of the hill looking down into Bath. Turn right again and a hundred yards to the south the woods ended abruptly and the park spread out before you, misty today in a grey-green haze.

Max could see now why Aitken was so proud of his domain. As a piece of real estate, it was quite astoundingly beautiful.

Turning left, he found himself in the orchards, beyond which was a low stone barn and the six-foot high wall again. He guessed that Elizabeth's cottage lay somewhere on the other side. Following the wall took him round to the pink granite obelisk which, according to a metal plaque, was discovered by Frederick Le Grice at Philae in 1817 and which arrived at South Harptree Manor in 1822 after various adventures.

Max stood gazing up at it in the cold, spitting wind and marvelled at the things people brought home as souvenirs of a good trip.

The Old Schoolhouse, built in 1839 as a philanthropic gesture by George Le Grice, was a hundred-yard walk from the obelisk along an avenue of plane trees. In early Victorian times, the children of South Harptree would have had a sharp, utilitarian education in that angular building.

Fifty yards beyond it lay the shrubbery and the portico of the big house. Max already had in his head a pretty good plan of the mansion. What interested him particularly at this moment was the position and the layout of the orangery, stuck on one end of the main house and communicating directly with it, instead of being placed separately at the end of the garden. A row of acorn-shaped urns topped its slate roof. In winter, it would have stored potted plants and palms. Still did now, from what he could see by squinting hard through the huge, Venetian arched windows. He counted two side doors, one practically hidden by the end of the shrubbery. Yes . . . it would be comparatively easy to slip unseen into what in the seventeenth century would have been known as the greenhouse, and thence into the main house, provided, of course, that the doors were unlocked.

The sky opened at the exact moment that he turned back towards the main gates. A small whirlwind sprang up out of nowhere to lash the rain sideways.

Max was no athlete, but he had to concede that the only thing for it was to cut and run.

Brenda Macmillan, watching from the corner of the drawing-room window, decided that perhaps Larry's young detective wasn't quite as green as he looked.

He wasn't bad-looking either, she thought. The shoulders not exactly powerfully built inside the jacket, but sinewy . . . 'Lithe,' she murmured in her neat, precise voice.

Brenda was edgy. Like a hen on a hot girdle, as they said back home in Scotland. She ran a finger along the window frame to check for dust. Found none . . .

Reached into the pocket of her cardigan for a peppermint to calm her stomach.

Lithe . . . yes. But he shouldn't be sneaking round the place thinking no one could see him. Her twitchy eye, staring out of the window, saw more than the heavy sky and the rain slanting down and the blowing trees. For her mind was running back over the events of the past few months.

It was the same old question that occupied her thoughts. A question that had been turning itself over in her mind for what seemed like an age . . . Did she tell Larry what she had found out or not? And if so, how much?

Would he say there was no need for her to concern herself with things like that? Tell her she was mad? Or would he lose his temper and . . .

The telephone shrilled and she gave such a start that she had to reach for another mint, before striding over to pick up the receiver.

12

At ten thirty exactly, Max tugged at the old-fashioned door bell of the Lodge. He was glad to be in the shelter of the porch and out of the rain.

He was about to give the bell another yank when the door abruptly opened. The man who stood there was of middle height, dour, unfriendly.

'Mr Le Grice?'

'Yes.'

Max handed him his business card. 'I'm a private investigator. Mr Aitken hired me to – '

'Aitken sent you here?' Le Grice barked, glaring at the card.

Well done, Max, up the chute inside ten seconds! Damage limitation was needed. 'Not exactly,' he said with his most charming smile.

'Well either he did or he didn't. Which is it?' Le Grice had the kind of face that looked as if it ought to belong to a surgeon. A gentleman of the highest reputation, but sceptical, on the whole, about his patients' chances. Fierce, bristling brows and piercing blue eyes sharply focused now on Max's person, eyed him up for the operating table.

'Well, I'm working for Mr Aitken, but he doesn't actually know I've come here.' Sounding confidential, Max added, 'I just thought you might know a few things about the Manor that he doesn't know.'

'A few? Hundreds, I should imagine!'

'That's what I was hoping. Only he hasn't lived there long and there are a lot of things he obviously hasn't a clue about. Of course I can't tell him that – '

'Why not? If you ask me, it would bloody well do him good.'

'Possibly,' said Max, 'but I have to keep my opinions to myself while I'm on the job. Anyway, he's desperate to find out who got into the house and doctored the whisky that caused Dr Wetherell's death.'

'I bet he is!' Le Grice gave a harsh laugh. 'Ruined his blasted image round here, hasn't it? Well, I don't feel sorry for him! Not in the least! He turns up here like some pop star and starts systematically wooing the villagers . . . trying to make them pathetically grateful for his presence among them . . . Have you seen those damned signed photos on the Manor guide? Thinks he's scattering religious relics, I shouldn't wonder! But you can't buy people's respect, you know.' And you can't buy breeding, his face seemed to suggest.

'Oh, I realize that,' Max said, agreeing with him.

'How d'you know he didn't doctor the stuff himself to get Charlie off his back? I wouldn't put it past him! Bought off the police, too, I shouldn't wonder. Somebody got a back-hander, or else they'd have charged him with poor old Charlie's murder.' Le Grice's eyes had an avid, intense look as they swivelled in the direction of the Manor and then back again.

'You really think that's possible?'

'Happens all the time these days . . . corruption everywhere. Saw a piece about it in the *Telegraph* only yesterday.'

'Mr Le Grice, I'd really like to hear more of your views about Dr Wetherell's . . . accident.' Max never enjoyed sucking up to people in order to blow their defence; but if it got you through to the truth of a case, then the end justified the means.

'Accident, my foot!' Le Grice's eyes flickered again. 'Look – how long will this take? Only my wife's – well, she's got a lot on her plate this morning.'

'Ten or fifteen minutes. That's all. I just wanted to ask a question or two about what you saw last Wednesday.' Max had his fingers crossed behind his back. Le Grice stared at him coolly, and Max smiled steadily back in what he thought was a hopeful way.

Le Grice was silent for a short while. He evidently couldn't make up his mind if Max was genuine. But then he said, 'You'd better come in then.' And stood aside to hold open the door.

The house was as dour and unwelcoming as Le Grice himself, with what Max could only define as a tombstone atmosphere, dampish, the mouldy smell seeming to emanate from the bare flagstones in the hall. The ground floor consisted of three octagonal-shaped rooms that ran into each other, none of them big enough to swing the proverbial cat. Rooms stuffed to suffocation point with what Max guessed were items brought from the Manor when they moved. And all far too big for their present environment.

There was a block-like mahogany sideboard, heavily carved, between the leaded windows. A huge, baroque mirror reflected the two or three ebony chairs and the green-striped sofa.

Le Grice took the chair by the empty fireplace and motioned Max into the one opposite. 'So – you've been visiting Aitken in his country house?' He laughed without mirth. 'What did you make of it? Were you impressed by the new décor?'

Max chose his words carefully. 'It's a trifle . . . florid for my taste.'

'Florid? Understatement of the year. They've ruined the place!'

'You've been inside, then, since you sold it to them?' Max asked casually.

Was that a flicker of unease in Le Grice's eyes? Suddenly he seemed dark and devious-looking. 'No, never,' he said abruptly. 'Swore I wouldn't.'

'Then how – '

'People talk,' Le Grice snapped. 'We've heard about it. Things get round.'

Max didn't say anything. Le Grice's best post-mortem voice sounded out again. 'They've destroyed all its English charm with their flashy notions. But the house will survive them . . . you'll see! It'll be itself again after they've gone. Which won't be long.'

Max wondered what grounds Le Grice had for this last statement. He shifted his backside on the hard ebony chair, trusting to some instinct that everything he wanted to know would emerge without being prompted, if he only waited.

Le Grice glared at the empty grate, which was thinly lined with newspaper. 'Aitken?' he said sarcastically. 'He's nothing! He'll sink without trace.'

His hands were shaking, Max noticed. Outside, the rain continued to slant down.

'Made a damned long-winded speech the other day . . .' He paused, looking over at Max. 'People get sick of the sound of his voice.'

'At the Eadfrith exhibition? You went, then?' Max asked.

'No. We didn't approve of it. Making a money-making circus out of a holy book . . .'

'Not even if it paid for the tower restoration?'

He made a dismissive gesture, shaking his head in disgust. 'The money would have come in somehow, without all that palaver. No, we didn't go to the blasted exhibition. Kept well away from it.'

'Would you mind me asking what you did instead?'

'Why should you want to know that? What's it to you?' Then, very slowly it dawned on him. 'My God, you think I slipped in there and poisoned the whisky! You think I killed Wetherell!'

'Of course not,' Max said; but he didn't let it sound altogether convincing. After a second or two had elapsed, he said, still conversationally, 'I just wondered what you meant by "kept well away from it"?'

'We went shopping in town,' someone said from the door-way. A female voice, quiet and hard.

Laura Le Grice shut the door behind her and came to stand behind her husband's chair. She was tall and dark, dressed in a greyish-blue jersey suit the same colour as the curtains and the rain.

'Who are you? What are you doing here?'

'He's a detective, Laura. Aitken's employing him.'

She stood there looking at Max silently for a moment. Then said sharply, 'Why should it make any difference where we were that afternoon?'

Her husband interceded before Max could open his mouth. 'They think we've been sending Larry hate mail. And generally being rather naughty.'

There was a pause before Laura said, 'Absolutely ridiculous!'

'Isn't it, but we'd better answer the young man's questions, or else he'll assume at once that we're guilty.'

13

Max gazed out of the Lodge window at the wild garden and the rain. He had a sudden impulse to take the conversation off at a tangent, so he said, 'I'm surprised that you sold to Aitken if you dislike him so much.'

Le Grice looked at him silently for a moment, but didn't take offence. Instead he said unexpectedly, 'He didn't seem so bad the first time the agent brought him. He seemed absolutely charming – and his wife was well bred. Well, I won't beat around the bush. You may as well know . . . we were in desperate trouble with the death duties and the income tax people. Then the roof wanted mending and I couldn't see any other way out of it at the time.'

'There wasn't one,' his wife said abruptly.

'You're quite right. There wasn't one.' Wearily, he said, 'So I instructed my solicitor to draw up the papers. Aitken came a second time – can't remember what his excuse was . . .'

'The cottages,' she reminded him.

He grunted. 'That's right. He didn't really want to buy the cottages. But I wasn't having the estate split up. He bought the lot or nothing, that's what I told him. The tenants depended on us, you see. I wouldn't have their homes sold piecemeal. Yuppies moving in and outpricing old Fred Salisbury and his like. Forcing them out into the street or into council places.'

'So you made him pay more than he wanted to?' Max asked.

A brief silence. Then Le Grice said, 'He could afford it.'

'And if he couldn't, too bad.' Laura met Max's gaze and her dark eyes were flint-like.

'He had the cottages done up, he tells me.'

Laura didn't have a response to that, but her husband said contemptuously, 'Brought jerry builders down from Swindon instead of using local people. Half the bathrooms are already developing mould . . .'

Max became aware of a snuffling, moaning noise somewhere

at the other end of the house. He glanced nervously round at the door, but no one else seemed to have noticed.

'So . . .' he said, fixing his mind back on the reason for his visit, 'you were shopping in town that afternoon? You didn't go to the exhibition?'

'No. We didn't.' Laura said it very quickly. Too quickly. With an almost physical sensation, Max knew she was hiding something.

'So how long were you in town, approximately?'

'We went in for lunch.'

Max saw Geoffrey look at her and grimace. For a moment, he seemed almost menacing. 'It was after lunch,' he corrected. 'Don't you remember? We finished up the beef.'

'The beef . . . Oh, yes.' Laura changed her story almost immediately. 'It was last week we had lunch in town. My mistake. This week we drove in at about two o'clock.'

'And which shops exactly did you visit? Would you be able to provide me with a list?'

'I think so. Let me see, we went to the antiques market opposite Bart's Bazaar. To Russell and Bromley, Liberty, Laura Ashley . . . And, yes, to Waitrose.' She looked at him with raised eyebrows. 'I've probably got the receipt somewhere if you actually need it.'

'It might be useful,' said Max. 'That's the entire list, is it?'

'That's all I can remember,' she said coldly.

'You didn't visit a chemist's shop? Boots, say?'

'No. Is there any particular reason why I should?'

'Amphetamines,' Le Grice said quietly.

'I don't imagine one can buy those over the counter, do you?'

Max was blatantly innocent. 'I wouldn't know,' he said. 'I was just wondering. You'll forgive me asking – ' Nice touch that, Max, he thought – 'but have either of you ever taken amphetamines as a stimulant?'

If anybody could do with it, he thought, it was these two.

'No, we most certainly have not!' Le Grice told him.

'So you wouldn't be familiar with their effects?'

'Not in the least.'

Another peculiar sound came from the next room. A high, agonized squealing sound that made Max's hair stand on end. The Le Grice ghost . . .?

'If you'll excuse me,' Laura said icily, 'I have to see to the dog.'

A dog! Max let out a long, inward sigh. Felt his pulse and blood pressure drop back down to normal.

'Ailing . . .' Geoffrey said when his wife had left the room. 'King Charles spaniel. We've had him for years. The vet's doing all he can – pills and such – but he's on his last legs. I don't know what Laura will do if he has to be put down. That dog's like a child to her.'

He got up abruptly and paced the room. 'Things might have been different – might have gone better for us – if we'd had a family of our own. But she can't have children. Lost three. Two miscarriages and a stillborn. A boy. We were going to call him William . . .'

Max looked down at his feet in commiseration.

'As it is . . .' Le Grice stood staring out of the window across the park to the Manor. 'As it is . . . well, it all gets a bit too much for her at times. I didn't say this while she was here. But she's under the doctor for her nerves. Had several bad bouts.' He said without turning round, 'Got nothing to do with all this lot, of course. Don't think that. But it's probably better that you should know.'

'Thanks,' Max said. He got up to leave. There didn't seem much else for him to ask at the moment. 'Keep my card,' he said. 'And if there's anything else you can think of that might be . . . useful, you can ring my office.'

Le Grice let him out and Max thanked him again for giving his time. As he walked down the path, he glanced back and up. Laura Le Grice was at an upstairs window, staring down at him.

No more expression on her face than on a peeled potato.

He knew one thing. He was glad to get out of the strange, dark atmosphere of the Lodge. He might be imagining it, but he'd felt a blackness there that was almost unbearable.

He was not surprised to find himself sweating, in spite of the sharp wind.

14

Laura picked up the pills that the vet had left for Fitz and
wondered why she had brought them up to the bedroom. The
detective, his eyes so darkly blue, had been very good-looking,
very charming, very watchful. And she felt physically sick –
sheer fear – now that he was gone.

Outside, it went on raining. She couldn't stand it when it hit
the windows like that. It made her think about the day they
had buried William. Must have a real funeral, the hospital had
said, with real mourning . . . otherwise you'll think you never
had him at all.

I wish I hadn't. At night, when I remember his little face . . .

Stop that, Laura. Stop it, do you hear?

She went into the bathroom and turned both the taps on
hard, so that Geoffrey would think she was cleaning. Then
stood for a moment at the top of the back stairs – there were
two sets, both difficult to manoeuvre, both dark and cramped –
to make sure that he wasn't going to come up. Shut up together
within such a narrow space, sometimes she felt like a penned
animal in a cage.

Not like when they had lived up at the Manor where, one
time, she had slept in each of the bedrooms by turns. Waking
up to a different view every morning for almost two weeks . . .

But now, all day long, Geoffrey clung to her with the tenacity
of an eel. And every day it felt as if someone had tied a new
knot in her stomach! And all the contents of this poky little hole
– socks, shirts, books, saucepans, a thousand *things* – came
pressing in on her . . .

'Laura? You up there?' His voice from below made her jump.
Made her pulse suddenly throb.

It required considerable effort to call back down, 'Yes. I'm
just . . . having a tidy.'

She was getting quite good at lying. Practice made perfect.

'This pie thing. Is it supposed to be in the oven?'

'I'll do it. In a minute. I'll be right down!'

She waited in the shabby, patchy light until she was sure he wasn't coming up . . . until her harsh breathing became easier. Then she moved swiftly across the landing and into the bedroom. The cupboard stood in the corner, high above the bed.

She had to force it open – everything here stuck with the damp . . .

It was the only place left to look. This was where it *had* to be.

Elizabeth liked the wind and the rain. They made the great trees thrash around, sent the yellow leaves flying out over the field. She watched them spinning now, as she picked up the phone.

It was ten minutes past one and she'd driven home to the cottage for a quick lunch. She didn't usually, but she'd had the feeling she might have left her spare keys in the front door. When she got back, she found that she hadn't. They were hanging on the board in the kitchen as usual; still, it meant that she could have a hot lasagne from the freezer for once instead of nibbling at a sandwich.

She dialled the number. It rang for a long time before anyone answered. She was on the point of putting the thing down when a voice suddenly said, 'South Harptree 224571. Rebecca Forbes speaking.'

'Mrs Forbes . . . my name is Elizabeth Blair. We've probably seen each other in the village. I run a patchwork shop – Martha Washington – down in town.'

'Oh, yes. The American . . .' Mrs Forbes sounded terminally bored. It was obvious that in her book Yank rhymed with septic tank.

'I wondered', Elizabeth said politely, 'if I might call and see you one afternoon? For a chat.'

'A chat?' For a moment, the line seemed to go completely dead. Then she said, 'Would you be trying to sell me something, by any chance?'

'Good lord, no.' Elizabeth was faintly amused. 'No. Actually, Max Shepard asked me to get in touch with you.'

'Max Shepard?'

'The young man who runs the detective agency above my shop. He's desperately busy this week and he's using me . . . well, a Man Friday, so to speak.'

After a long pause, she said, 'How long will this take?'

'Not longer than half an hour, I assure you. How would this afternoon suit you? Say four o'clock?'

'I suppose it will have to. Do you have my address?'

'The Beeches. It's at the bottom of Rectory Hill, isn't it?'

'I can see you've been doing your homework, Mrs . . .'

'Blair.'

'Mrs Blair.'

Elizabeth said, 'Actually, it's Max who does the homework. I'll see you at four then . . .'

'I'd be grateful if you were punctual,' Rebecca Forbes told her. 'I have to go out at four thirty.'

Elizabeth put the receiver down thoughtfully and went to fetch the lasagne from the freezer. She popped the plastic container into the microwave and wondered if it was just because of the surprise element that Rebecca hadn't sounded more curious. Hadn't once asked what this was about . . .

Porcelain-pale, Rebecca put down the receiver.

On the other side of the wall, the radio was talking to itself. A BBC voice read out the weather forecast. Spoke in sepulchral tones about a depression approaching from the south and variable winds.

The voice went on sending out messages, but she could no longer hear it . . .

The day had been odd and disjointed from the beginning. All morning she had had this unutterable longing to be back in Sydney. Back where the bay stretched for mile after mile . . . She could see it now when she closed her eyes. The shimmering silver sea . . . the blue sky and the oleander bush outside the long windows. Larry with his sweater knotted over his shoulders bending over her as she lay on the bed.

But memory couldn't hold her in the past. She always had to come back here to the deadly dull grey of the present tense.

She'd been convinced he was tired of Julia. Instead, he'd gone back to his *dear* wife and daughter! I deserve amnesia, at least, she told herself. Then, viciously, *he* doesn't deserve anything at all except a dose of the thumbscrews.

And now this awful Yank wanted to come and see her! What the hell were they on to?

She wished she could stop having nightmares about Wetherell. Nightmares in which he still lay there on the floor at her
feet, sweat running down his face into his open mouth.

She thought: I didn't feel sorry for him at all. The more he
suffered, the better really.

She looked at her scarlet fingernails for a while and then into
the middle distance. Told herself, 'She's only a damned American! Frightfully stupid, I shouldn't wonder.'

Of course you can put one over on her.

15

Max had been glad to get away from the Lodge, but once he
had shut the wicket gate on the Le Grices, he felt the claustro-
phobia evaporate. He would take a look round the orangery
while he was up there.

The rain seemed to be easing now as he sprinted the hundred
yards or so up the carriage sweep to the Manor. There was a
red Metro parked over on the far side of the house. Brenda
Macmillan's . . . tucked in at an angle where the steps led from
the terrace down to the formal Italian garden. The car was
spotless. Even the hub-caps had been polished until they
gleamed. Two floral cushions were propped at forty-five
degrees one each side of the rear window.

An obsession with cleanliness, Max thought, equals sexual
problems in childhood . . . Freud had said so. Or else some
television pundit almost as important. Jonathan Miller or Kilroy-
Silk . . .

As he approached the orangery from the shelter of the great
Turkey oak, he was struck by the fine proportions of the
structure. The three round-headed windows divided by Tuscan
columns, frostwork keystones ringing the main door. *The greenhouse*, Elizabeth's guidebook had informed them, *was an absolute
necessity for the fine gardens of the period, if only to store the orange,
myrtle and bay trees during the winter. During the summer, when
empty, it would become an airy garden house, adorned with pictures
and statues* . . .

'Feel free to come and poke round at any time,' Larry had said. 'I've told the staff who you are.' Nevertheless, Max felt somewhat of an intruder as he pushed open the end door and heard it give a long, ailing creak.

He closed the door behind him and shook the rain off his jacket. It was darkish over here in the corner. Half-hardy plants had already been brought in for the shelter; dahlia tubers lay in rows in a box. Julia was the gardener, or so they all told him . . .

Yes, he could imagine her sitting there in the tall-backed wicker chair, sorting out seed packets and instructing the boy on how, precisely, to clip the hedges. They'd have to have a boy or an old codger in to help. No one pair of hands kept gardens as extensive as these looking . . . well, like something you saw in the National Trust magazine.

He moved across the stone-flagged floor to the left-hand side of the orangery, where a wooden hay rake leaned ornamentally against an ancient wheelbarrow. There was an old pine cupboard for seeds, fertilizers, string and flowerpots. Vine fronds clung to the vaulted ceiling. Yes, thought Max, Julia would sit there and quietly direct things and Larry Aitken ('A bloody fortune I paid for this place!') would ponce in and try to lord it over her and Emily.

Emily! Here, Max's heart gave a distinct lurch as he remembered the layers of pure gold in her hair, the delicate pointed face almost like a boy's. Though there was nothing in the least bit boyish about that figure! He felt a pulse start to beat in his temples and succumbed to a long, sensual daydream about himself and the fair Emily . . .

At last he came back, albeit with some reluctance, to the real world. There was a particular door he was interested in – the door that must lead from the orangery into the main house.

He had one or two false starts before he found it. The first door in the left-hand wall led him into the murky recesses of a deep cupboard hung on both sides with hammers and trowels and fruit nets and shallow seed boxes. The second opened on to a tiny room hung top to bottom with dried flowers. Roses and honesty, larkspur and hydrangeas – it smelled like a hay harvest. The third door, however – the one at the far end, next to which, like a sentry, stood a very old, very shaggy palm tree

65

– gave him what he wanted: entrance to the main corridor that bisected the house.

Here was the cool, broad passageway he had walked down on his first visit to the Manor. Green carpet, heavily panelled walls and a double line of doors.

Max stood there and listened. The house remained silent as the grave. There didn't seem to be anyone about. Not that he felt any real guilt about being there – he was on Larry's pay roll, after all. But he'd just as soon take his second look along the ground floor unaccompanied by the tiresome (and tiring) Macmillan woman.

He made his way up the steps and along the passage, opening doors silently as he went. Found himself once more in the billiards room and then the small breakfast room with its grey-marbled fireplace. The study was, as before, entirely lined with books (were they read?). There was a glass-fronted cupboard containing double-barrelled shotguns, a bust of Charlie Chaplin and rather a garish portrait (Julia's?) of Aitken himself hanging over the chimneypiece.

The walls of the dining-room were cherry-brandy red flock. Two large, gold Buddhas guarded the bulbous mahogany sideboard. Max grimaced when he saw the elaborate chandelier ponderous enough to grace the palace of Versailles. He muttered to himself, 'A bit over the top, *old son*, don't you think?'

The drawing-room was at the far end on the left, but that was one room that he didn't need to re-examine. He made the return journey to the orangery as silently as he had come. Congratulated himself for proving the theory that it was perfectly possible to slip into the house via the orangery and leave again without being spotted.

But it was as he was passing back through the door into the orangery that Max made the most interesting discovery of the morning. In fact, he felt so delighted with his find that he allowed himself a spot of lunch at the Barley Wagon before going back to town.

He was not so delighted with life at two thirty that afternoon when Phoebe refused to start and he was forced to manhandle her down the road to the garage for first aid.

'More holes than a string vest, mate!' was the mechanic's candid opinion of Phoebe's radiator.

'Surprised you're still here!' he said of her brakes.

But Max was damned if he was going to abandon her on the advice of a biased little mechanic who played Bros tapes.

He said, 'There's miles in her yet! She's a long way from giving out on me for good and all.'

By three thirty that afternoon, Brenda Macmillan had finished most of her work. She was sitting in her box-like office knitting.

Larry's demands on her were not really too arduous. This morning she'd finished typing up the second chapter of a book of backstage misadventures that he was compiling.

'It's a fascinating project,' she'd commented when a publisher had suggested it.

'It's a load of old cobblers, darling,' Larry had told her. 'But as long as it brings in a few bob . . .'

That was the thing about Larry. He was so down to earth, in spite of his fame and fortune.

All morning it had been raining. But now, although the light was still dingy, a tranquil sun was beginning to break through. She picked up what she thought was her pattern, but found that it was the poster advertising Emily's mid-term production. *As You Like It* in Edwardian dress with Emily playing Rosalind. Well, let's hope she's better than the last thing we saw her in, she thought, giving her wool a sharp tweak. Emily! It was as though someone had stuck a sharp hatpin into Brenda's heart. The little madam had but a hundredth part of her father's charm and talent. Did she think Larry's name would open all doors for her? No one's going to hand you success on a plate, she'd informed Emily once – and had been told for her trouble to mind her own business.

Positively nasty, that girl could be when she felt like it. Oh, yes, a real spoiled brat! What she needed was discipline . . . Julia tried now and again. Had positively mounted guard, the other night, outside Emily's bedroom door. Refused to let her out of the house until she would say where she was going and with whom – but it was too little and too late. Emily had eventually supplied the necessary information, but then she could lie to her mother in the most calculated way when it suited her.

Brenda's thin lips pursed as she found her pattern and turned the page. How she would like to take the girl down a peg or two!

What was it that Emily had said to her a month or two back? She had been suffering somewhat. Had poured herself a *tiny* medicinal nip from the decanter in the drawing-room. Emily had walked in unexpectedly.

'Caught you, did I? Does Daddy know you pinch his whisky?'

'I'm not feeling too well,' Brenda had told her. 'A touch of flu, possibly . . .'

'And did you have flu last week as well? And the week before that?'

Damn the girl's insolence! Well, what if she did have a little nip now and then, Brenda asked herself. She deserved it, didn't she, for keeping this great place ticking over?

At this point a thought struck her. What if it had been Emily who had tampered with the decanter and caused old Wether-ell's death? What if . . .

It was then, as she sat there thinking, that she heard the sound from the passage. The soft click of a door.

Strange, she thought. They're all out.

Larry and Emily were in town. Julia had driven down to the gallery for the afternoon.

It came again – someone moving softly, furtively, down by the orangery.

So who could it be? She picked up a heavy book. Tiptoed down to look.

No one was there. But the orangery door was slightly ajar.

16

Elizabeth had that minute come to the conclusion that Rebecca Forbes was the kind of Englishwoman she disliked most of all.

The kind who made you feel round-shouldered and inferior. Her accent ladled out with a Georgian silver spoon . . . hall-marked, of course.

They stood facing each other across a small, square coffee table. Rebecca had perfect bones and she wore a black suit with an ivory blouse and extremely high heels. 'Get down, Bambi!' she said. 'There's a good girl.' The white poodle had come yapping at the door as soon as Elizabeth rang the bell. A nasty-looking little thing that scratched everything it touched.

'Get *down*, Bambi! I won't tell you again.'

Bambi? Summed up the whole place, Elizabeth thought. Itsy-bitsy ornaments and a salmon pink velvet sofa. A Greek urn thing full of heavily arranged flowers stood on the glass-fronted bookcase. On the table in front of them lay a mushy novelette and a copy of *Good Housekeeping*. When did women like Rebecca ever keep house, for God's sake?

'Let me take your coat.'

Elizabeth slipped off her tweed jacket and watched Rebecca lay it on the back of a mock Chippendale chair.

'It's not a Burberry,' Rebecca said with the lightest of laughs.

'I'm sorry?'

'I said you're not wearing a Burberry.'

'Is it obligatory?'

'My little joke,' Rebecca explained sweetly. 'It seems to be the uniform for most American tourists. A Burberry worn with trousers and comfy shoes.'

'I'm not a tourist,' Elizabeth pointed out in a mirror-image of Rebecca's tone. No offence taken. Just light amusement.

'So you're not. I forgot,' Rebecca said with the merest touch of acid. 'Do sit down.'

OK, honey, Elizabeth thought. So I've got your number. You're a pussy-cat with claws. A pussy-cat who knows all the rules of the game and has no qualms about breaking them. But actually I quite like it when people are rude to me. It liberates something inside me . . . lets me have fun being rude back. She leaned over and picked up the pink-covered book. '*A Heart in Torment . . .*' she said brightly. 'I didn't think anyone read Barbara Cartland in this day and age.'

Rebecca said, 'I was sorting some stuff for Oxfam. It . . . must have got left behind.'

Elizabeth laughed. 'No one will ever admit to reading her. Isn't it amazing?'

'What was it you came to see me about?' Rebecca snapped.

Elizabeth explained why Larry Aitken was employing Max.

'We . . . wondered how much you knew about this hate campaign against Mr Aitken.'

Rebecca hesitated. 'I know he's been getting letters and phone calls. Julia told me.'

'Did she go into detail?'

'No. All I know is that it's been going on for a while. But then, everyone gets funny phone calls from time to time.'

'Do they?'

'Oh, yes, it's quite common. We had a heavy breather a few years back. Most people have been through it, only you don't realize until it happens to you.'

'So Mr Aitken never spoke to you about it?'

'No. I don't think so.' Rebecca gazed at her without batting an eyelid.

'I was just curious,' Elizabeth said neutrally, and then decided to bring in the big guns. 'Only . . . certain rumours seem to be flying round about you and him.'

'What sort of rumours?' Rebecca's bold-eyed gaze twitched with nerves for the first time. 'I don't particularly like your prying questions, Mrs Blair. I'd like to know what any of it has got to do with you. If Mr Shepard's on the case, why didn't he come here himself?'

'Max and I are in partnership, Mrs Forbes,' Elizabeth heard herself saying. 'And he asked me to say that you'd do better to talk to us now about the . . . relationship between you and Mr Aitken rather than have the police involved. We're much more discreet, you know. That's why Mr Aitken employed us.'

'Well, he does usually know how to control the publicity.' You could see the ice thaw and something else begin to take its place. A flow of charm. Apparently, she had decided it was better to co-operate. 'Tea . . .' she said, springing up with a suddenness that almost overturned the coffee table. 'I'm forgetting my manners. Would you like some tea?'

'That would be very nice . . . if it's no trouble.'

Rebecca promptly escaped to the kitchen, probably glad of the chance to work on her story. When she came back, five minutes later, it was to play the gracious hostess, bringing in a silver tray, fluted china cups and a Marks and Spencer's chocolate cake. Elizabeth sat there for a while amused by it all.

She sipped her tea. 'I believe you're quite a committee lady?' she said.

'I am actually. Who told you?'

'My neighbour, Miss Marchant.'

'Ah . . . Dottie.' Rebecca made a face. 'Yes, I'm on several committees, as it happens. The Dogs' Home. Save the Children.'

'The St Swithin's Roof Fund . . .'

'The St Swithin's Roof Fund.' She shrugged. 'You have to do something with your time.'

'You don't have a family? Children?'

'No. They never happened. I'd have been a lousy mother anyway. Far too impatient. And you?' Rebecca cooed. 'Do you have a family back in the States?'

'Three sons and a daughter.'

'Gosh! You must miss them!' She was settled in the corner of the sofa, cup in lap. For the first time, she looked completely at her ease. She must have got her story absolutely watertight.

Her grey-shaded eyes were bright as she gazed at Elizabeth over the top of her cup. 'You wanted to know about my relationship with Larry,' she said.

'I think it would be as well.'

'He seduced me in Sydney. Oh, I know that sounds melodramatic, but it's exactly what happened. I think he was quite simply bored that night. He didn't have anything else to do, didn't have any other female interest lined up, for once, so he made up his mind to bed me. I'm sorry to say he's like that.'

'Was it a pleasurable experience?' Elizabeth asked drily.

'At the time, yes. I have to admit it.'

'That sounded rueful. Do I take it that the affair's now over?'

'Good God, yes! But I'll admit something else. I didn't want it to end – at the time.'

'He finished it?'

'Dropped me like a hot cake as soon as we got back to England. Too dangerous, he said, to keep it going in a place this size. He daren't upset Julia again.'

'Again?'

'Didn't you know? She caught him in bed with their secretary a year or two back. Threatened to leave him and sell the story to the papers if he wasn't a good boy from now on.'

71

'Brenda Macmillan?' Elizabeth's cup slipped and she almost had her tea in her lap. Trying to recover her sang-froid, she thought, so you got one over on me this time, but you don't have to sit there like the Cheshire Cat looking so goddamned smug.

'Oh, I know you wouldn't believe it.' Rebecca helped herself to a slice of chocolate cake and began cutting it into tiny squares with the bone-handled tea knife. 'Brenda's as clumsy as a carthorse with a face to match. But Larry's immensely vain, you know. He'd hate any female to escape his clutches. And I mean *any* female.'

'But – surely Julia would never have let her stay on? The secretary, I mean?'

'He begged her not to take it out on Brenda apparently. All his fault, he said. Completely stupid of him. Wouldn't happen again, he promised. And Julia being Julia . . .'

'Forgave and forgot?'

'Forgave anyway.' Rebecca said, 'So you see I was only one from a long line of women he loved and ditched.' There was a brightly coloured artificiality about her voice. 'Oh, I had dreams of romance, I'll admit that. Dreams of him getting rid of Julia and installing me as his new wife at the Manor. Wouldn't you?'

Elizabeth didn't think so somehow.

'I was so damned stupid! I honestly thought it would carry on when we came back to England. If he'd wanted to break the news to Julia gently, then I was prepared to wait. I'd have met him in London for a while. He's got a flat in Kensington, you know. He calls it his bolt-hole. Says he uses it for business . . . But Larry never had any intention of forming a serious relationship.' She gave a hard, brittle laugh. 'I was just a bit on the side.'

Elizabeth put her cup down.

'I can't imagine how he could ever have married Julia in the first place, can you? A dowdy, namby-pamby clergyman's daughter . . . but I suppose she attached herself to him like a trailing plant . . .'

How you hate her, Elizabeth thought. And Larry. She said, 'The day Dr Wetherell died . . . the day of the exhibition. Did you go to the Manor? Actually into the house, I mean?'

'I knew you were going to ask that when we got to the bottom

72

line.' Rebecca was gazing at her no longer with animosity but almost with resignation. 'Yes, I was in the house. But not during the exhibition hours. I went up there earlyish in the morning and slipped in.'

'What time exactly?'

'Let me see. I got up at about eight. Bob had left the house by then. I opened the post. Made coffee . . . Then I took the dog out, but that didn't make me feel any better . . .'

'You felt ill?'

'No. Just savage. I'd woken up feeling savage and it wouldn't go away. So in the end, I made up my mind to go up there and see him. Larry. And I walked up to the Manor – it must have been at about nine thirty – through the woods. There's a track. I had to see him. I didn't even bother to put on my glad rags. I was in slacks and flat shoes. Bob mustn't know this, you realize? I don't want it to get out.'

'Of course,' Elizabeth said. 'And when you say "slipped in" . . . What exactly do you mean?'

'I went in by the side door. The one that leads in through the orangery. Well, I wasn't going to use the front door, was I? I knew Julia had gone down to the studio to light the wood stove.'

'You're familiar with their movements then?'

'Everyone knows Julia spends a lot of time down there. Larry broadcasts it. Not because he likes what she paints, but because he likes people to know his wife is an artist.' A sarcastic laugh. 'Anyway, I went in by the side door.'

'Did anyone see you? Say the secretary . . .'

'Brenda? No. She'd gone off to post some letters in the village. I waited round the back of the Schoolhouse until she'd gone.'

'So the coast was entirely clear?' Elizabeth wondered how often Rebecca Forbes had tucked herself away and watched the house.

'Yes. And then I went straight to Larry's study.'

'You're familiar with the house?'

'Yes.'

'And Larry was waiting for you?'

'Good lord, no! I took him entirely by surprise.'

'Was he pleased to see you?'

73

'Not exactly. He told me to go and take a running jump. His actual words were, "What the hell are you doing here? I'm expecting someone."' A hard laugh. 'He's like that, you know. Hard as nails once you've exceeded your sell-by date.'

'So you had a row?'

'A bloody awful one, I have to admit it.'

'And?'

'And in the end he practically threw me out on my ear.' She picked up a square of chocolate cake and popped it into her beautifully shaped mouth. Elizabeth thought, either you're the coldest woman I ever met or the most accomplished liar. I wish I knew which.

She looked for a moment into Rebecca's well-insulated face and then she said, 'Did you go anywhere near the drawing-room while you were there?'

'No. The drawing-room's on the other end of the house. Way past the study . . .' Rebecca's gaze was needle-sharp. 'And if you're asking me – I probably would have put something in his whisky, the mood I was in, if the thought had occurred to me. But it didn't. I can't prove it, though. Anything else?'

'One more thing. Did you have . . . have you ever had in your possession any amphetamines?'

'*I* didn't. No.'

Now what did that mean? The extra emphasis on the *I*? Elizabeth watched the other woman's face unsmilingly. 'Are you implying that you know someone who did?'

'I'm not implying anything. I'm telling you.'

'Telling me what exactly, Mrs Forbes?'

'That Larry took them. Didn't he tell you?'

'Not that I recall. Are you sure of your facts?'

There was triumph and amusement on her face in equal measure. She said, 'He kept quiet about it then, did he? The devious sod! He took amphetamines – pep pills – to help him get through his *onerous* schedule of engagements. To keep him awake when he had to work into the small hours. To zap himself up when he was feeling like death. I've seen them in his hotel room. I know he took them.'

17

Geoffrey Le Grice forced his wife to sit down and fetched her a
brandy. He had dealt with her in this kind of state – panic
mingled with hysteria – many times. Unless he got her to talk it
out of her system at once, she was liable to cut herself off from
him for weeks.

'So tell me, Laura. Spit it out. What's wrong?'

At last she did.

She had plunged out of the Lodge quite suddenly at three
that afternoon, while he was taking his nap. Suddenly she
couldn't stand it any longer. Couldn't bear sitting there worry-
ing, with the clock ticking and her mind racing on past it . . .
overwound and overcharged. She'd run out of the Lodge so
quickly, she'd forgotten to change into her outdoor shoes and
bits of gravel kept getting into her light leather slippers and
cutting her as she ran.

At least it had stopped raining, though the trees were still
dripping.

She'd gone round by the path that looped its way round the
kitchen garden and back to the orangery. There was less danger
of being seen that way. She heard a rumble of thunder in the
distance as she got to the Turkey oak.

Something had snapped over by the french windows, but
when she glanced over her shoulder, it was only a thrush with
a snail in its beak, smacking away with it on one of the
flagstones. Crack, crack, crack . . . Poor snail. Fractures all over,
then a messy end.

None of the windows had a face at them. They might be in
there or they might not. But she had to take the risk. She didn't
have an option.

There was a gap of ten feet or so between the oak and the
Tuscan column at the end of the orangery. Too easy, she
thought, slipping like a shadow from one round-headed
window to the next, counting as she did so. *Two, three, four* . . .
She had already made up her mind what she was going to say

if she were caught. She'd lost Fitz. Had seen him go in through the half-open door. Had to catch him before he did any damage to the orchids . . .

The door creaked as she let herself in.

The orangery had always had unhappy memories for Laura. There she had told Geoffrey that there was no chance at all of her ever having children. There, in the corner, he'd sat trying desperately not to look as if he cared. Just the smell of the place – glassed-in heat and potted earth – made her feel nauseous. But she took a hold on herself and concentrated on the job in hand.

She had to find what she'd come for – and get out fast! She would have sworn that the palm tree was bigger last time she had seen it. Bigger and much more spiky than this moth-eaten thing . . . The earth in the pot was dry and crumbling. She imagined it holding little bits of bone and dried-up dead insects and shrank as she thrust her trembling fingers into it . . .

Dear God, it was no longer there!

As she began to search the upper branches, a confusion of voices began in her head. 'It was here, I know it was.' *Find it and they won't be able to prove anything.* I know they won't. Only a matter of keeping mum then, no matter what any of them say. *And not letting anybody else into the place to ask questions.*

But it had gone.

Now, for the first time, her stomach truly cramped with the realization. Someone else had found it. Someone else knew. And sooner rather than later, would be knocking on the door . . .

Max crossed into the narrow passage that led to Pierrepont Mews and tossed a 10p coin at the busker who was playing Vivaldi. He had forgotten about the exorbitant bill for Phoebe's medicine. He was walking on air.

He stopped briefly at the fudge shop, bought a quarter of rum and raisin and bit contentedly into one. It was late afternoon and the buildings had turned that deep, improbably yellow ochre only to be seen when the sun comes out after rain.

He couldn't wait to tell Elizabeth. She'd never believe it! Max took Elizabeth's joshing about the half-baked way he ran his business pretty well, on the whole. But deep down he had this urge to solve just *one* case in a manner that would rock her back on her all-American heels.

He let his mind run back over the events of the last twenty-four hours. He'd had the most incredible stroke of luck. For under a tacky old palm tree in the orangery, he had found a small, antique bracelet. Twisted gold with the most exquisite clasp in the design of a bird, very distinctive . . . He was certain he'd seen something similar somewhere before, but couldn't place where. Of course, the proper thing would have been to take it straight to Larry – but instead he'd chosen to tote it round one or two jewellers' shops in the city.

He'd drawn a blank at first, but at last a select, old-fashioned establishment in New Bond Street had recognized it. The proprietor was a squat little man with gold-rimmed half-moons. Yes, he could look up the name and address, if Max wanted to return it to its owner . . .

Max couldn't wait to see Elizabeth's face.

He was going to enjoy her expression.

Elizabeth was right in the middle of her sales talk when Max burst into the shop. 'The Broken Star design is an eight-pointed star, sometimes known as the Double Star or the Dutch Rose,' she explained to the customer, warning Max off with a frantic spread of her hand behind her back. 'It really is the loveliest quilt I've had in for months. Made by Ellen Thompson in Turkey Creek, Virginia. Mrs Thompson is one of the finest craftswomen on the mountain . . .'

Max was still mouthing something to her, but she continued to ignore him. 'Mrs Thompson quilts and keeps chickens,' she went on cheerfully. 'She's eighty-one years old now and lives in a white board house on the site of the dug-out of the original homestead.'

'I've got something to tell you,' Max said in her ear as she leaned over to turn up the gas. She'd had a fireplace put in when the shop was renovated. For safety reasons, it was one of those artificial jobs with mock logs and an everlasting flame; but it was set high in the wall and had a pretty ironwork grate round it and people seemed to like it. You could see them admiring it. It put them into a good, *buying* mood.

'Ditto,' she hissed. 'But it'll have to wait.' She could see the

77

customer fingering the quilt lovingly and had this gut feeling she was going to make a sale.

'How much?' the woman asked.

'I'm afraid it's rather expensive – but what you're really buying is an heirloom, don't you think? I can deliver,' she promised, after foraging for the price tag. 'It's no trouble at all. In fact, I like to bring them myself to make sure they get to their new homes safe and sound . . .'

It was twenty-five minutes to six when the customer left. Max managed to tear himself away from a less than absorbing *Dictionary of Textiles* and hopped over to put the catch down.

'So what is it, you nuisance?' Elizabeth said.

He smiled sweetly and told her to be patient. 'So how did you get on at the Forbes residence?' he asked.

'I've had better afternoons,' she told him. 'The lady followed a good old English tradition. You can be infinitely rude to someone as long as you don't raise your voice . . .'

'She gave you a hard time . . .'

'Stop grinning, you jerk. She has this way of looking down her nose at you.'

'That wouldn't be hard,' Max said, eyeing Elizabeth's five foot two inches.

'A kind of insolence . . .' Something struck her. 'I'm beginning to talk like the English. I'm wrapping things up instead of coming out with the straight, unpalatable truth . . . Rebecca Forbes is a bitch!'

'She was very nice to me,' Max said, po-faced.

'You realize it's the reason you have so many good actors in this country?'

'Rebecca pouring herself all over me?'

'No. The way the English hide their emotions behind pretty phrases. Tell lies as a polite reflex . . . "Yes, I *will* have another cup of tea, thank you," when you're spitting inside.'

She decided to tell him about Larry's affair with La Macmillan.

At first he didn't believe her. 'She's lying.'

'I don't think so. I figure she's an accomplished liar, but not on this one.'

'Did she have anything to do with the hate mail or the whisky?'

'It's possible. She can be vicious.' Elizabeth sounded momentarily thoughtful. 'And she knows her way up to the Manor via a track through the woods.'

'So she *could* have laid the poison that killed his dog?'

'She *could* have. Though I'm not absolutely sure. She belongs to the Kennel Club, you see, and judging by the way she spoils that nasty little lapdog of hers, she's nuts about our canine friends.' She changed the subject. 'So . . . what's this secret you were bursting to tell me?'

'Oh . . . nothing much.'

Playing hard to get, she thought, and picked up her keys. 'OK – time to go home,' she said on her way to the door.

That did it. 'I found a bracelet in the orangery,' Max said quickly. 'It belongs to Laura Le Grice. Matched the brooch she was wearing the morning I called on them. I *knew* she had a twitchy look in her eyes when they were answering my questions. I knew she was hiding something! They said they hadn't been inside the Manor since they sold the place – but this proves that they're lying.'

'How do you know she didn't drop it there when they lived at the Manor?'

'They moved out two years ago,' Max said. 'It would have been caked in dust and cobwebs by now. But it was in good shape and shining. Besides . . .' His eyes gleamed. This was obviously his *pièce de résistance*. 'She had it mended only two months ago. The catch had a weak link, the jeweller said. So what do you think of that?'

He sat there grinning at her. She caught some of the excitement behind his words and smiled at last. 'OK, Max, you've got me. So, what are you going to do about it?'

'I'm going back there to confront them with the evidence, of course. Tomorrow.'

18

Laura Le Grice, unable to sleep, lay beside her husband listening to the dawn chorus and remembering the early days of their marriage. The Le Grice family had been on its way down even then, she recalled, but she hadn't cared. She'd been very much in love with Geoff and it was the young Guards officer she was marrying, not the ancestral home.

How he'd loved the army! Military glory – trumpets and great armies and glittering squadrons wheeling on the parade ground . . . that was what the Le Grices had stood for, century after century. Geoffrey hadn't actually faced combat, of course. Not like Charles Le Grice (1599–1643) who had raised a troop of horse at his own expense for the King and been killed by a Roundhead colonel at the battle of Stamford Hill. Or William Le Grice (1789–1815), a superb and reckless horseman, who fell at the Battle of Waterloo while leading a charge.

No battle honours for Geoff . . . *His* years in the army had been spent directing tank exercises and regimental dinners in post-war Germany, but they'd been happy there in the early years of their marriage, just the two of them . . . Until what she had come to think of as the dark and gigantic forces had started to move against them.

Geoff's father had been selling priceless objects from the house even then, to try and keep his head above water . . .

To keep the house going for the next generation.

But it was a useless effort; he may as well not have bothered. The debts had been out of this world and there was to be no next generation. She didn't know how Geoff had remained calm through it all. But that was his way. Even last night, he'd assured her that everything would be all right.

No one would ever be able to pin anything on them. He'd make sure of that.

But still she felt the black crows settling on her spirits.

At 8.15 a.m. Geoffrey brought the porridge from the kitchen into the tiny dining-room. A wood fire slowly smoked in the grate. Outside, all the clouds had cleared away. It was going to be a clear day if not a fine one.

Fitz had stopped whining and lay exhausted in his basket. Geoffrey thought: Have to be the vet in the end, I suppose. The last sad trip . . .

He gave a split-second glance in his wife's direction. Poor old Laura! He gazed at her once-lovely oval face across the table, at her brooding dark eyes. That piercing glance of hers, once so lively . . .

He hadn't wanted it to end like this.

But the game could turn rough unless he acted.

He pressed a napkin to his mouth and put down his coffee cup. 'I think it has to be today,' he said quietly, and watched Laura's face give him a sick look in return.

At eleven that morning, he came out of the front door carrying a bundle wrapped in a blanket. He took a furtive look round before leaving the safety of the latticed porch – but only the statue of a small Roman god with a chipped nose stared back at him from the overgrown lawn.

All around him was the raw smell of rotting leaves and yesterday's rain. A wood-pigeon called from the top of the horse chestnut on the edge of the woods. There was no other sign of life.

He risked the short distance between the porch and the station wagon and stowed the bundle in the boot.

Locked it firmly before returning to the Lodge to dig out an overnight bag from the hidy-hole underneath the stairs.

19

At the library in the Podium, Elizabeth waited at the enquiries desk for Angela to return from showing another reader where to find 840.72 (biographies of Pavarotti). At eleven fifteen in the morning, the place was already busy with browsers and a good number of old dears who had come for the conversation.

She looked forward to her weekly encounter with Angela. The girl was, in Elizabeth's opinion, ever so slightly loopy. Well, it takes one to know one, she thought as she rummaged in her bag for the name of the book she wanted to order. Me and my crazy thing about Robert Lightfoot. Angela and her paranoia about the boss . . .

'Mrs Blair! Sorry to keep you waiting.' Angela wore her

flowered corduroy blouse and her kilt. Her enthusiasm showed in the way she adjusted her glasses and her smile.

'Hi. How're you doin'?' Elizabeth said. She never ever addressed anyone else in this way, but Angela expected it. It was their little private joke. Elizabeth always said, 'Hi, how're you doin'?', and Angela always replied, as she did now, with a little giggle, 'I'm doin' fine, thank you, Mrs Blair. I'm having a good day.'

'How's Mr Brown?' Elizabeth enquired next.

'Don't talk about him!' Angela said. So they did. Mr Brown, who had only been put in charge of the place six months ago, and who was making Angela's life hell, had taken it into his head to ban her Friends of the Earth collecting tin. And yesterday he'd told her off for making an emergency phone call to the vet about her cat, who had a very nasty stomach infection.

'Never mind,' Elizabeth said. 'Perhaps he'll decide to emigrate like I did.'

'Fat chance!' Angela said inelegantly. Then, gazing at the piece of paper Elizabeth had given her, 'Your other book came in.'

'Which one's that?'

'*Bristol Emigration Records of the Seventeenth and Eighteenth Centuries.* Not many laughs there, Mrs B.'

'You might be surprised,' Elizabeth said. She looked round as if to check that no one was listening. 'Can I trust you, Angela?' she asked.

'Course you can. Why?' Angela looked a mite apprehensive.

'There aren't many laughs,' Elizabeth said confidentially, 'but I'm told that in Chapter Five there are a number of naughty bits . . .'

'Gosh! Really?' Angela said, and viewed the tome – and Elizabeth – with a new eye.

It must have been her day for loopy people, because when she got back to Martha Washington, she found Dottie Marchant prowling round the shop.

'I thought I'd like to take a squint,' she said. 'This place used to sell corsets, you know, in the old days. You spent half the morning here, what with all the measuring and fitting . . .'

'How fascinating,' Elizabeth said.

'There was a pastry-cook's across the way. Crabby old soul owned it. How much is this cushion cover?'

Elizabeth told her.

'As much as that?' Dottie was shocked. 'Then I rather think it's a good thing I make my own! We were taught embroidery as children, you know. I'm not *fond* of it, but one has to do something in the winter evenings.' Leaping from subject to subject with gay abandon, as usual, she said, 'My dear father died when I was very young.'

'I'm so sorry,' Elizabeth said.

'No need. We children scarcely ever saw him when he was alive. We were in bed when he went off early to his office in the City and in bed again by the time he came home late at night. The only time we got a sighting of him was on Sunday at luncheon.'

Elizabeth said thoughtfully, 'I guess it still happens.' Her mind hopped to Larry Aitken and Emily. How much time could a star give his daughter, between the plays and the TV shows and pantomimes and charity events . . .?

'That's a jolly colour,' Dottie said, touching the red calico of an Album quilt.

'Isn't it? Turkey red. The dye reached America in 1829 and red and white quilts became very popular for a while.'

There was a moment's pause and then Dottie said in a complete non-sequitur, 'Have you had any trouble with mice? I only ask because I've got a plague of them! I'm convinced that they're coming in from those old stone sheds on the other side of the Manor wall.'

'Mice?' Elizabeth looked startled.

'The end shed butts on to my outhouse, you know. That's where they're coming from! I shall have to go and see him.'

'His Nibs . . .?'

'Exactly! I've been thinking . . . It all began the night after that Emily girl had her party. Don't you remember? Disco lights, music blasting out till all hours – and the language, my dear . . .!'

'I missed that particular episode,' Elizabeth said. 'I was in London visiting a friend, remember?'

'It's my belief that they left bags of refuse in the grounds,' Dottie said. 'Students, His Nibs called them. Not much studying

83

going on that night, I told him! Sex mad, if you ask me. I could see it all going on from my bathroom window . . . I heard the Macmillan woman describe the girl as *unbalanced*,' Dottie confided. 'But then, I dare say it takes one to know one . . .'

She took herself off to catch the bus home. A plague of mice! Elizabeth gave a gentle shudder. What would it be next, she wondered. Frogs or locusts?

Twelve noon. Max was suffering from a hangover as he sat staring at his computer screen. Shouldn't have celebrated last night, he thought. Definitely shouldn't have started (God, his eyes!) on the Budweiser.

He pressed the EXIT button, followed by ENTER and waited for the document to finish editing. Thank God he only had one call to make today!

The office was a bare, longish room with a creaky floor. Apart from his second-hand desk, the furniture consisted of two chairs and an old upright piano inherited from the previous occupants. Presumably they hadn't been able to think of a way to get it back down the corkscrew staircase. How anybody had got it up here in the first place beggared all thought. But a piano did add that vital touch of . . . well, class!

On the window sill there were three Mars bars and a box of aspirin. He thought about taking a couple, but couldn't face levering himself up out of the chair.

He tapped a few paragraphs into the Aitken file. Entered a description of the antique bracelet . . . the name and address of its owner. But then the damned machine bleeped at him and started to speed backwards, without warning, to the top of the document.

He decided to close his eyes while it went on its travels.

He didn't actually hear the door open behind him until Elizabeth's voice said, 'You *are* up here! It was so deathly quiet . . .'

'I think I'm here,' he told her. 'I may yet be proved wrong.'

'Bad as that, eh?' she said drily. Then, 'This place smells like a brewery! I'll open the window.'

'No – don't!' It wasn't that he minded the fresh air, which might have done him good. It was just that he couldn't face, at this particular moment, the thumping and bumping it would take to force the sash up. 'Hangover,' he explained in a ghost of his normal voice.

'Try raw egg and oatmeal,' Elizabeth told him. 'It'll shift it in minutes – one way or the other.'

Sometimes she was just plain sadistic, he thought as he rapdily vacated the premises.

Coaxing the reluctant Phoebe out into the traffic, he waited for the pressure filling his head to evaporate. Last night he'd been dying to get on with the job. Now he was dreading it. It was the same old story . . .

'Too sensitive, my son!' old Ackroyd, his ex-boss, had said. Max could see the bastard's eyes now, bright and hard, boring into his own. 'People are crazy, nasty, perverted liars,' he had said. 'We prove it over and over. But it doesn't mean you have to piss yourself every time you tell them so.'

It was true. Nevertheless, Max's nerves continued to jump.

He arrived at the Lodge just in time to catch Geoffrey Le Grice on his way out.

20

Julia Aitken, trailing back to the house for lunch from her studio, noticed Max's heap of rust parked down by the Lodge and wondered vaguely if it was time for the Pilton pop festival.

But it wasn't May or June, she told herself. It was October. Charles Wetherell's untimely demise was playing havoc with her memory and her nerves. Plus all those blood-sucking reporters surrounding the house . . . They had no shame, no pity, no morals, any of them! Yesterday one had got as far as the front door and stayed there for ages hauling away at the bell.

She dragged off her smock, bundled it into a tight ball and hugged it like a baby. If there was one thing she'd always hated about being married to Larry, it was living your life in the full glare of publicity.

Hearing the sidelong whisper, 'That's Larry Aitken . . .' wherever you went. People staring and nudging each other in restaurants, egging each other on to ask for his autograph. 'It's for my mother, actually. She thinks your show's *wonderful!*' How many perfectly good meals had been ruined in that way?

It was inescapable. It was like living as some rare zoo animal!

She still couldn't believe Charles Wetherell was dead. She'd been scared witless at first that they were going to arrest Larry and charge him with murder. They'd kept him at the station an unconscionably long time and asked a mass of questions. But it hadn't happened, thank goodness. In time, perhaps, the rumpus would blow over. She tried to make herself believe it, but this morning it felt like being on the inside of a nightmare. Macabre. Oddly telescopic . . .

She stopped by the herb border. Behind her, the woods and the fields spread towards Bath. Doves called in the trees. A wan smile passed over her face as she admired the thyme and wild marjoram and a late clump of lavender at the bottom of the terrace steps. All those tiny seed heads . . . beautifully ridged and jagged . . . a deeper mauve down towards the stems.

Temporarily she felt comforted by the plants.

But then the sense of displacement came back. With a cold feeling round her heart, she thought: The garden will never be the same again. Whatever peace I found here has been destroyed. And all at once there swept over her a sudden, swift nostalgia for the world of her childhood, for her father's tranquil world of books and sermons. For a household in which any kind of excess, emotional or material, had been heartily frowned on . . . Pa had been dead five years now and she missed him. He'd been tough on her when she was younger -- not at all the indulgent father that Larry was to Emily – but of late she had begun to appreciate his quiet wisdom, his dry humour . . . The evenings spent reading and studying together which seemed, in retrospect, such an important part of her teenage years.

She had fallen out of favour with Pa when she brought Larry home. With all the thoughtlessness of an eighteen-year-old, she had blithely announced that they were going to get married. No wonder he had been against it! She hadn't given him one ounce of warning.

'An actor?' he had said, horrified. 'A fly-by-night without a single brain in his head? Is that what you want, Julia? You disappoint me!'

'And what are you intending to live on?' he'd asked next.

Pa had done his damnedest to discourage the relationship; but the more he'd tried, the more determined she had become. And that was when he'd turned from a considerate parent into quite a different character. He hadn't spoken to either of them for the first ten years of their marriage.

Yes, love at first sight could sometimes be destructive . . .

She fingered the small pearl brooch at her neck that had belonged to her mother. That meant more to her than the glittering stuff that Larry bought her. No, thought Julia, it wasn't so surprising that Pa had disapproved of Larry. A man who had spent ten years researching the Second Catilinarian Oration, who wore a battered old straw hat and stuffed bundles of lecture notes in his pockets, was not likely to be impressed by a handsome face and a charismatic smile.

Pa and Larry? Chalk and cheese! Pa had invariably lived with the utmost austerity; whereas Larry . . . well, when she first knew him, he had owed money right, left and centre. She remembered him making a silly joke about it once. Sitting there in the dining-room at Oxford . . . 'I can't afford *not* to spend money!' he'd said. 'In the theatre, image is everything.'

Pa was not amused.

Yes, Larry had been extravagant in those days. He still liked to spend on clothes, she reminded herself, and on antiques. But of course circumstances were quite different now . . . weren't they? Anyway, he didn't go mad any more like in the old days. He was was less foolish, more judicious, surely?

Julia pondered the issue as she leaned over to touch the lavender. There were times when she wished he would tell her more about their financial affairs. Let her know what exactly was going on. Anxiety twisted her face as she remembered Pa's warning on his death-bed. He'd opened his eyes just the once, before he went, and whispered, 'Julia – don't feel you have to stay with him. There's my money, if the going gets tough . . .'

With an enormous effort, she hitched her mind back to the present. To the phone call from David Crichton at nine thirty that morning. She was reacting badly to the phone at the moment. Had sounded, she feared, more dithery even than usual.

'Julia,' he'd said. 'It's David. Is Larry there?'

'Y . . . yes. Yes, he is. Somewhere.' Her heart was still beating at double speed. 'Well, I mean, he's here, but he isn't. I'm not sure . . . He's down at the stables. I think . . .'

'Ah . . .' The long pause had made her feel terribly uncomfortable. That and the cool formality of the tone he was using this morning. What did he want? What did she say now? The oak chest she was sitting on creaked as she moved suddenly.

'So how are . . . things?' he asked.

Her breath tightened. 'Oh, so-so. You know.'

'I suppose all this has been pretty hellish for you?'

'No much fun,' she said faintly. Why couldn't she tell him what she really felt – that her nerves were screaming . . . That there was, within her, a Sahara of shifting sand emotions.

She wondered what the cool young accountant would do if she burst into tears and went to pieces on him.

But she didn't, of course. Pull yourself together, Julia. Deep breath, hold it . . . Now! She gripped the receiver hard and said, 'Do you want me to give Larry a message?'

'Yes, if you would. Tell him I've got to see him this evening. It's urgent. Tell him I'll come up at eight, if that suits him. No – tell him it'll have to suit him. We've got to have a talk.'

Terse and hard. She'd never heard that particular edge to David's voice before. What did it mean?

'I'll make sure he gets the message.' Feeling a little peculiar, as if a touch drunk, she had picked up the pad they kept on the table to write Larry a reminder note. And in that moment had come a memory of the last time David had come up to read Larry the riot act. Six months ago now, almost to the day.

Her legs didn't seem to want to work at all now.

They were made of kapok.

The world shifted . . . There were voices over there behind the Old Schoolhouse. A car engine starting up and a sharp shout as a door slammed. She managed to put a small smile on her face as Brenda came out to tell her lunch was ready.

21

Laura had led the way into the poky sitting-room. Max had followed her, still half dreading the interview or at least wishing that it could take place in a more cheerful venue. He had placed the bracelet very carefully on the table in front of him.

Laura was saying, 'When we sold the Manor, Geoffrey did a deal with Aitken. A bad one as it turned out, but we weren't to know that. There were three or four important Le Grice portraits that had never left the house, had for as long as anyone could remember always hung on the staircase. Aitken promised to let them stay there where they belonged. It caused Geoffrey distress to leave them . . . but we didn't want them crammed into some tacky corner at the Lodge.'

She had the profile of a sharp nun as she stared out of the window. Max looked at her curiously. Extraordinary how she seemed suddenly to have taken charge. To have taken up a stand in defence of her husband.

She said abruptly, 'You can see what would have happened to them if we'd brought them here.' She waved a hand towards the two portraits over the fireplace: a pale Regency officer superciliously smiling and a handsome but stout, white-haired dowager, two feet square, in a hideous gilded frame. 'Two minor Le Grice portraits,' she said abruptly. 'Already spotting with the damp . . . Dying slowly for lack of light or anyone to admire them!'

Geoffrey was standing by the bookcase, his greying hair brushed smooth, his expression hangdog.

Laura said, 'We didn't feel it proper to remove the others from the Manor where, after all, they belong. We felt very strongly that they're part of the history of the place. So we had it written into the contract that they should remain there hanging on the staircase in perpetuity. But then Aitken went back on his word.'

'He moved them?' Max said.

'Oh, very cleverly. Not all at once. Not so anyone would

notice.' Her voice sounded bitter. There was a delicate pallor on her cheeks and she looked almost haggard. 'But one by one, they were taken down and stacked away in a cupboard. The woman who goes there to clean told me. He kept them in that dark little store room in the passage that leads to the orangery. And do you know what he replaced them with?'

'No idea. Tell me.'

'With his wife's fearful flower paintings! Have you ever seen one?'

Max said he wasn't much into art, he preferred photographs, that Fifties couple in Paris kissing, that kind of thing.

Laura looked at him as if from another world. 'Drab!' she said. 'That's what I hear he called *The Brown Boy*!'

'*The Brown Boy*?' Max didn't understand.

'It's the best of all the pictures. The one we were fondest of. An elegant little eighteenth-century portrait of William Le Grice, painted when he was ten years old.'

Max said, 'I see.'

'Do you?' She stared at him with such intelligence and feeling that he shifted awkwardly in the chair. 'Well, we fretted and fumed and I even had a go at him about it, but I got nowhere. He'd taken them down for cleaning, he told me quite brazenly. It was an out-and-out lie and we both knew it. But we couldn't prove him a liar, you see. Well, not until a certain amount of time had passed without them being put back up. And then we heard – the last straw, this – that he'd called in old Griffin, the auctioneer, and was thinking about sending them up to Sotheby's for evaluation. He was going to sell them! Our family portraits!'

'You could have taken him to court,' Max said.

'By which time, they'd probably have disappeared and he'd have pocketed the money!' Geoffrey had decided to join the conversation. He seemed to have no control over the nerves of his face; they were twitching with anger. 'So . . . Laura decided to take in into her own hands. On the day they had the exhibition at the Schoolhouse . . .'

'The day Wetherell died?'

'The same.'

'You went up to the Manor . . .?'

'Yes,' she said briefly, exchanging a look with her husband.

'I slipped in through the side door into the orangery. I knew I probably wouldn't be noticed with all those people milling round.'

'And?'

She smiled remotely. Her long, white fingers worked nervously. 'And . . . I removed *The Brown Boy* from the cupboard and brought it back here to the Lodge. I thought, at least we shall have *one* of them! They belong to the Le Grices – not to some little philistine who welched on a gentleman's agreement! I mean, he hasn't even noticed, yet, that the picture has gone! That's how much he cares about the history of his precious Manor!'

Max thought of the square package that Geoffrey had hidden in the boot of his car. It stood now on the floor resting against the wall.

Geoffrey's eyes knew what he was thinking. He got up and uncovered it softly, with swiftness, so that the Brown Boy's eyes fell on Max frankly, confidently, without any warning.

Extraordinarily beautiful little face . . . almost alive really. Fine, dark hair gathered in a tail above a snuff-coloured cotton jacket . . . Max was startled not so much by its beauty as by the considerable emotion that it induced in him.

'You like it. Thought you would,' Geoffrey said gruffly. 'Better than the vulgar stuff *they* thought right for the place . . .' His voice conveyed the contempt he had for the Aitkens' sense of décor.

Laura said, '*The Brown Boy* is a treasure! It shouldn't be stored carelessly in a back cupboard – or sold for gain. It belongs to the Le Grices.'

But would the law think so? For the moment Max repressed the urge to seek Geoffrey's opinion on the subject and concentrated on the matter in hand. 'So you dropped your bracelet in the orangery on your way through?'

'On my way out,' Laura told him. 'In my hurry to get away with the portrait, I caught my arm on the palm by the orangery door. The faulty catch on my watch must have given way – but I didn't miss it until a lot later.' There was a longish pause while she went back over it all in her mind's eye. 'I couldn't remember for a while where I'd last worn it. But it suddenly came back to me in the middle of the night that I'd caught it in the palm tree.

91

Your mind does things like that, when you're half asleep and half awake. I remembered . . . And I knew I had to go back there and find it before someone else did. But I didn't make it.'

Max felt some sympathy for them in their predicament, but he knew he couldn't let it cloud his judgement. 'So where were you taking the picture when I arrived?'

'We have a friend down in Penzance. We decided to ask him to look after it for us for a while. Until all the hoo-ha was over.'

'Hoo-ha?'

'Let's face it, Aitken was bound to find out in the end. That it was missing . . . And who's the first person he'd suspect?'

Max regarded them steadily with a hint of regret. 'I shall have to tell him. You realize that?'

'I suppose you will.' Geoffrey's hands were clenched tight in his lap. 'There's no chance . . .?'

Max shook his head. 'None at all. Sorry. I'll do my best to get him to treat it . . . well, leniently.'

'If you would.'

But I wouldn't bet on my powers of persuasion, Max thought with some cynicism: Larry will have the pair of them exactly where he wants them. And won't he just enjoy turning the screw?

On the dot of five o'clock, Max rang the great man from his office. 'I'd like to have a talk with you,' he said.

'Is it urgent?' Larry sounded rattled, for some reason.

'I'm afraid it is.'

'Can't we deal with it here and now on the phone?'

'I don't think that would be advisable. I'd rather come and see you.' Max looked out across the mews, where the rain had come and gone and dusk had come to settle over the tall flower stands. He had debated whether to tell Aitken immediately and had decided against it because to flip the Brown Boy story straight out at him would do the Le Grices no good at all.

'Well, I suppose so, if you must! What time can you get here?'

'Seven thirty suit you?'

'Not really, but I suppose I've got no choice. Don't be late, though. I've got another appointment at eight.'

Max put the receiver down not caring whether he had upset the great man's social arrangements or not. He began to ransack through the desk for the print-out of the Aitken notes and stuffed them into a blue folder together with a transcript that he'd made of the Le Grice interview. Then kicked the drawer shut and stretched himself.

The fuzzy feeling in his stomach was not fully gone, but he felt better. He grabbed a Mars bar from the window sill before haring down the stairs.

At a quarter past six, Julia lifted the receiver of the upstairs extension. She stood there listening for no more than two minutes, but her dark grey eyes seemed stricken, her fingertips whitened as she pressed the edge of the bedside table.

She was shivering. There was a chill wind that October evening. She could not bear to listen any more, so gently, very gently, she put down the receiver.

He had pulled the carpet from under her feet. That's what he'd done! And it wasn't simple vanity, but a form of greed that was the underlying motive . . .

A huge hole like a shell crater was forming inside her. Her legs would no longer hold her. She had to sit down on the bed.

At ten minutes past seven, when Max came haring into Martha Washington, Elizabeth was still working on the month's orders. She had loaded the Broken Star quilt and a couple of wall hangings into the back of the Citroën parked outside the shop and was scrabbling to get the paperwork in some sort of order before setting out on deliveries.

'Betsy! You're still here. Thank God! Listen – I've got a problem . . .'

'Tell me something new,' she murmured. 'No, Max, I can't lend you any money. My purse holds precisely thirty-two pence.'

'It's nothing like that,' Max said.

'It isn't?' She sounded amazed.

'Of course not!'

'What is it then?'

'It's Phoebe.'

'Phoebe?'

'She's taken to her sick-bed. She's given up the ghost.'

'You don't say . . .' Her eyebrows rose.

93

'She won't start. And I've got this appointment with Aitken at seven thirty and he warned me not to be late. So . . . I was wondering if you could lend me yours just for half an hour?'

'My what?'

'Your car.'

'No,' she said flatly.

'I'll give him twenty minutes. No more. I promise.'

She spoke with firmness. The Citroën was packed, the invoices in a neat pile and her customers had been notified that she was on her way. 'Sorry, Max. I've just loaded her up. I'm off on deliveries – '

'But I'll be back in two shakes of a lamb's tail! Before you're even ready to lock up.'

'Max – watch my lips . . .'

But it was never a good idea to be subtle with him. His brainbox wasn't up to it. Already he was blowing her a fat kiss and reaching towards the desk. 'Thanks, Betsy . . .' he said. 'You're my favourite woman.'

'Max!'

Too late. The little schlep had gone through the door with an airy grin and her car keys. Elizabeth swore softly. Then with more fervour. 'The lame-brained idiot!' she said. 'I'll kill him when he gets back!'

22

Aitken had just come in from the stables. He was wearing a green, quilted waistcoat and a tweed cap. His green gumboots had, presumably, been left at the back door.

'She came here and helped herself to the painting?' he said incredulously. 'Bloody cheek! I'll have them for that.'

'You intend reporting the matter to the police?' Max said.

There was a touch of cold fury in Larry's voice as he momentarily lost his plummy tones. 'Too right I will. The thieving gits! I'll teach them a lesson.'

Was there a hint of sadism behind the famous blue eyes? Outside, a gale was blowing.

Max cleared his throat. 'They . . . were rather hoping that you might overlook it. After all, *The Brown Boy* has been returned.' It stood now against the wall at the far end of the drawing-room, covered with a light wrapping of brown paper and knotted with string.

'No chance! I shall ring Manvers Street in the morning.'

So that was that.

'Theft, pure and simple. That's what it is.' There was a brief silence. Then Aitken moved to the window, stood glowering out into the darkness almost as if watching for someone. The old house seemd to creak and groan around them. Finally, he yanked the heavy curtains across.

Max cleared his throat and said, 'The business with Mrs Forbes . . . I may be wrong, but I don't think she had anything to do with the poison pen letters – though she seems very bitter.'

'Can you be sure?'

'No. It's just . . . a gut instinct,' he said rather grandly, Elizabeth's phrase coming back to mind. Another pause. Then, 'However, there was one subject I wanted to ask you about.'

'Fire away.' Aitken's look was piercing, but wasn't there some sort of guardedness about him as he stood there waiting?

From the vase on the table Max inhaled the musk of bronze chrysanthemums. He flipped back the page of his notebook. 'Why didn't you tell me you were in the habit of taking amphetamines?' he asked.

There was a heavy pause. Then Larry answered. 'Who told you that? The Forbes woman, I suppose?'

'Let's just say it came to my notice.'

'It has to be Rebecca. No one else knew.'

'Not even your wife?'

'OK, Julia knew. And Emily. But they wouldn't say anything.'

And Brenda Macmillan, Max wondered?

Larry looked at the dial of his watch. The golden hands of the carriage clock on the mantelpiece said that it was eighteen minutes to eight.

'Look – there's nothing sinister about my hiding the fact that I occasionally . . . *occasionally*, mind . . . take the odd pep pill. OK, so I should have told you earlier . . .'

Max said nothing.

'But I thought . . . well, I knew you'd assume . . . people would assume it was me that doped the whisky. And it wasn't. I promise you.'

The curtain moved as a gust of wind hit the house. 'Do the police know you kept these pills in the house?' Max asked.

'Yes. I told them. I had to.'

But you didn't tell me, Max thought. He said, 'So the amphetamines probably came from *your* supply? Not from an outside source?'

'Yes. Look – I'm employing you to trace the sources of the hate mail, not – '

'It may all be connected,' Max said. 'I have to know the facts. So where did you keep the amphetamines? Were they locked up?'

Larry looked uneasy. 'Well, usually I keep them in the bedroom. In my bedside cabinet. But I must admit that I'd been careless that day. I was tired. I'd got a script to learn and the exhibition and I was due to drive to London straight after the sub-committee meeting . . . I took a pep pill after breakfast that morning and I must have left them out on the bureau. At least, Emily informs me that they were lying there for anyone to see when she went to grab an envelope before she went out.'

'Were there any missing when you opened the packet that morning?'

'No. I don't think so. But I was tired and in a hurry. I probably wouldn't have noticed.'

'But you must have had a count-up after Wetherell died. How many went into the whisky?'

He shrugged. 'Not many. Two or three perhaps.'

'And were they still lying openly on the bureau while your committee meeting was going on?'

'No. They were in the bathroom cabinet. Brenda tells me she found them and put them away.'

'When?'

'Some time that afternoon. You'll have to ask her.'

'Fine. I will. Er . . . while we're on the subject,' Max said, 'I wondered if you could confirm or deny reports that you and Miss Macmillan have, shall we say, rather more than the normal employer/employee relationship?'

A spiteful wind howled down the great chimney behind

them, then Aitken said explosively, 'Who the hell told you that?'

'It's probably better that you don't know.'

'Damned right it is, old son!' Aitken looked furious.

Max kept his voice steady. 'But if you could just confirm or deny?'

Aitken said: 'Does my secretary look the type of woman one would have an affair with?'

'Not . . . on the surface of things, no.' Max had to admit it.

'Good God – can you imagine getting between the sheets with Big Mac?'

'Then it's not true?'

'Of course it's not true! I've had some stories spread about me, but that just about takes the biscuit!' He said, 'Listen, sunshine, when I asked you aboard, what I had in mind was that you should stick to the task in hand, not run round the place raking up every little bit of muck you can find. Now – if you've finished asking your damned silly questions . . .'

The interview was obviously terminated. Out in the hall, Aitken flicked a switch that put on the outside light.

Asked me aboard? thought Max. Who does he think he is? The bloody admiral or something? Captain of a sinking ship, more like. If I didn't need you to get the bank manager off my back . . . *sunshine* . . .

'Filthy night.' Larry's voice had assumed its former *bonhomie*, but he still seemed anxious to rid himself of his guest. 'Would have offered you coffee, but my wife's at her art class and I'm afraid I can't tell one end of a kettle from the other.'

'Er . . . Emily not here either?' Max asked with some nonchalance.

Aitken smiled as if half expecting the question. He said, 'My beautiful daughter is painting the town red, as usual. She'll be home in the small hours, I presume – if at all.'

If Max found the answer disappointing – frustrating even – he didn't show it. 'Well, I'll be in touch . . .'

'Do that. Give the door a heave. It sticks in this weather.'

He wasn't kidding! The heavy door finally yielded, but only after much tugging. Outside, the trees were soughing in the darkness. Larry said, 'Mind the steps. They're steep.'

But he didn't bother to wait while his guest negotiated them.

The door banged shut and the light went off almost immediately. Max was left stranded in the pitch darkness of the portico.

Groping his way out like Blind Pugh, Max thought, 'That's OK, Larry, we all understand if you're so hard up you have to save on the electricity. Just save enough to pay my bill, that's all, *sunshine!*' His fingertips touched something cold . . . stone and fungus . . . A thick pillar. Behind him were blue shadows, the arch of the fanlight. In front, a loose step which wobbled . . .

That black shape must be Elizabeth's rather plush Citroën.

His shoelace felt loose but he didn't stop to tie it.

At least, he thought, I can let the Citroën rip all the way down the hill. Talking about letting rip, he supposed Betsy would, very probably, when he got back to the shop.

Let rip? She'll kill you!

The bottom step. Thank goodness! For an instant only he hesitated, then stepped out. But suddenly the ground wasn't there any more . . .

He fell heavily. Damn it, there must have been another step! The wet gravel hit him. My best trousers! he thought desperately.

The Aitken file had flown out of his hand. It took a full five minutes of cursing and swearing in the darkness to retrieve the contents – those that the wind hadn't blown away – and cram the whole sodden mess back in again.

Elizabeth, however, had not an ounce of sympathy. 'I'll swing for you!' she said as, twenty minutes later, he sloped into Martha Washington. Then, 'Max? What the hell have you been doing? Playing at mud pies?'

Max explained.

She shook her head mutely. 'Serves you right for stealing other people's cars.'

'It's all in one piece,' Max said contritely. 'You can borrow Phoebe any time . . . when she feels better. Feel free.'

'Who in their right minds would want to borrow Phoebe? Right, seeing that you *are* here, you can work for your keep! Pick up that box – the big one – and help me shove it in the trunk.'

'Boot.'

'Trunk. And quit answering back! If anything's happened to

my Broken Star, I'll have you for breakfast. It's worth a small fortune.'

The Broken Star was still in the boot of the Citroën, but not exactly in the same pristine state as when she had loaded it.

She examined it under the Victorian street light.

Made a most unpleasant discovery.

'Blood? My God . . .!'

Gingerly she lifted one corner of the quilt. The body lay in a heap under the Broken Star. The face stared up at her with a hideous expression.

'Crichton?' asked Max's voice from behind her.

'Crichton,' said Elizabeth. 'Call the police, Max.'

23

Elizabeth still hadn't recovered from the shock of the events of the night before. She paced up and down in the sitting-room at the cottage trying to persuade herself that it had really happened.

Twenty-four hours ago now, almost to the minute . . .

The mews, charming by day, had so suddenly appeared menacing, the Broken Star a bizarre prop for a bizarre scene . . . a scene from a New York cop film. Yet it had all happened in the centre of beautiful Bath.

She saw it all for the umpteenth time in her mind. The flowers in the window-boxes lit eerily by the police arc lights . . . lobelia and geraniums and trailing pansies. The woman in the flat opposite leaning out of her window to see what all the fuss was about.

The police had sealed off the mews with tape, had brought in a Land-Rover with a generator and set up lights to flood the corpse where it lay huddled in the back of the Citroën. Suddenly, in spite of the warmth in the cottage, Elizabeth shivered and wished the images would leave her head. Crichton's grey jacket and trousers dark with blood . . . his skin turning waxy. A frenzied attack, they said. The fatal blow had gone four inches into the heart, but there were fifteen or twenty other wounds as well.

She thought of the Lab Liaison Officer bending over the body. Of Detective Sergeant Johnson, half-way between the Force and the forensic people, correct, calming, even mildly jovial. He had taken charge, had told her to go in and put the kettle on, love . . .

Max had had to accompany them to the station. He was still there, as far as she knew. What the hell would they do with him? If only she hadn't let him take her car! If she'd stopped him, he wouldn't have been able to go and he wouldn't be in this mess.

The worst thing was that there was something about the blood and the open back of the car and the flashing lights at night that had brought back Jim's death. The memories seemed to flood over her with an intensity she could never have expected. It was five – no, six years ago now. Jim had taken himself off on a fishing trip with his friend Joel Gilchrist. Had even joked with her that he might just forget to come back on Sunday evening. Well, the joke had turned out to be grimly prophetic. They were on their way back through the Smokies when this other car had hit them. A young drunk driver . . .

No death was ever easy to accept, but when it came like that, so suddenly and without warning – one night to be playing chequers with you on the porch and the next consigned to oblivion – well, that was something else.

She started to clear away the supper things. If she didn't do something useful, she would certainly cry. Then she poured herself a stiff whisky and took it upstairs . . . Crossed the splintered Victorian floorboards to sit in the window overlooking the garden and tried to combat the old night terrors by gazing out over the fields to the faint gold that was Bath in the frosty distance. It was very still out there. No sound at all, except for the owls, somewhere out across the dark landscape. On the chicken sheds at Church Farm, probably, hunting for mice.

Tawnies, she thought. There were two of them holding a conversation with each other; one said tu-whit, the other tu-whoo. Owls were birds of ill omen, some said, but Elizabeth didn't think so. How could beautiful creatures like that bring trouble, for heaven's sake? Or at least more trouble than was already on her plate!

For a few minutes more she sat quietly listening to the owls and the wind in the tall trees in the quiet of the evening.

Quiet? She thought: Only on the surface of things. The tranquillity of this village is a mere façade. There's a dark undertow of hypocrisy, lies, greed . . . And now murder.

Holding a Socratic dialogue with herself, she sipped at the whisky.

Should you still try to have faith in humanity no matter how badly people behave?

Of course. What else is there to have faith in?

Yes, but doesn't that make you a bit of a mug?

Perhaps it does. But I'd rather be a mug than lose my sense of optimism.

The world's full of suckers like you, Betsy Blair.

Maybe so. But you are what you are and you can't do much about it.

When Jim Junior rang, early next morning, she found herself trying to play down what had happened.

Jim said, 'You found a stiff in your car trunk?'

'Well . . . yes.' She couldn't deny it.

There was a protracted silence, then he said, 'Ma – you'd better come on home.'

'I don't want to come home, Jim.'

'I thought you said this was a civilized place?'

'It is. I promise you.'

'Then what the hell is a stiff doing in the trunk of your car?'

'It probably had something to do with Max,' she told him.

'Who's Max?'

She told him. 'He's investigating this other murder, you see. Well, it wasn't exactly a murder. More a case of accidental poisoning.'

'Another stiff?' The line crackled for a moment, then all hell broke loose. 'Another stiff? That is *it*! That is most definitely it! I didn't like you going over there in the first place, but now I can assure you that you're coming home – '

'Jim. It's perfectly safe. This is Bath. Not Dodge City.'

A resounding 'Huh!' echoed all the way across the Atlantic.

*

Dottie Marchant had heard the news on Radio Bristol. She was lurking over the hedge to give her commiserations as Elizabeth came out of her front door at eleven that morning.

'My dear – you must have been quite shocked when they found him! Not very nice for you! Not very nice at all . . .' Her eye was avid. 'Poor Mr Crichton! He did so much for the church, you know. I saw the Reverend Silk first thing at the post office. I must say he looked quite dazed by it all. He was taking his cassock to be dry cleaned, but he walked off and left it in a bag on the floor. I had to chase after him with it. I think I gave him quite a fright.' She dropped her voice almost to a whisper. 'Between you and me, he's run down. Needs a holiday. Not that he's likely to get one! Poor as church mice, you know! But then, I've never met a parson who's good over finances. Do they know how the corpse got into your vehicle?'

'Max left it parked outside the Manor. He thinks someone shoved it in there while he was inside with Mr Aitken.'

Dottie nodded. Then, 'Evil spirits,' she pronounced darkly.

'Evil spirits?'

'The Manor's always been disturbed by them. Do you believe in the supernatural, Mrs Blair? I'm a great one for the spirits myself.'

Elizabeth thought, I shall need a very large measure of spirits if I don't get out of here. She said, 'You'll have to excuse me. I must catch the bus.'

'Catch the bus?'

'My car has been impounded,' Elizabeth explained wearily.

'We used to walk it in the old days,' Dottie informed her. 'Three and a half miles via Rectory Hill. Kept you very trim.'

Well, I don't intend to walk it, Elizabeth thought. I could if I had to, but Man has now invented the wheel, Miss Marchant!

Max's office was still locked when she got to the shop, but at twelve thirty he stuck his head round the door. 'I'm back,' he announced. 'A free citizen again.'

Elizabeth was immensely relieved to see him. With a dry mouth, she said, 'Is everything all right? I kept ringing the station, but all they would say was that you were helping with their enquiries.' She noted that he was wearing the same mud-stained trousers. 'You look bushed,' she said.

'I am. Come and eat with me, Betsy. I need to talk.'

102

'Eat?'

'It's OK. I shan't put you through the ordeal of my beans on toast. Let's try Pasta Plus. My treat.'

'In that case,' said Elizabeth, 'I'll get my bag.' It wasn't often that Max bought you lunch.

In the restaurant, she ordered tagliatelle in a creamy mushroom sauce. 'So what happened at the cop shop?' she asked.

'Oh, questions, questions and more questions.'

'But they were satisfied with your answers?'

'Obviously . . . for the moment . . . or they wouldn't have let me go. I gather they grilled you for a while as well?'

'For a couple of hours. Until I convinced them that the body wasn't in the car when I last saw it. So what time was he killed?'

'Approximately ten minutes to eight.'

'While you were in the house?'

'Yep. According to Larry, Crichton had an appointment with him at eight. He must have arrived early.'

'And he was killed out there on the drive?'

Max said, 'Apparently. They found his car parked by the Old Schoolhouse. No signs of blood or any struggle there . . . but the gravel was a mess in front of the shrubbery, which is where they think the attack took place.'

'Right in front of the house?'

'It was very dark.'

'And you didn't hear anything?'

'Not a thing. Mind you, the way the wind was howling round, it's not surprising. As Andy said, you could have had a pitched battle out there that night and the wind would have drowned it.'

'Andy?'

'PC Andy Cooper. My inside man at Manvers Street. We drink together at the rugby club every Friday night.'

'Useful . . .' Elizabeth said drily.

'Yeah. Andy's all right. He bought me a coffee after they gave me my freedom. He thinks it's dead funny, me being hauled in. Driving the corpse all the way down to town . . .' He shuddered slightly at the memory of it.

'Well, there's one thing . . .' Elizabeth said.

'What's that?'

'If Crichton was killed at ten minutes before eight, you and Larry are each other's alibis.'

'True. We walked out of the station practically together. Well, until I bumped into Andy. He didn't look too pleased at being there for the second time in a few weeks. Larry, I mean, not Andy.' The pasta arrived. The strain that had been on Max's face was beginning to subside.

'Actually,' he said casually, 'I squeezed a very interesting snippet of information out of Andy. Apparently, they found papers in Crichton's briefcase suggesting that he was investigating discrepancies in the Roof Fund figures.'

'Fraud?'

'That's about it. Certain sums had been siphoned off into another account.'

'So Wetherell may have been right after all. Into whose account?'

'I don't know. Andy wouldn't give me any more details'. More than his job's worth, he said. Or else he didn't know any more. But it seems likely that Crichton was murdered because he found out about the fraud.'

Elizabeth frowned with renewed concentration. 'He was going up there to tell Larry what he'd found out? And somebody knocked him off before he could do so . . .'

'It's a strong possibility.'

'So who had access to the Roof Fund? Who could handle the cheques?'

'I made enquiries about that last week. Larry. Forbes. Brenda Macmillan. And the Reverend Silk.'

'We can cut Larry out. He was with you.'

'Unless, of course, he got someone else to do the dirty deed for him – set up an appointment with me to give himself a watertight alibi.' He thought again. 'But that's no good. *I* rang him to fix the appointment. He wasn't at all keen.' He sat there, still frowning. 'But I suppose he had enough time to set up a killing *after* I rang him.'

Something struck Elizabeth. 'The Rector was taking his cassock to be cleaned this morning,' she said in a strange tone.

'You don't think *Silk* did it?'

'Whoever killed Crichton must have been covered in blood.' Elizabeth poured them both more wine and said, 'What I don't understand is why they did it right there by the front door, when they could have lured him into the trees or a more secluded part of the grounds where the body wouldn't have been discovered for ages. Why would anyone choose to hide it in your . . . in *my* . . . car? They must have known it would be found almost immediately.'

'I think the killer was interrupted in his task. He saw the light go on in the outer hall as Larry prepared to let me out and he – '

'Or she.'

'He or she panicked and chose the nearest hiding-place – the boot of your car. Betsy – I'm sorry about the quilt.'

'So am I.' But then she relented. 'So . . . what's a £350 quilt among friends?'

'That much?' His face was a picture.

'That much.' A thought struck her. 'Is finding a stiff in your car an act of God or serendipity?'

'Haven't a clue. Why?'

'I was wondering if I can make an insurance claim, you dumb turkey.'

At four o'clock, she popped next door to see George Godwin, who owned The Music Box. In the continuing absence of the Citroën, she needed a lift home. George had big, kind eyes behind his gold rims. 'I knew the crime rate would go up when the Yanks moved in,' he said.

'George, don't you start.' She perched herself on the edge of a leather-topped stool. 'It's been a hellish long day.'

'I see you had some press interest.'

'Uh-huh. I am sick and tired of being asked to pose in the rocking chair!'

'All good publicity,' George said.

'Then I'll send them over here tomorrow. You can have a taste of it.'

They sat there for a while discussing Crichton's murder. 'If one of them is fiddling the fund,' said Elizabeth pensively, 'which would you plump for?'

George wrinkled his brow. 'The Macmillan woman probably.'

'Why her?'

'It seems to me the others all have too much to lose if they were found out.'

A long pause. Then he said, 'Of course, the Roof Fund committee may not be the only ones who could get at the money.'

'Who else could?' she demanded, puzzled.

'Well, a lot of transactions are done on computers these days. Ever heard of hackers?'

She hadn't thought of that. But it only seemed to make the whole thing more difficult.

'Anybody could do it,' George said, 'providing they had the know-how and access to the right kind of computer.'

'Thanks a bunch, George,' Elizabeth told him. 'You've widened the field almost to infinity.'

'No. Not infinity . . . Just include computer experts with a great big grudge against old Larry.'

At five thirty, she went up to tell Max she was leaving. She found him frowning at his computer screen. Frowning at the last name on the list Larry had given him.

Tabernay.

Oxford – some time back.

No further details.

'Something wrong?' she asked.

Max said, 'Larry didn't want to go into detail unless he was forced to. Well, perhaps it's time somebody applied that force to him, Betsy.' Then, 'Your phone's ringing,' he said.

She tore down the stairs again to answer it. 'I'm so sorry to trouble you,' the caller said. 'This is Barbara Rushmore. You sold me the Broken Star quilt . . .'

'Yes, Mrs Rushmore. I'm sorry I wasn't able to deliver it. Er . . . circumstances beyond my control, I'm afraid.'

'Well, yes. That's why I'm ringing. I read about it in the papers. And . . . well, under the circumstances, I feel I must cancel the order.' Her voice was cultured, but not too happy. 'I hope you'll understand, Mrs Blair. It's not that I'm squeamish or anything . . .'

But you'd always see a body wrapped up in it, Elizabeth thought. 'I could order you a replacement,' she offered hopefully. 'It might take a few months, but . . .'

'No – really.' Mrs Rushmore sounded faint. 'If you don't mind, I'd rather just have you cancel my cheque.'

Damn it all, Elizabeth thought as she put the phone down. Murder's bad for business.

24

Sally Stewart was not having the best day of her whole working life at the Bath and Wessex office in South Parade. Old Forbes was in a vile temper this morning. She knew where she'd like to tell him to stick his job, only it might shock the customers.

'Miss Stewart . . .' he had said. 'May I suggest that you keep your mind on your work – and not on whatever girlish plans you may have for this evening?'

His eyes were always piggy nasty when he looked at you. Spooky . . . like something out of a sex and horror film.

It was rumoured that he had marital problems. Sally couldn't honestly say she was surprised. She'd never understood how an elegant woman like Mrs Forbes could have got herself hitched to an overweight, balding, sarcastic sod like him in the first place.

I needed this morning like a hole in the head, she thought, feeling for the chocolate bar she had hidden in her pocket. She'd stuck to her diet for almost ten days now. One little Mars bar wasn't going to hurt. And she wasn't going to let that moron get her down . . . no fear! She didn't know exactly how she was going to get her own back on him, but she'd find a way . . .

'He'll kill you if he sees you eating,' Gill said.

'Who cares?' Sally let the chocolate ooze deliciously round her mouth.

'You're mad, you.'

'May as well be mad as miserable!' Sally took another surreptitious bite.

You had to do more than just exist, she had decided soon after her parents' divorce had messed up her GCSEs. She'd never accepted that she'd be stuck for life in her terminally boring job at the Bath and Wessex. What she really wanted to do was something creative. Something artistic . . .

She glanced at the clock. It was only twelve fifteen. She didn't know how she was going to get through the rest of the day. Usually she could manage by switching to automatic pilot, but today it didn't look as if that was going to work. Today as she stood behind the counter, a sensation of pure panic kept washing all over her. It felt as if someone was winding her nerve strings tighter and tighter and any minute now they would explode into little pieces.

She couldn't see him until nine thirty that evening . . . Nine whole hours to wait, five of them to be spent here in this dump!

Time stretched ahead like an endless waste.

Sally Stewart thought to herself: It's because we quarrelled. That's why I'm in this state.

She could see him now, standing there with the lamplight catching his thick, crisp hair. (Vain about it, he was). Smiling brilliantly like he did when he was in a particularly bad mood.

'I'm not trying to get rid of you, Sally,' he had said. 'I just think we ought to be careful for a while.' The bed all in a mess still behind him . . . his shirt half done up.

They would never had had the scene if she hadn't been so stupid. She always got too possessive . . . Wanted too much, too soon. Wanted the moon and the stars and everything else besides.

Oh, she knew it was a difficult situation for him. He had a wife and family. Nothing could be done quickly. She understood all that. If only things could be right between them again – it was all that she wanted . . .

Mr Forbes' door banged open and he barked an order. Gill made a face and shot off to make him coffee.

I'd put arsenic in it, Sally thought. He's probably been losing on the gee-gees again. He was always 'nipping out to see a customer', but it was common knowledge his shoes could have made their own way down the road to Ladbroke's.

At least, she hoped it was the horses.

'He had Mr Hollywood on the phone,' Gill said when she came back.

'Aitken?' Sally tried not to react. Sounded merely casual.

'Sir Lawrence himself. Doesn't seem to have done much for

108

his temper. I wanted to stay and listen, but he practically threw me out.' Gill looked at the Mars wrapper in the bottom of the bin. 'Got any more of those?' she said. 'You've made me feel hungry.'

'Sorry.' Looking pale, Sally found a smile for the next customer.

'Lyn saw him outside the Pump Rooms yesterday. Larry, I mean. She says he swore at a photographer who was following him.' Gill laughed. 'Funny, I thought he liked having his picture in the paper.

Sally didn't answer. Whatever had Larry said to Forbes to throw him into such a temper? Something to do with the fact that David Crichton had spent three days shut in the back office checking certain figures . . .?

And now Crichton was dead.

A female voice, she recalled, had answered when, scared and uneasy, she'd tried to ring him on the night of the murder. She'd put the phone down almost at once. Had rung a second time an hour later, but he'd seemed totally unconcerned by what she had to tell him. Stop getting yourself into a panic, he'd said. Calm down. Look, go and have a drink with one of your girlfriends. You're getting neurotic.

Suddenly . . . Sally had a stomach ache.

The policemen – two of them, one young, one older – came at four thirty that afternoon.

'Could we see the manager, please?' one of them asked her. 'Mr Forbes . . . Mr Robert Forbes, I believe? Will you tell him it's a matter of some urgency?'

25

Elizabeth walked down to the police station in Manvers Street on a bright autumnal afternoon. The office to which she was escorted was down a long corridor, the interview room adorned with pin boards and tatty piles of paper.

The telephone message had, according to Caroline, been

polite and almost casual. 'Ask Mrs Blair to pop down to the station some time today . . .'

'Any time?' Elizabeth had asked.

'That's what they said.' Caroline had a queer look on her delicate face. 'Er – I'll hold the fort if you like.'

'I'll be right back,' Elizabeth told her. 'I shouldn't *think* they'll lock me up.'

'Oh, right,' said Caroline.

Sergeant Brent Dando was an earnest young man with roast beef cheeks. 'Sorry to drag you down here, Mrs Blair,' he said. 'Only there are one or two things that require clarification . . .'

'Fire away,' Elizabeth said.

'You mentioned that you knew Mr Crichton . . .'

'I didn't know him personally.'

'But well enough to recognize the body?' he said.

'Yes. I knew him by sight.'

'Could you elaborate on that?'

'Certainly. I'd seen him at Dr Wetherell's funeral.' Outside the morning sun slanted down in the yard. Sergeant Dando looked young, about nineteen years old. Did he shave? She doubted it.

'You went to Dr Wetherell's funeral . . .?' That seemed to surprise him.

'Yes. I happen to live in South Harptree.'

He tapped his pencil against his teeth. 'So you *were*, shall we say, acquainted with Mr Crichton?'

'No.' She decided to shoot straight. 'I'm an old Nosy Parker. I didn't want to miss anything. Are you going to write that down and use it in evidence against me?'

His brown eyes crinkled at the corners. 'I shouldn't think so.'

They went through one or two other matters. No, Elizabeth said, she hadn't known Max long but she could swear to his honest, upright character. And Phoebe had been truly sick that night with what she could personally testify to be a terminal illness.

'Phoebe?'

'I'm sorry. Max's own car. He calls her . . . it . . . Phoebe because she's yellow.'

Sergeant Dando didn't follow, not apparently having studied classical literature at his seat of learning.

'Phoebus was the sun god,' she said. 'The sun's yellow . . . do you follow? Of course, I told him that, strictly speaking, he ought to call the car just that – Phoebus – because Phoebe is someone quite different . . . the goddess of the moon, you know. But he says she's definitely female, very changeable, and that the moon's yellow as well, so it hardly matters.'

'Er . . . to get back to the matter in hand,' said the Sergeant, 'have you ever visited the Manor, Mrs Blair?'

'No,' said Elizabeth. Something about the way his hair stuck up in a quiff reminded her of her great-nephew, Henry. Any minute now, she thought, he'll reach into his pocket and produce some bubble gum.

'But you can see it from your cottage?'

'Only just.'

'But if your garden adjoins the Manor wall . . .?'

'My neighbour's garden does. Miss Marchant . . . I'm on the far end. I can just about see the yew hedges from my end bedroom window, but it hardly makes me a close neighbour.' She thought of something else that had been lying dormant in her mind. 'You know what's been puzzling me?'

He gazed at a corner of the desk and said resignedly, 'What's that, Mrs Blair?'

'Why, on such a foul night, didn't Crichton drive his car right up to the house? Why leave it by the Old Schoolhouse and get wet?'

'Because your Citroën was already parked in front of the house?' he suggested.

'But Max says there was a whole bunch of room in the driveway. The Aitkens have three cars and they're frequently all parked there at once. No, it wasn't for lack of space . . .' Thoughtfully, she said, 'He may have wanted to sneak up on Mr Aitken unseen for some reason. Wanted to catch him doing something that he shouldn't . . .'

Sergeant Dando was not to be drawn.

She decided to try another tack. 'I'd call a successful young man like Crichton a high-flyer, Sergeant, wouldn't you? And possibly pretty ruthless . . .'

There was a pause. But before the Sergeant could speak, the door opened and an older officer came in.

He said, 'Sorry. Didn't know you were here.'

'It's all right.' Sergeant Dando got up from his chair. 'We're just about through.' He seemed relieved to have an excuse to end the interview.

I can't imagine why, Elizabeth thought.

The shop was full. From the floor above came a sound which might have been the deep boom of a mighty drum.

Elizabeth said, 'For heaven's sake, Max – '

She launched herself upstairs.

'Max – stop that row!' she bellowed. 'Some of us are trying to run a business down below!'

'Betsy!' He swung round on the Victorian piano stool. His rendition of 'Good Morning, America' came to an abrupt halt. 'Sorry,' he said. 'Forgot about your customers. It helps me think.'

'Well, if you could just knock off thinking until about five thirty . . .' she said acidly.

'I would – but I got hold of another tasty little snippet last night.' He got up from the stool and strolled over to the desk.

Elizabeth said nothing.

'How about this then? It seems that the money missing from the St Swithin's Roof Fund has been systematically transferred, over a period of months, into a certain mysterious acount number in Oxford.'

'How on earth did you find that out?'

Max tapped the side of his nose and tried to look mysterious. 'Impeccable source,' he said.

'Your friend Andy, I take it? So who's been transferring it?'

'That he wouldn't say. I'm not sure they know themselves yet, actually, but old Andy wouldn't admit it. All he said was that it was under investigation.'

'Larry Aitken mentioned an Oxford connection when you first went to see him.'

'He did, didn't he?' Max sat down in the swivel chair. 'I had a phone call from him this morning, actually. He's buzzing off to London to do some filming, it seems.'

'The police are willing to let him go?'

'Seems so, for the moment. But I hear it's with the proviso that he leaves his passport with them and stays for the whole time at his flat in Kensington.'

'I don't suppose you mentioned the account in Oxford to him?'

'I asked, but he wasn't very keen on talking about it. Just insisted rather hurriedly that it had nothing to do with him.'

'Did *he* know whose name the Oxford account was in?'

'He rang off while I was in the middle of asking him . . . Train to catch, he said. But it doesn't really matter.'

'Why doesn't it matter?'

'Because I've got a little lead of my own on the Oxford connection.'

'You have?' Elizabeth felt surprised. She probably looked surprised as well.

'Uh-huh!' He sat there beaming away at her. 'You'll never guess', he said, 'what I found.'

'Probably not, Max. So you'd better tell me.'

'Well, if you're really interested . . .' Opening the top drawer of the desk, he pulled out what looked like a small black diary. He handed it to her. She opened it curiously. Written inside the front cover was the name David Crichton, followed by his address, telephone number and various other personal details.

'Where on earth did you get this?' she asked, amazed.

'A-ha!'

'Max . . .'

'All right. All right . . . It was tucked away in the folder that I dropped on the Manor drive the night we found Crichton's body. I didn't find it before because I shoved it into my desk drawer as soon as I got back and didn't open it again until this morning. Don't you see, Elizabeth – it must have fallen out of Crichton's pocket when the murderer was loading him into the boot of the Citroën!'

'And the murderer didn't notice?'

'It was pitch dark out there. A foul night. He would have been in too much of a panic to notice anyway.'

'And you happened to scoop it up with your papers when you dropped them.'

'Exactly.' Max looked triumphant. 'Clever, eh?'

'Lucky!' A thought struck her. 'Do the police know you have it?'

'Not yet.' Max looked triumphant.

'You'll have to hand it in, you know.'

'Of course – but only when I've had a good squint at it . . . and photocopied it, of course.' Just this once, Max was enjoying being one step in front. Then he said, 'You'd better take a closer look. There are some interesting entries.'

Against the entry for 21 October was scrawled 'Tabernay. Oxford 21315 748–6'.

'It's not a telephone number,' Max said. 'I've tried it.'

'The Bath and Wessex account number then?' Elizabeth guessed.

'Possibly. There's only one Tabernay listed in the telephone directory for Oxford. Mrs B., 119, Bower Street. I'm going down there tomorrow to see the lady. Find out if there's a connection between her and dear old Larry.'

'Lucky it's an unusual name,' said Elizabeth thoughtfully.

'Yes.' Max still looked as if he'd found the key to a fortune. He nodded towards the diary and said, 'Keep reading. There's something else that's quite interesting.'

The letters REB were entered at regular intervals, two or three times a week, from August right up until October. The last of them were against the date of the night that Crichton was killed. Elizabeth felt the blood tingling in her veins.

'Interesting, eh?' Max said softly.

'He'd been seeing Rebecca Forbes?' Elizabeth's mind was whirling.

Max said. 'You have to be wrong about her, Betsy. She's tied in here somewhere . . .'

She said, 'But he can't have been seeing her for three weeks in August. She was in Sydney with her church cronies. She's a smart cookie, but I can't see how she could nip back here for a date with Crichton!'

'Hadn't thought about that,' Max admitted.

'Of course, he may have marked in a block booking regardless. Those nights are to be kept free for Rebecca, whether she's here or not . . .'

'You think so?'

'It's possible.' Elizabeth said, 'And to think she was reading Barbara Cartland! She needed escapism with a love life like hers?'

Max was thinking. 'I suppose there's a possibility they were meeting, but not having an affair. If Rebecca knew Larry was

114

fiddling the fund – well, she might get her revenge by telling tales to Crichton . . .' His mind went off at a complete tangent as he asked, 'So what are you going to do with the Broken Star?'

'When the police finally let me have it back?' She shrugged. 'Have it cleaned, I suppose, if that's possible. Ship it back home again to Virginia, if it can be restored to its original state.' Her eyes lit up with a mischievous sparkle. 'Jim Junior can get rid of it for me in one of the local craft shops. He won't dare tell them about its lurid history.'

'You mean you won't tell whoever buys it about the murder?'

'Don't be a schmuck. Honestly, Max, you're no businessman!'

'And you're as tight as hell sometimes.'

'You think I'm mean?' She gave a chuckle. 'You should have spent an hour or two with my pa-in-law.'

'Don't tell me – he was a tough old backwoods boy with a heart of gold . . .'

'Guess again.' Elizabeth shook her head, smiling back at him. 'Hiram G. wasn't any cute old pop. He was a skinflint who kept his money tied up so tight, we had to count every god-blasted dollar to run the family business. Well, we beat him in the end, but perhaps some of his cheese-paring notions rubbed off. Sorry if it shows.'

On the way downstairs, she thought: An affair between Rebecca Forbes and Crichton? Did she throw me off the track deliberately?

Did Larry find out they were on to his fraud and kill Crichton?

So many scenarios – but all so thin at the moment. Castles on cobwebs . . .

The phone rang the minute she put a foot back inside Martha Washington. 'Mrs Blair?' a voice said. 'This is Julia Aitken.'

'Hello, Mrs Aitken.' Elizabeth thought: What on earth . . .?

'I . . . heard about your car. And the quilt. It . . . must have been a dreadful shock for you.'

'It was rather.'

'I'm . . . most dreadfully sorry that you should have been involved . . .' A pause. 'You may not be interested, after all that, but . . . Well, I wondered if I might ask you a very small favour?'

'Ask away.' Elizabeth was intrigued.

'It's just that . . . Well, I'm besieged here by all these wretched reporters. I don't feel like braving them yet – but I can't seem to concentrate on my painting or any of my usual pursuits. I suddenly thought of those cushion kits that you have in your shop. I don't suppose – don't feel you have to do this – but I don't suppose you could bring one or two up to the Manor for me to choose from? I wouldn't ask, but . . .'

'It's no trouble at all,' Elizabeth told her.

She sounded immensely relieved. 'You're terribly kind.'

'Would tomorrow morning do?'

'That would be lovely.'

Elizabeth had had her share of being harried by the press. She felt a sudden spurt of sympathy for the woman. But there was something else . . . She was *dying* to see inside the Manor. To know how they were all reacting in such difficult times.

Briefly she felt thoroughly ashamed of herself.

26

Max drove her home that evening. At first he said he wouldn't come in, but at the mention of Maryland fried chicken, he changed his mind.

'Of course, there's one person', he said suddenly half-way through supper, 'who could manage to kill two birds with one stone in this affair.'

'Who's that?'

'Forbes. Trouble is, I can't somehow see Fatso as a murderer.'

'Everyone's a potential murderer,' she said, 'if they're pushed hard enough.'

Max didn't agree. '*You* couldn't kill anyone,' he said.

She thought about it for a moment. 'I could have killed my pa-in-law, I think, at certain times of my life.' Then, 'So you've got a theory about Forbes. Spell it out . . .'

'Well . . . say Forbes found out that his wife has had affairs with both Larry and Crichton. He kills Crichton right in front of Aitken's front door so that Larry will cop the blame. Let's assume for the sake of argument that it's Forbes who's been fiddling the fund, not Larry.'

'*Ergo* Crichton finds him out, sets out to tell Larry and then Forbes does for him . . .'

'Pardon?'

'*Ergo*, Max. It's Latin for therefore.'

'They teach you Latin in the colonies?'

'My husband was a lawyer. I guess some of it rubbed off.'

Max said, 'Well, speak English from now on. I only went to St Bernard's Comprehensive. You never told me he was a lawyer.'

She said, 'He wasn't really.' Then she explained. 'I mean he wasn't a lawyer deep inside. Jim was a pretty simple guy who wanted to buy a farm and raise crops . . . but he finished up running the old man's law firm.'

'You sound cheesed off about it.'

'I didn't mind him turning lawyer. There were bits he positively enjoyed – and he made himself damned good at it. But Hiram G. wouldn't let him do it his own way; stuck his oar in at every opportunity. Once or twice, Jim nearly quit.'

'So why didn't he?'

'Because he was too goddamned nice to go off and ditch the old so-and-so. That's why.' She carried on thinking for a moment and then said, 'Are we to assume also that Forbes is the one responsible for Larry's hate mail?'

'Why not? He perhaps started off with the petty stuff – the letters and the phone calls. He poisoned Larry's dog, and that gave him the idea of drugging the whisky. Forbes was, after all, at the exhibition earlier in the day. He could have slipped into the Manor and dropped the stuff in the booze. Remember', Max went on, 'that our Bob, quite uncharacteristically for him, asked for a beer at the sub-committee meeting. And he was terribly eager – you might say maliciously eager – to pass the stuff to Wetherell and get Larry into trouble. Of course, he wasn't to know the Doc would snuff it. Probably regretted it, but couldn't put the clock back.'

Elizabeth said, 'It's a bit risky, isn't it? Would Forbes be prepared to put his own career on the line for the sake of a petty revenge?'

'But if he could make it look as if Larry himself had moved

the money . . .' Max sat gazing out through the uncurtained window with a glass of Budweiser in his hand. He looked totally comfortable – and his theory was growing. 'It would be his *pièce de résistance*, don't you see? The culmination to his campaign. What would disgrace the Lord of the Manor more than anything? Vain old Larry? Easy – arrange it so that it looks as if he'd been filching sums from the Roof Fund and stashing it away in an account number in Oxford.'

'We're absolutely sure that it wasn't Larry himself embezzling the fund?'

'For a measly few thousand?' Max scoffed. 'Would he risk his fame and fortune for that kind of sum?'

'You're probably right,' Elizabeth said. 'So go on. I'm still listening.'

'Well – Forbes has the necessary expertise and access to the office computer when all the rest of his staff have gone home in the evenings. He makes sure there's no way it could be traced back to him. Who's going to believe that the manager of the Bath and Wessex would be doing it? Larry, on the other hand,' he was growing more excited, 'has this . . . female . . . an old flame . . . called Tabernay tucked away in Oxford. He's told Bob about her in an unguarded moment while they're playing golf together. Guffaws all round and good for you, old son – don't know how you do it! Then . . . let's see . . . Forbes nips down to Oxford, opens an account in her name and sets it up to look as if Larry's filtering the folding green stuff into his mistress's account.'

'I don't know.' Elizabeth sounded doubtful. 'Forbes is as thick as thieves with Larry. Everybody knows it.'

'He *pretends* to be thick with him. But the evidence is in the diary, Betsy, in black and white. I'd take a bet that Rebecca had been hitting the sack with both Larry and Crichton – and Forbes couldn't wait to get his own back on both men. He drives up to the Manor that evening at about a quarter to eight. He hides his car somewhere, stays lurking in the bushes until Crichton arrives, then knifes him . . .'

'But why stuff the body into the Citroën if he'd planned to have it found on Larry's doorstep?'

'Panic at the last minute, when we disturbed him? I don't

know. Either way, he shoved the body into the Citroën and made off back to his car via the woods.'

'It's all possible. And he'd have the motives. But I'm not entirely convinced about the computer thing. Would Forbes be clever enough to shift the payments without letting anything be traced back to him?'

'Possibly not. But if he wasn't . . . well, all the better. He thought he could do it, but Crichton's a clever chap and spotted the fraud. Don't you see, the mistakes help prove the theory. Crichton had to be silenced.'

Elizabeth shook her head. Somehow she felt as if they were trying to carry the theory instead of it carrying them. 'I'll sleep on it,' she said. Then told Max about Julia Aitken's phone call.

'You might ask her if she knows anyone called Tabernay,' Max said.

Elizabeth said, 'She won't if it's one of Larry's fancy women.'

'Even so. You might ask.'

27

When Elizabeth arrived at the Manor, Brenda Macmillan opened the door to her.

She said, 'Mrs Aitken is on the terrace, I believe.' She wore a putty-coloured jumper and looked like home-made sin and for the life of her, Elizabeth couldn't imagine her in the sack with Larry.

Julia was sitting on the steps talking to a fat tabby cat. She jumped when Elizabeth called out a greeting. 'What a beautiful fellow! We used to have a big tabby back home.'

'Really?' Julia put down the cat and got to her feet. 'I'm sorry about the pack of vultures out there.' She nodded in the direction of the front gates. 'I expect you had a fight to get in.'

'Worse for you, I should think.'

'I do feel . . . battered by it all. We'd better go in.'

'No – really. I'm quite happy to sit here and admire your garden.'

'Are you quite sure?'

'Absolutely.'

'Well, if you're positive . . .' She had the perfect manners of another day and age. 'I thought perhaps the patchwork might soothe me. I've been sleeping badly.'

She looked hollow-eyed.

'Have you seen your doctor?' Elizabeth asked.

'Yes. He gave me some pills, but I'd rather not take them,' she said. 'Larry's not sleeping either. He's even talking of moving. We both love this place, but I don't think it'll ever be the same again . . .'

'Wouldn't it upset you to leave?' Elizabeth asked.

'I'd hate it. I loved it here.'

Past tense. Elizabeth said, 'I expect you're more attached to the house than your husband. I mean, I expect that he's away a great deal.'

'Yes. He works far too hard,' Julia said. 'Partly because his is a precarious profession and partly because of the way he was brought up. His mother was very puritanical, you know. Methodist. Very stern and rigorous, or so he tells me. I never met her. She died when Larry was seventeen.' There was a long pause, and then she added, 'She committed suicide. Drowned herself. Left a note so that no one should be in any doubt but that it was her own choice.'

'How dreadful,' Elizabeth said, a little surprised at Julia's sudden revelations. Unwise revelations? Perhaps. But then the woman was probably still in a state of shock.

'Yes.' Julia's lips were slightly trembling as she said it. 'Not a very nice thing to have to remember all your life, is it? Of course, the press had a field day when they found out. About fifteen years ago, one of the tabloids did a spread on it. "Aitken Mother Horror". All this seems like a nightmare repeating itself.'

'I can imagine.' Elizabeth hesitated. 'Do you know why she did it?'

'Oh, there was always some mental instability. But I believe she was very unhappy in her second marriage. Larry had left home by that time. Didn't get on with his new stepfather. They had a most terrible row, I believe. They got into a fight and Larry knocked him out. He has a bit of a temper, when he's roused. He thought he'd killed him . . . Anyway, he ran off

120

and joined a repertory company. He used to meet his mother now and again, but always in some neutral place.' Silence. 'I think he sometimes blames himself for her death . . . He thinks he should have done more to protect her. The stepfather used to knock her about, you see. That's why Larry went for him in the end.'

So Larry had a temper – and a violent one at that.

'I couldn't make out why he had this bitter streak. You'd never guess, to see him now, but . . .' Julia's voice trailed off. Then she said, 'Life would be so much simpler if there were no messy, incalculable things like emotions, don't you think?' There was a wistful note in the remark. 'They're a great hindrance sometimes.'

'And sometimes a great pleasure . . .' Elizabeth suggested.

Julia didn't seem to be listening.

After a moment, Elizabeth cleared her throat and said, 'I . . . brought a few cushion kits for you to choose from. I tucked in some made-up samples.'

Julia came back to the present. Slowly she drew the samples from the Martha Washington bag and laid them on her lap. Her fingers touched the quilted feathering. First the Sunburst, then the knotted Nine Patch and finally the Crazy Windmill. 'They're so beautiful,' she said.

'Aren't they?' And useful, Elizabeth thought. She had noticed before that patchwork relaxed people, made their eyes soften . . .

Julia touched a square of blue calico. 'I wasn't much good at school, but I liked art . . . making things . . .'

'You run a gallery at Wells, I believe?'

'Yes. I wouldn't say it's highly successful yet, but it's doing OK.' She gave the tiniest shudder. 'Dreadful American expression!' When she realized what she'd said, she looked smitten. 'Oh, I'm so sorry. I wasn't thinking. I didn't mean . . .'

Elizabeth laughed. 'It's all right. Don't worry.' She wasn't patronizing, like Rebecca Forbes. It had just slipped out. 'A lot of American expressions *are* ugly,' she said. 'Do you enjoy running a gallery?'

'It's absolutely liberating!' Julia's eyes turned eloquent. 'It gives me an occupation. As you said, Larry's away a lot. Sometimes for longish spells, when he's doing a play. He always seems to be away on occasions like birthdays and anniversaries . . .' She picked at a loose thread on the Nine Patch. 'Do you know what I'd like most of all in the world? I wish we could be . . . an ordinary family. I think I'd be happy living in one of those little cottages down by the church. Doing the garden, minding my own business, having everybody else mind theirs . . . You won't tell anyone I said that, will you?'

Funny question, Elizabeth thought. But she was probably terrified of what might get into the papers. 'Of course I won't,' she said.

'It's not easy being married to a famous TV personality, Mrs Blair. In fact, sometimes I think I can't bear it any longer. It's difficult to make real friends, you know, in this business. People are always after something. It's difficult to tell the difference between who's real and who's not.'

Elizabeth made no reply, so she went on, 'We had real friends in the early years. But we've moved around a lot. And you just lose touch with people . . .' There was another long pause while Julia combed at the fur on the cat's sleek back. 'Larry doesn't seem to mind too much. He says you have to take people at face value and not worry. But I do.' Then she laughed. '*He* rather likes showing off to the villagers, if truth were told.'

Yes, vanity helps, Elizabeth thought. It gives you a thicker skin.

'I didn't really mean showing off.' Julia suddenly realized the phrase might be disloyal. 'It's a term Emily uses when she's teasing him. "Showing off to the yokels again, Daddy? Really, how embarrassing!"'

Elizabeth smiled. 'You can always rely on your children to point out your faults.'

'Can't you just?' It sounded heartfelt. 'They have your entrails all over the floor by the time they're finished with you.' Julia went on gazing at the Nine Patch. 'I had a terrible time with Emily in the spring. She wanted to go and live in London. She has a lot of friends there, but . . . Well, some of these young-sters are into drugs, you know. Larry would have given in. He's far too tolerant with her. But I said no.' In a little rush, she said, 'It didn't make me very popular, I'm afraid. Was I right, do you think?' She answered herself. 'I'm still not sure. Brenda says she was fending for herself in Geneva at Emily's age.

Working for some computer firm . . . Do you have children, Mrs Blair? Are they married?'

'Two of them. The others are still hunting like crazy.'

Julia said abruptly, 'Whoever tries to marry Emily will have to be some sort of Superman. Larry dotes on his daughter. I'm not sure any young man will be good enough for him.'

'Jim was like that with Holly. My daughter. They get jealous, you know.'

'I suppose so.'

Elizabeth thought, jealousy was old Hiram's trouble, too. He was afraid of being left out. Afraid of a new wife who had power over his only son's heart. She waited for a moment, then said, 'I wonder – would you have any knowledge of a friend of your husband's called Tabernay?'

'Tabernay . . .?' Her voice sounded puzzled. 'No, I don't think so.'

'It's an unusual name.'

'Yes. I think I'd have remembered it if I'd known whoever it was. Is it important?'

'Probably not. It's just that Max Shepard wanted to know.'

'Ah, yes. His office is above your shop, I gather?'

'Yes.'

'And that's how he came to borrow your car . . .?'

'Unfortunately, yes.'

Julia said, 'It may have been someone Larry knew before we met. I've never heard him mention the name.'

'Oh, well . . . Talking of names, does your husband use his real one or is Aitken a stage name?'

Julia hesitated, glanced at Elizabeth just once, then said, 'Larry Aitken isn't his real name. I've got used to calling him that now – but it was very odd when he first changed it.' Then with a laugh, she said, 'All right . . . I can see you're itching to know. His real name is Roy Hodges. Doesn't quite have the same ambience, does it?' Another quick, flicking glance was followed by a question. 'You won't tell anyone, will you? Larry would be cross with me.'

'Of course not.' Watching her, Elizabeth wondered if Larry bullied her.

'This dreadful business about David . . .' Julia was almost embarrassed. 'I understand the police interviewed you, too.'

'I guess it was pretty inevitable, seeing that someone dumped him in my car.'

'Yes.' Julia shuddered. 'I couldn't stop shaking. It was worse than when poor Charles went.' She hesitated, then asked, 'Have they any idea who might have done it, do you think? Or why they should wait until he was outside our door?'

'I don't think they have a clue at the moment.' Elizabeth tried to keep her voice light and casual. 'You knew Crichton reasonably well, didn't you? Did he have any enemies that you could put your finger on?'

'I honestly can't think of anybody,' Julia said. Her face turned thoughtful. 'He wasn't the type to make enemies. He was just . . . a nice boy. Everyone liked him.'

'So what type was he, exactly?' Elizabeth persisted. She saw the look on Julia's face and responded immediately to it. 'I'm not prying, you realize. It's just that Max and I were chatting about it the other day and we decided that Crichton was really a very . . . self-contained young man. No one knew very much about his private life.' She laughed. 'Oh, hell, I suppose I'm just curious. That's what it boils down to.'

Julia didn't seem to mind, now, talking about Crichton. But she didn't have many answers either. She said, 'I think his biggest interest was probably history. It was his subject at university, he once told me. But apart from that . . . Well, he was a very good accountant. And he worked hard for St Swithin's. That's about what it amounts to.' She looked worried. 'I'm sorry I can't help more.'

Walking out through the Manor gates, Elizabeth wished she'd had the nerve to ask just one more question.

Are you aware that your husband had a little fling with Rebecca Forbes, Mrs Aitken?

But the fact was, she already knew the answer.

You didn't live with a man for twenty-odd years and not know . . .

Now, would Julia be capable of dropping dope into the whisky to teach her wandering husband a lesson?

No point really. Larry didn't drink. And Rebecca's tipple was gin . . . so you finished back where you had started. In the middle of a maze without a map.

28

Number 119, Bower Road turned out to be a neat semi-detached with a few neglected rose trees round the front lawn.

'Mrs Tabernay?' Max asked when the woman came to the door. 'Mrs B. Tabernay?'

'Who wants to know?' She peered suspiciously out with the safety catch still fastened. A sharp old biddy in her seventies.

'My name is Max Shepard, Mrs Tabernay. I'm a private detective.'

'A what?'

'A private detective.'

'Inspector? You don't look like an Inspector.'

'No. I'm a private detective!'

'You'll have to speak up. I don't hear like I used to.'

'Here's my card,' Max bellowed. 'Examine it at your leisure, why don't you?'

She held the card a long way away from her and stared at it hard. 'Private Detective?' she said at last. 'You expect me to believe that? I wasn't born yesterday, young man. You buzz off and try your tricks on somebody else.'

'No – really. It's the truth. All I want is to ask you a few questions.'

'You'll ask them on the doorstep then. There was some chap on the telly last week as had all a widow's savings when he told her he'd come to read the gas meter.'

'Look – I'm not a con man!' Max yelled. 'Do I look like a con man?'

After twenty seconds or so, she said, 'I can't say as you don't.'

'I've come to ask you about Larry Aitken,' he said. 'You've heard of Larry Aitken?'

'*Take Your Chance*. Course I have. Watch it every week.' But her eye continued to glare balefully at him from behind the chain.

'Well, he's in a spot of trouble, you see, and I'm making enquiries for him. You may have seen it in the papers.'

'The body under the bedspread . . .' she said with relish. Then peered with renewed interest at the business card. 'Bath, wasn't it?'

'That's right.'

'Went there on a coach trip once. Everything cost too much. Well, I suppose I could let you in. Walls have ears,' she said, jerking her head in the direction of next door's twitching nets. 'I can give you five minutes. No more.'

The house was your normal semi-detached, with a bricked-up fireplace, a bay window and heavy furniture. 'Do I know Larry Aitken?' Mrs Tabernay said blankly. 'Do I know the King of Siam! Don't be daft! What makes you think I hobnob with TV folk?'

'So there's no connection at all between you and Mr Aitken?'

'Chance would be a fine thing! Any more daft questions?'

'Er – could you tell me if you have an account with the Bath and Wessex Building Society?'

'If I did, I wouldn't tell you about it.' Now her defences were up again and suspicion crackled in the air.

'Look, Mrs Tabernay, I really don't want to see your book or know how much money you have . . .'

'I should think not!'

'I'm just trying to establish if you save with the Bath and Wessex? A plain yes or no . . .'

'You're selling insurance!' She was up in arms in a minute. 'That's what you're up to! Well, you can just clear off out again. I warned you – '

'No. No, honestly . . .' Sweating profusely, Max wondered why he was stupid enough to do this for a living. (What living. an inner voice promptly demanded.) 'A simple yes or no will suffice,' he said for the second time. 'Then we'll leave the subject.'

'No, I haven't got an account with the Bath and Wessex. Just the post office. That's all.'

He felt his spirits sink.

'So can you tell me if there are any other Tabernays in Oxford?'

'Any other what?'

'Any other Tabernays,' Max bawled across to her.

'No need to shout, young man. Why would you want to know?'

'I'm just trying to trace a person called Tabernay who may have links with Mr Aitken's case.'

'I don't know of any others. No.'

Patiently, Max began to question her about other members of her family.

Yes, she'd been married, but her husband had died ten years back.

No, they'd never had children, though they'd both been fond of them.

Yes, her husband had had one brother, name of William. Three years younger, but he was gone now too, the cancer took him.

Yes, William had been married, to a lovely girl called Evelyn. Hadn't seen her for years, though, she'd gone off to Australia.

Yes, William and Evelyn had a family, a boy and a girl. No, they weren't in Australia with their mother.

'So do either of them live here in Oxford?' Max asked with some desperation.

'That depends.'

'On what, Mrs Tabernay?'

'On what you call living.'

The silence lengthened. Max cleared his throat. 'I'm sorry?' he said.

'You would be, if you could see her.'

'See who, Mrs Tabernay.'

'Poor little Sammy,' she said.

The clock struck eleven. They sat there one on each side of the empty fireplace like a pair of bookends.

'Sammy is . . . your niece?'

'That's right. But you won't want *her*. She's got no need of building society accounts where she is, poor little soul.'

'And where would that be, Mrs Tabernay?'

'And she can't talk to you neither. Can't talk to nobody. She's at the Geriatric Unit at the Infirmary. Francis Road.'

'Geriatric Unit?' He didn't understand. 'But she's . . .'

'Barely forty years old. Yes, I know. But there's nowhere else to put her. They closed the other place . . . the place for the mentally handicapped. Nice, it was there. Quiet. Lovely gardens to look out on and paintings and such . . . but it didn't pay, they said.' She gave a hard laugh. 'Now when did the mentally handicapped ever make a profit, you ask yourself? But they seem to expect them to these days! Oh, yes. Poor blighters . . .'

'So Sammy – your niece – is mentally handicapped?' Max said.

'No.' She sat there looking at him implacably out of dark boot-button eyes.

'Then what – ?'

'She wasn't born that way, young man. She's brain-damaged now. But she was a lovely girl . . . until she had the accident.'

'Accident?'

'She was badly injured in a car smash twenty years back. Nineteen years old, she was then. A real beauty, as I said. Been like a cabbage ever since. No, you won't talk to her, my lad. And no amount of money would put her right.'

She gave him the full story in detail over coffee and biscuits. They'd been on the way to some rock concert in London, but they'd only got as far as that bad bend on the bypass. There had been five of them in the car, but Sammy – Samantha – had been the only one thrown out. The chap who was driving got off with a stiff fine instead of jail. Drunk as a lord, they said, but he'd run off and not reported it until the morning and then of course they couldn't prove anything.

Max glanced up from his notes. 'Can you remember the name of the driver?'

'You must be joking! All that time ago. It's all I can do to remember what day it is.'

'What about Sammy's parents?' Max said.

'Well, William's dead now, as I said, and Evelyn – well, she's pretty well an invalid down there in Perth. Diabetes, they tell me, but in my book it was grief that brought it on.'

'You mentioned that Samantha had a brother . . .'

'Iain. Yes. Clever boy. Clever with his computers . . .'

Max felt his stomach give a lurch. 'Computers?'

'Computers. Spent hours and hours playing with them up at that college. He was a doctor, you know. Not the hospital kind. A scientific doctor. *Dr* Tabernay . . .' she told Max with a fierce kind of satisfaction. 'He and his friend from the college set up in business together.'

However tiresome the interview was proving, there was something about Sammy Tabernay's sad history that intrigued him. He couldn't as yet connect any of it directly with Aitken, but he had a hunch that it fitted somewhere into the jigsaw.

'And where does Dr Tabernay live?' he asked, his pen poised. 'Could you give me his address?'

'I could.' An odd smile on her face. She was going to demand a fee, the crafty old witch!

'I'd be very grateful.'

'I'm sure you would.'

Still the long pause. Max started to reach for his wallet. He supposed it was worth it . . .

'Won't do you much good, though.'

Max groaned inwardly. God, she was tedious!

'Why's that, Mrs Tabernay?' he said patiently.

She gazed back at him, her expression almost triumphant. 'Because he's in the churchyard at St Mary's!'

'You mean . . .?'

'He committed suicide five years back. They said it was overwork, but I know better. The poor boy never got over the shock of what happened to his sister.'

29

The offices of Logos (UK) Ltd were located behind a band of tall trees on a half-finished industrial estate ten miles from Oxford. Max parked Phoebe in the small, bare parking bay in front of its smoked windows and climbed out.

Storm clouds were sailing across from the direction in which he had come, great black, bulbous affairs that somehow made the day feel ominous. Or perhaps it was just that the Tabernay story was beginning to get to him. It was odd how some families seemed to get more than their share of tragedy, he thought as he passed in through the silently-opening glass doors to the reception area.

The girl behind the desk looked up and smiled as he came in. Nice! Max thought, swiftly changing moods, taking in blond hair, a scattering of freckles on her pretty nose and the single strand of pearls round her elegant neck.

'Good morning. Can I help you?' she said with a heart-twisting smile.

'I've an appointment with Dr Moran. Three thirty. I'm Max Shepard.'

'Yes, Mr Shepard. If you'd just like to wait a moment . . .'

I'd wait a year or two, Max thought, with someone like you in my line of vision. She did something to the keyboard in front of her and spoke into the telephone in the quietest and easiest manner. He thought: there's something about the way women move (well, some women at least) that doesn't need words. It's a language of its own, when you come to think of it . . . more perfect than mere speech.

'. . . don't you think?'

'I'm sorry?' She'd said something to him and he hadn't even heard her.

'I said there's a storm brewing.' Her voice was laughing. 'You were miles away, weren't you? A penny for them.'

'Er . . . I was wondering where the nearest hotel was around here.'

'The Cherry Tree. I love your car.'

'Phoebe?'

'She's absolutely beautiful.'

'You think so?'

'I do.' Max's pulse went into a good, rattling gallop as she smiled at him again.

'There's only one trouble,' he said.

'What's that?'

'She happens to leak.'

'Oh, dear.' A rumble of thunder was even now growling round the building and almost directly it began to rain. First, great heavy drops that splashed off the pavement. Then a positive deluge that came thrashing against the windows.

'Well, you can't have everything,' she said simply. A statement so wise – so profoundly sensible – that it blew his brain.

And not only his brain. Other parts as well.

Dr Tim Moran stood up and shook hands with him as Max

entered his office. He was a tall, spare man of about forty, dressed in a grey tweed jacket and sober tie. The office was neat and functional with a view across fields to a small man-made lake.

He was mildly surprised to be questioned about Iain Tabernay, but soon settled down into quiet recall of the necessary details. 'Iain and I shared a room at Oxford for almost three years,' he said. 'We were friends as students and when we got our doctorates, we set up in business together.'

'A successful business, obviously,' said Max, taking in the expensive high-tech equipment on the desk and the American-style loose-weave drapes.

'It was dodgy for a year or so, like most new businesses. But then it just took off. We forged links with two American firms that I'd had contracts with. I did a year over there in Seattle. We were pretty excited about the future. But then . . .'

'Then . . .' Max waited.

Moran's face looked troubled. 'You know about Sammy? About Iain's sister, I take it?'

'Yes. His aunt told me.'

'It was tragic. Iain and Sammy were so close. It knocked him for six. He had a couple of nervous breakdowns while we were still in college. And he was under psychiatric treatment when he took his own life.'

'How?'

'Rigged a hose to his car exhaust. He drove it up to a secluded spot in Mere Woods and – that was it.'

'Tough on you, too. I should think.'

'It wasn't easy. I suppose you could say we were like brothers.'

'How long ago was this? His suicide, I mean?'

'Oh . . . five years ago.' They sat there for a moment. 'Anything I can help with?'

'I wish you could.' Then abruptly, Max said, 'I don't suppose you know Larry Aitken?'

'Larry who?'

I knew you wouldn't be into TV games shows, Max thought – but he still got out the Manor brochure with Larry's picture on it.

Moran must have been the only person in the whole of

England not to recognize the great man. He took it and looked at it impassively, then shook his head. 'Sorry.'

So here they were in another blasted cul-de-sac! Max stuffed the brochure back into the folder and stood up to make his polite thank-you speech. Oh, well, can't win them all, he thought. He wondered if he would ever win even one of them . . .

'I suppose you could always track down Sammy's boyfriend,' Moran said suddenly. 'If you wanted information that badly.'

'Her boyfriend?' Max stared at him. 'A steady boyfriend?' he asked. 'Important, I mean?'

'Very important, I think.'

'And this was at the time of the accident?'

'Hardly likely to be after,' Moran said laconically.

'Sorry. Stupid question.'

'Iain used to bring him to the pub for a drink sometimes. That's how I know about him.'

Max sat down again. 'So what was he like, this boyfriend? Can you give me a description?'

'Chestnut hair, thin – good-looking, I suppose.'

'What else can you tell me about him?'

'Not a lot.' Moran thought for a bit. 'He liked a pint, was reasonably good company. Quite athletic, I seem to remember. Used to do a bit of jogging . . . quite often turned up in a track suit.'

'And he was upset about what happened to her?'

'What do you think?'

'I'd say he was.'

'Right first time.' Moran sat there rubbing the tip of his slightly hooked nose. 'I seem to remember he was a student at the Polytechnic.'

'What was he studying?'

'Wouldn't know.'

'And his name?'

'Can't remember that either.' He saw Max's face. 'Sorry.'

'Can't be helped, I suppose.' Max reached something out of his pocket. 'Look – if you should remember his name, or anything else that might help me trace the boyfriend, could you give me a ring on this number?'

'Can do.'

As he got to the door, Max turned. 'And I don't suppose you remember the name of the chap who was driving the car? The one Sammy was injured in?'

'Shan't forget that in a hurry,' Moran said. 'Iain kept on and on about it whenever he got drunk. Hodges. Roy Hodges. That was his name.'

30

'OK, Max. A re-run . . .' Elizabeth said. 'Let's see what we have.'

'I hate women who organize,' Max said gloomily. 'Let's have a coffee.'

When he'd opened the door to her at a quarter past one – lunchtime – she had found him pale and pink-eyed from lack of sleep.

'So how are we today?' she had asked drily.

'Frazzled.'

'You should try getting to bed early now and again.'

'You sound like my mother.'

'God forbid I should be your mother, Max. Why weren't you at work?'

'Heavy night,' he said.

'Here or in Oxford?'

'Oxford.'

'So don't tell me – you were getting yourself a spot of much-needed education . . .'

'You might say that.'

She gave him a shrewd, all-embracing glance. 'That kind of education, huh? Blonde or brunette?' she asked.

'Blonde.' A far-away look now appeared in his bleary blue eyes. A look that made Elizabeth wish she was twenty-six years old again and capable of such fine rapture. 'You'd better ask me in,' she said. 'And get the coffee on.' Someone was going to have to drag him back to the real world.

Now, a whole half-hour later, he was showered and dressed – if a Greenpeace T-shirt and track suit bottoms counted as dressed – and they had recapped on the activities of yesterday and were pondering the implications of Roy Hodges and Larry Aitken being one and the same man.

'Of course, we all do stupid things occasionally,' Elizabeth said.

'Some of us more stupid than others. Well, it explains why he doesn't drink any more.'

'Yes,' said Elizabeth. Presumably there had been some sort of road-to-Damascus effect after the accident. How, she asked herself thoughtfully, did one reconcile the two Larry Aitkens? The unknown actor who, roaring drunk at the wheel of a car, had maimed a girl for life and Aitken the rich philanthropist? Was the relentless charity work an attempt to atone for what he had done to Sammy Tabernay? His own form of self-punishment? Or just another means of heightening his popularity among his mass audience?

Max asked if she took her coffee black or white.

'One sugar, no milk,' she told him.

He disappeared through a stripped pine door into the tiny kitchen. The flat was your typical bachelor pad. A pile of socks (clean, Elizabeth hoped) littered the oval table which also held a haphazard arrangement of old newspapers and music tapes. A whiff of something exotic and spicy hung around the small, striped sofa and the Turkish rug. Presumably it emanated from the foil dish on the bookcase, which held the remains of yesterday's chicken tikka. The debris apart, it was an elegant room with its large-paned window looking out on to black Regency railings and a below-stairs view of disembodied legs as they tramped to and fro outside on a level with your head.

How extraordinarily peaceful it was in these side streets! Oh, there were traffic snarl-ups out on the ring road and in the one-way system that snaked through the heart of the city. Hordes of tourists up and down Milsom Street . . . But here where perfectly proportioned town houses gazed each other out across slabbed pavements almost as wide as they were long . . . here the only vibrations to be found were from an age when two Georges, one mad and one randy, had ruled the shires and life was conducted in a remarkably civilized manner.

Within the few square miles that were ruled by Nash, she quickly reminded herself . . . Filth, disease and penury had abounded elsewhere in Regency England. And no doubt the seven deadly sins had flourished even within the delightful city created by Wood the builder, Allen the quarry-owner and Nash the social organizer.

As they still do now, she thought. Greed and jealousy and hatred as savage as anything to be found among primitive tribes. Whether you liked it or not, they existed and would go on existing.

She wondered suddenly where Max had got to. 'Where's that coffee?' she called out. 'What's taking you so long?'

'The washing up,' came the reply.

She went to help – and promptly wished she hadn't. The pile of dishes in the sink stood two feet high. There was a silence while she studied the film of mould on the top mug, then she said, 'I'd accept alcohol instead . . .'

'I've scrubbed two mugs. We'll have both,' Max told her. He was measuring out coffee grains with unusual concentration. Suddenly he said, 'So what if Sammy's boyfriend decided to get his own back on Larry?'

'We're heaving out Fatso?' Elizabeth asked.

'For the moment. Let's take a new scenario. Let's suppose that Sammy's boyfriend – call him Mr X – somehow found out that Roy Hodges is now the very famous Larry Aitken.'

'Spotted him on television perhaps?' Elizabeth looked thoughtful.

'Something like that.'

'And even twenty years on, he still has this immense anger and resentment that Larry got off scot-free and poor little Sammy's lying in some kind of limbo.' She took the coffee that Max handed her. 'He decides to deal out some punishment himself. So he finds out where Larry lives . . . comes to Bath . . . and starts to hassle him with the letters and the phone calls. He poisons the dog. And then, one day, he gets into the house – '

'Came up to the exhibition and took his chance?' Max conjectured.

'It's feasible. He sneaks into the drawing-room when the house is deserted; sees the pills lying on the bureau and drops them into the decanter.'

'Exit Dr Wetherell,' Max murmured.

'Does it seem OK to you so far?'

135

'Carry on, ma'am,' Max said. 'I'm all ears.'

'Well . . . say in the mean time, he's read about the Roof Fund. There was a big splashy article about it in the *Chronicle* in the summer . . . remember? That huge photo of Larry posing with the Eadfrith Gospel. Say he's read that Aitken's on the committee and sometimes deposited cheques into the fund himself. Mr X has this doozie of an idea about making it look as if Larry's fiddling the fund.'

'Doozie?' Max murmured with a pained look.

'Same motive as when we decided it was Forbes doing the plotting. Mr X is all out to get Larry disgraced in the eyes of the good people of South Harptree . . . to destroy his image of being the good guy and charity fund-raiser.'

'Yes, but *how* would he manage it?'

'Not sure yet.' She went on thinking. 'Iain Tabernay might have passed on a few tips. He was a computer expert.'

'Yes, but how could our friend gain access to the Bath and Wessex computer?'

'George says you could hack your way in . . . Trouble is, you said Tabernay died five years ago.' She stopped as she remembered an interesting piece of information. 'Brenda Macmillan did a year with a computer firm in Geneva.'

'So she did. Can't see a motive, though. She's nutty about old Larry.'

'She might be hard up. Have debts . . .'

'A Scot?' Max said incredulously. 'Anyway, if she set up a false account somewhere, she'd hardly be likely to use the name of Tabernay. I doubt she'd know about Sammy. She'd call it something like Burns or Stewart.'

Elizabeth said, 'The thing is, I can't see her doing anything to hurt old Larry. I mean, she hero-worships the guy. But it'll bear investigation.' She passed him a newly opened packet of biscuits and said, 'Let's try another tack. How about if our Mr X made friends with somebody in the Bath and Wessex office?'

'Forbes?'

'Forbes or . . .'

Her face had an expression of particular concentration. Suddenly, she said, 'He was good-looking, wasn't he. Dr Moran said so. Presumably he's still pretty attractive twenty years later. Maybe . . . he got to know one of the girl clerks.'

Max agreed that it was a possibility.

Elizabeth still sat there with this rapt expression in her eye. She helped herself to a chocolate wheatmeal and took a tentative nibble. 'Max – can I use your phone?'

'Be my guest.'

Five minutes later, the gleam in her eye was even brighter. 'That's it,' she said, as she came back in from the hall.

'What's what?'

'Well . . . suppose our Mr X had an accomplice at the Bath and Wessex who fiddled the computer for him.'

'Right.'

'Put yourself into the accomplice's shoes. The police have turned up at the office to investigate a possible fraud. What would you do?'

'Scarper?'

'Exactly. So . . . I just rang Bob Forbes.'

'And?'

'And I told him I'd sold this wall-hanging to one of the young ladies who works in his establishment. Only she wasn't there when I tried to deliver it to her at the office this morning.'

'Did you?'

'Did I what?'

'Sell her something?'

'Oh, Max, for God's sake – I'm inventing a little story! I wanted to know if any of the girls didn't turn up for work today. Anyway, I asked if he could possibly give me the girl's home address, so I could deliver it to her flat.'

'But how did you know who – '

'I didn't even have to give him a name. He was in such a filthy mood that he blasted it all right out to me there and then. He doubts if I'll find young Sally Stewart at her flat in Monfort Street, as she appears to have done a bunk. She hasn't been at work since Tuesday and if he chose to, he could give you a very good reason why!'

When he went into the office at three that afternoon, Max found a message on the answerphone. 'Mr Shepard? This is Tim Moran. From Logos. Listen – I just remembered the name of Sammy Tabernay's boyfriend. Well, half remembered . . . I don't know if this will be any help or not, but it was something like Cox. Or Fox. I'm sorry, but I still can't remember his first name.' A little cough then a short pause. 'Well, I hope it's some help. If you need anything, you have my number.'

Rebecca Forbes strongly denied, when Max called on her at four fifteen, that she had ever had an affair with David Crichton. Not even if her name *had* been found in Crichton's diary! There must be some mistake, she told him.

And stood there watching him – a smile curving her cheeks – as he did a three-point turn in the road outside. But the smile did not quite reach of the green of her eyes.

31

Sally Stewart had not slept. She stared down into the green depths of the river as it flowed under Pulteney Bridge. All night she had huddled miserably under the colonnades in the damp and the cold.

Where the waters met the bridge, they looked as calm as a millpond, but the effect was illusory. Close to, there were all sorts of nicks and swirls on the surface, points at which the deeply sucking eddies centred as the wind or the current caught them. Nearer was the thunderous roar of the weir . . . A boy had been drowned there a week or two back. He had leapt from the parapet for a bet and caught his head on the sunken remains of some girders.

Beyond the sluice gates, the river broadened. She wondered how deep it was where the boats were moored opposite the Parade Gardens.

At one point, last night, she had thought they were on to her. Footsteps had approached from the direction of North Parade. Slow, secret footsteps slithering a little in the darkness. On all fours she had crawled back into the wall until the stone dug into her back. Had waited, almost choking with fear. But then she'd heard a trickling stream directly to the right of her. It was only a midnight reveller, relieving himself on his way home.

When first light came, the slope below Orange Grove lay under a listless, spiritless mist. The bandstand stood surrounded by cold flowerbeds. A pair of sparrows had come to peck at the crumbs left from last night's supper – a vegetable pie that she had bought from the market.

Her body felt stiff, but her mind moved endlessly. So what now, she thought, her face turned towards the puppet theatre set into the walkway from the bridge. The air was very still. Below the weir lay a band of rubbish, a long murky tail of it. Dead Coke cans, old rope, two washing-up liquid bottles . . .

What now?

A leap from the bank?

She was a lousy swimmer. Yes, that would finish it all. But she knew she wasn't brave enough for that.

She had lost her job. She couldn't go back to the flat in case the police were waiting. Her hands kept breaking out into a clammy sweat.

What if she pleaded that she'd been taken in by him entirely? That she was sorry now that she'd ever got involved? She really did feel sorry . . . and that was the truth.

Fear – absolute panic – kept rising inside her.

She could see again his face when he'd opened the door to her. She'd gone running up the stairs in such a state that she'd almost knocked over the palm thing on the landing.

He had stood there staring at her as if she were quite mad. Had said coldly, 'I thought I told you never to come here.'

'I had to see you! It's urgent. I'm frightened.'

Even then he hadn't asked her in. His eyes had stared at her as if she was someone . . . something . . . he barely recognized!

And then came the movement from behind him.

There was someone with him . . . a girl all wet and dripping, wearing nothing but a towel, her blond hair curling in tiny tendrils . . .

How easily all your most precious dreams could be shattered!

All he had said was, 'Well, I told you never to come here. It's your own bloody silly fault.'

'You . . . bastard!' she had whispered, shaking all over. And bolted back down the stairs while her legs would still carry her.

*

Eight fifteen. Bath Spa station. The south-west wind had brought up a billow of rain clouds and washed Beechen Cliff a soft, greyish green.

Sally walked in a kind of daze into the buffet to get herself a coffee. She caught her reflection in the misty door pane. She didn't look as haggard as she felt. Just as well, perhaps!

She'd had a wash in the Ladies' room, dragged her make-up from the zipped compartment of her hold-all, applied a dusting of shadow to her puffy eyelids. The thought of food nauseated her – yet she knew she needed something to settle her stomach.

Black coffee and biscuits, she thought.

As she waited in the queue, she turned her head and gazed at the newspaper stand. The door opened again behind her to let in a swirl of wind. Two teenagers had been shot dead in a bar in Belfast. A one-armed man had saved a child from drowning in Weston-super-Mare.

And then she saw it! ACTOR ARRESTED ON FRAUD CHARGES. ACCOMPLICE SOUGHT.

She swallowed. Felt sudddenly sick . . .

Yes, it was her name underneath. Sally Stewart, aged twenty-seven, of Monfort Street, Bath.

But no photograph as yet, thank God! That at least was something.

32

Bob Forbes mopped a brow in his over-heated office and let his thoughts pass from the two-thirty at Newmarket to that dark horse, Sally Stewart. No matter how he tried, he still couldn't quite believe it.

Silly Sally . . .! Someone had happened to call her that once, and the name had stuck. Silly Sally, of all people, with her clumsy feet and hands, her stumpy figure. A bit dim, he'd thought her, quite honestly. It just went to show that you never could tell.

Of course, they'd known about Larry's sexual prowess. Bob supposed he'd been bedding her . . . but he couldn't really imagine that either. Silly Sally? It didn't bear thinking about, but it was the only explanation.

What Bob couldn't get clear in his mind was the point of it all. I mean, for such a paltry sum. A couple of thousand . . . Small change, surely, to a man like Aitken?

And then there was this other party that he'd got stowed away in Oxford. Female, no doubt! Some hot little filly he hadn't wanted anyone to know about.

How the hell did the clever sod do it?

Wouldn't do him much good if he landed up in jail though.

Bob Forbes thought: It's Julia I really feel sorry for. Taking one blow after another . . .

His mind went back to the first Christmas the Aitkens had spent at the Manor. Larry had brought a crowd of them back for drinks without forewarning her. She'd been standing in the hall, small and slim, wearing this old painting smock, splashes of blue and green all over it . . . But the triangular blue mark at the corner of her left eye hadn't been paint! More like the remains of a whopping great bruise.

She'd walked into the studio door. That was what she'd told them, swift as a bird. But Bob had seen her face as she turned to run upstairs and get changed. Fear . . . apprehension . . . that was what he'd seen in her blue-grey eyes.

Could Larry have done that to her? Clocked her one? Bob wasn't sure, but he'd seen the famous temper now and again . . . and the thought *had* indisputably crossed his mind.

Sitting there with his tie loosened a little, his august shape wedged into a chair that was several sizes too small for him, Bob told himself that you could never tell about people. You never knew what secrets were hidden behind closed doors.

And talking of secrets . . . He braced himself to ring his home number. Last night, watching her smooth cream into that round-boned face of hers, he had been tempted to say, 'I want to know, Rebecca. No – I *demand* to know why the police keep hauling you in! What exactly did they find in Crichton's diary? I'm your *husband*. For God's sake, I've a right to know!'

But all she ever said was, 'They just wanted to check some times and dates. It's not important.'

A shutter, like the leathery eye of a lizard, always flickered in Rebecca's gaze when he tried to wrestle the plain truth out of

141

her. That beautiful, poppy-coloured mouth of hers smiled and uttered bland phrases . . . But suddenly, tapping out the digits on the phone on the receiver in his hand, Bob knew that he wasn't going to let her get away with it for much longer.

He wasn't looking forward to the next five minutes, to a certain conversation he was about to have with his wife, but chickens had to come home to roost . . .

'Rebecca?' he said. 'Can you meet me for lunch? It's time we got a few things straight.'

Sally Stewart's room faced the front on the second floor of number 18, Monfort Street.

'Feel like a spot of breaking and entering?' Max had asked Elizabeth. But getting in there had actually been quite easy. They'd had a stroke of luck. A small removal van had been parked outside the house when they arrived – students moving into the ground-floor flat, it seemed – so the front door had been wedged wide open. They had simply walked in past the wooden crates as if they were residents. And once on the second floor, Max's bunch of magic keys had done the rest.

The room smelled stale. From the street below came the sound of young voices and distant laughter. Elizabeth hadn't exactly approved of what Max termed a careful little afternoon reconnoitre. But on the other hand, if he intended to go right on in there anyway . . . well, there wasn't any point in being left out of the proceedings. And two could search more quickly than one, she reasoned.

'What does it remind you of?' Elizabeth asked.

'A jumble sale?'

'Or the Old Curiosity Shop. How can anyone live in such a clutter? It's worse than your place, Max.'

'Thanks.'

'You're very welcome.' A thought struck her. 'Perhaps the police left it in this state.'

'Looks pretty authentic to me,' said Max. 'Which half will you take?'

'I'll do from the wardrobe to the window. You go the other way.'

The door of the wardrobe stood half-open. The half-dozen shelves on one side were stacked with casual gear, shoved in at all angles, sweaters, socks, cardigans. On the left-hand side hung what seemed to be working clothes, slightly better kept. Skirts, half a dozen mumsy blouses with bows, a good tweed coat and a blue poplin mackintosh.

Wherever Sally Stewart had gone, Elizabeth reflected, she hadn't taken much with her.

At the back, on the floor, behind the jumble of shoes, was an empty wine bottle – Santa Rita, a bag stuffed with old Christmas paper, a man's tie (red silk with an imprinted paisley pattern), and a bundle of empty carrier bags. Everything smelled faintly of TCP. Or was it seaweed . . . a long, frilled strand of which Elizabeth found hanging over the back of the dressing-table mirror? Dried bladder wrack, if she wasn't mistaken.

'It's going to be fine tomorrow,' she observed, brushing the stiff greeny-yellow stuff with her finger.

'Seaweed?' Max said.

'Souvenir of a good day out?' she suggested as she checked her way through the pile of magazines, the old make-up bag, the china ring rack, the tights and the assortment of scarves on the top of the dressing-table.

'Think this is her?' asked Max, finding a snapshot in an oval frame on the shelf over the fireplace. A plain girl with mousy hair and glasses smiled out at them . . . A girl with her arm linked into that of an older woman. Her mother? Same eyes, same rather heavy nose . . .

'I reckon,' said Elizabeth. 'Not the kind of girl you'd expect to be wearing these,' she said, fishing out a pair of very frothy and probably expensive French knickers from the top drawer. The other drawers yielded nothing very interesting: except, in the bottom one, folded with a care missing in the rest of the room, a paper napkin enclosing a dried rose.

'Looks vaguely familiar,' Max said when he saw the green embossed napkin.

Two views of the Scottish glens, clashing with the yellow roses on the wallpaper, obviously came with the room and offered no clues as to the personality of the occupier. The contents of the long bookcase, however, held more interest. Solid yet flimsy tomes like *Cashelmara* and *A Woman of Substance* stood side by side with books of quite a different kind. Virginia Woolf's *To the Lighthouse*, heavily annotated. 'Symbolic' under-

lined next to the passage about the table in the pear tree . . .
and 'Crusty old sod!' next to a description of Mr Ramsay. There
was a copy of *The Writer's Workshop*, a second-hand volume of
Tess of the D'Urbervilles and *The Oxford Book of Modern Verse*.

'Interesting . . .' murmured Elizabeth, pulling out a copy of
Nicholas Nickleby. There was something sticking out of the top
of it, a slip of notepaper being used as a bookmark. Unfolding
it, she saw the date 17 May at the top. No address. The note
read briefly: *Sally. I'm on late tonight. Make it 11 o'clock, not ten. L.*

'Larry?' Max suggested.

'It's possible.' But somehow, she had her doubts. 'Doesn't
seem altogether his style.'

'Not florid enough?'

'Exactly.' And the paper was too . . . mean. Anything Aitken
wrote on would have to shout money. He'd buy it from that
shop that sold hand-made Venetian stuff in Broad Street.

Still, the letter L intrigued her . . . you couldn't *positively*
dismiss Larry from your mind.

Over at the makeshift desk – two hardboard shelf units
supporting an old table top – Max found a pink folder, A4 sized,
marked: *Sally Stewart. Creative Writing. City of Bath College 1990/
91.*

'Very neat,' said Max.

One hell of a lot neater than the rest of the place, Elizabeth
thought. She fished out the dozen or so essays and stories and
sat down on the bed to take a quick look. They were of average
standard . . . An essay entitled 'A Room I Know Well'. A set of
scribbled notes about imagery.

Elizabeth recognized a quotation and read aloud.

> *The sculptur'd dead, on each side, seem to freeze,*
> *Emprison'd in black, purgatorial rails:*
> *To think how they may ache in icy hoods and mails.*

'Keats . . .' she murmured.

'Pardon?' said Max.

'Just airing my literary knowledge, Max. Don't you ever read
poetry?'

'Not if I can help it.'

She flicked over the pages in Sally's neat, sloping handwriting. A page of Haiku verse, decorated with doodles of birds. A story entitled 'Fog', in which a ghostly car dissolved on the M4. *Ingenious, but watch your commas*, the lecturer had commented.

Max handed her a *What's On In Bath* pamphlet he'd found on the desk. 'Page four,' he said.

On page four someone had ringed a mini-marathon to be started in Great Pulteney Street on the third Saturday in March. 'She's athletic?' Elizabeth said, surprised. The girl in the snap-shot looked . . . well, clumsy, if not lumpen.

'Perhaps she decided to get fit,' Max said.

'But I can't honestly see her in running shorts and a vest,' Elizabeth said as they emerged ten minutes later.

They were half-way down the top stairs when they met someone else coming up: a girl in a red jacket with brown, curly hair. There was something about the way she looked at them . . .

Under the pretext of fastening her shoe, Elizabeth let Max go on down.

The girl crossed the upper landing, glanced round, then rapped on Sally's door.

Rapped once again, more urgently . . .

'She's not there,' Elizabeth said, straightening up.

The girl gave a start and turned.

'We've already tried,' Elizabeth told her. 'Are you a friend of Sally's, by any chance?'

The girl said briefly, 'We work together.'

'At the Bath and Wessex?'

'Yes. Why?'

'Oh, just curiosity,' Elizabeth said. 'I don't suppose you'd happen to know where she is?'

'Why should I?'

'Oh, no reason.'

'So – you've no idea where she might be?' Elizabeth prompted.

'What's it to you, anyway?'

'Well, I wanted to know when she's going to collect some-thing she ordered from my shop.' It wasn't exactly comfortable to be telling white lies to a stranger, but . . . 'Is she a friend of yours?' Elizabeth probed gently.

145

'Sort of.'

A cagey answer. Elizabeth looked at the girl for a moment before deciding. Then she said, 'Look – if you *do* hear anything of her, perhaps you'd be kind enough to contact me?' Fishing into her pocket, she produced her business card. 'I know she's . . . in a spot of trouble, but I'd like to help her. Perhaps if we could find her before the police . . .'

The girl scuttled across the landing and rushed back down the stairs.

'Well, I blew that one, Max,' Elizabeth said as she joined him in the street.

Stupid of her. But it couldn't be helped.

33

Elizabeth sat in Max's old armchair, totally absorbed in the essay that she'd filched from Sally Stewart's folder. The one entitled 'A Room I Know Well'.

It was not a very long piece of work, but it was heartfelt! The room was spacious and seemed to have a bar in one corner, glowingly described. *Plump, delicious, golden bottles hang like ripe fruit, upside-down on the tree. A radiant light shines from that corner, a honey-coloured brightness . . . a golden dream from an enchanted world!*

'An alcoholic would know the feeling,' Max murmured when she read the passage out to him.

'I don't think it's the alcohol that's she's raving about,' said Elizabeth. 'Listen . . . *My body feels heavy with longing. I'm going quietly crazy as he lifts the sparkling crystal with one hand and pours with the other, smiling at me as he does so, gazing at me as if across some Aladdin's cavern. My heart dissolves as he –* '

'Fetches her another gin and tonic?' Max suggested.

'Shut up, Max. This is serious. Where was I? Right . . . *My heart dissolves as he smiles at me. Just the pleasure of sitting there in the loose-covered chair – cabbage roses rampaging over English chintz –* '

'Cabbage roses rampaging?'

146

'I said shut up, Max! . . . *knowing that he absolutely must come over in the end, after so many rapacious glances.*' Max was doubled up by this time, but she kept on reading. '*There is an immense glass ashtray on the table in front of me and a bowl of blue statice, lots of lovely old furniture and a picture of a woman with a fan on the wall opposite. A Gainsborough goddess in a heavy gilded frame; two smaller portraits on either side of her. I'm in such a foolish state of mind . . . half intoxicated; I think the pictures are watching me. Elegantly, timelessly, in a golden aura that floats balloon-like across the centuries . . . I've forgotten about the cold outside the three long windows; Jack Frost silvering the pavements and the obelisk in the garden in the middle of the square;* She's obviously having a go at semi-colons this week. *I've forgotten everything except the grip of his eyes on mine, the warm mobility of the emotions inside of me . . .*'

Max said, 'Warm mobility? Oh, God . . .' and vanished into the kitchen. She heard him falling around the place, helpless with laughter.

Elizabeth sat looking at the paper on her lap. It seemed to her not so much funny as touching . . . pathetic. like the secret confidences of a fifteen-year-old's diary.

Only Sally wasn't a child. She was a grown woman. Gauche, naïve, floundering in a tide of emotion . . .

When Max came back, he brought two glasses of red wine. 'I'm sorry,' he said. 'I'll behave myself now.'

'Yes . . . well, sit down and concentrate. Let's suppose our Mr Cox or Fox, who had a grudge against Larry, has followed him here. I want you to tell me everything we know about him. I want you to be Sherlock Holmes.'

'Watson might be more appropriate.'

Elizabeth said, 'Probably, but just this once let's pretend you've got a razor-sharp brain.'

'Right,' he said cheerfully. 'Mr Cox or Fox . . . Well, he's thin with brown hair.'

'He *was* thin twenty years ago. And his hair may have gone grey.'

'Or been dyed.'

'And maybe he's equipped himself with a Groucho moustache and plastic glasses. Don't bother using your very vivid imagination, Max. Just stick to the facts.'

147

'OK.' He put his head to one side, considering. 'Well, he used to jog.'

'Reckon he still does?'

'Possibly.' Max's face lit up. 'That leaflet in Sally's room.'

'The mini-marathon. You think *he* might have been the one taking part, not Sally?'

'Perhaps she went along to cheer him on.'

'Or met him there. Not bad, Max. Carry on.'

He thought. 'His initial might be L. There was that note.'

'Might stand for Larry, though. It might have been Larry she fell for. He might have been the one who coaxed her into fiddling the money.'

'Can you imagine Larry in bed with her?'

'Nope.'

'Neither can I. Forget that one.'

'She might have attracted him with her vibrant personality, Max.'

'I wouldn't bet on it,' he said gazing into his glass. 'She writes like a Mills and Boon lady and she had a pink bunny rabbit on her pillow. Scrub the vibrant personality.'

'You think so?'

'I think so.' He paused, then added, 'I read a Mills and Boon once.'

'Was this in your ill-spent youth?'

'I found it on a train.'

'Did you enjoy it?'

'It shocked me a bit. All that . . .'

'Soft porn?'

'I was going to say "warm mobility".'

She laughed. 'I forgot how impressionable you are, Max. So – do we know any more about our man?'

'He's good-looking. That's about it, really.'

'Right.' She handed him the essay. 'Now . . . I want you to read this again and tell me what you think about the room.'

He read for three or four minutes: the clock ticked and Elizabeth sipped at her wine.

'Well?' she said finally.

'Well . . . it sounds pretty plush, as rooms go.'

'Doesn't it just? Ever come across such a room before?'

He hesitated. 'I'm not sure.'

'In general terms, I mean.'

Max took another sip of wine and gave the essay another puzzled glance. 'In general terms?'

'Yes. Think, Max. Lots of splashy chintz armchairs. Thick carpet. Draped chintz curtains with matching ties. All the tables . . .'

'And the bar with the sound of glasses clinking in one corner. Sounds like a hotel bar or a restaurant.'

'Right! Then there are long windows looking out on to a lovely old square. Know anywhere like that, Max?'

He sat up suddenly. 'Wood's Hotel?'

'The lounge that looks out over Queen Square. Good boy! That's exactly what it reminded me of, too. It's too big for an ordinary room. All those portraits – and I knew you'd recognize the bar in the corner.' There was a pause. 'And there's something else that's very, very interesting.'

If there was, Max couldn't think of it. He shook his head.

Elizabeth took the sheets from him and began to read. *'He holds the crystal in one hand and pours with the other . . .'*

'Haven't got a clue, Betsy. She's in love with the barman?' he said jokingly.

'Exactly! I think our man *might* work at Wood's Hotel, Max. I have this gut feeling.'

For some reason or other, Elizabeth found sleep that night hard to come by. The moon was bright. She lay under the duvet gazing at the thin, white light on the wall and thinking about the young Robert Henry Lightfoot.

Yesterday she had found him in *Bristol Emigration Records*. His name, place of origin, trade and destination. Well, you couldn't be absolutely positive that it was him, but it seemed unlikely there would be *two* Robert Lightfoots leaving the village of Little Gurney for Virginia in 1744.

Or, as it turned out, leaving the confines of a Bristol jail . . .

Robert Lightfoot. Joiner. Parish of Little Gurney. Aged twenty. So horrifically young! *Four years for stealing two shillings' worth of goods from the shop belonging to Sarah Cottle.*

Delivered to the quayside to be transported to Virginia, on a fine autumn morning, with a nip in the air. A young man with a taut face and the uncontrollable urge to cut and run, like poor

Sally. Only the shackles on his legs would have prevented it. Why had he stolen two shillings' worth of goods? Because he needed tools for his trade? Because he needed to help feed his seven brothers and sisters? Elizabeth liked to think so. For after he had served his term in bondage at the Wilson Plantation, hadn't he turned out to be of sterling character? Set himself up in business, bought land . . . brought his old mother over to join him . . .

'Great going, Robert!' she said softly.

She'd like to tell young Sally that it was possible to come through a bad business and make something of your life.

But very probably she wouldn't have the chance . . . Elizabeth closed her eyes and drifted off at last.

34

The coffee shop at Waterstone's bookshop in Milsom Street was packed. It was just on lunchtime. Elizabeth seemed to have been sitting in the corner by the window for ever, but in fact had only been there ten minutes.

The conversation over the counter at the Bath and Wessex earlier that morning had for a time been disappointing. At first, Sally's friend with the brown eyes had been hostile, seemingly terrified by Elizabeth's presence there . . . by her invitation to have a chat over a snack lunch.

She had refused point blank. But then, at the last minute, some other impulse had jerked out of the girl. 'I . . . I may have to work through,' she'd said. 'I can't promise anything . . .'

Elizabeth went on gazing down into the street. It was a blowy autumn day and the shoppers were having to fight against the wind. China teacups rattled behind her and the smell of home-made carrot cake, chocolate fudge slices and apple and almond bars pervaded the place.

She was wondering how long to go on sitting there when something caught her attention. She turned away from the window and saw that there was a familiar red jacket in the self-service queue.

The girl took almost five minutes to load her tray with apple cake and a pot of English Breakfast tea. She wove her way through the crowded tables to where Elizabeth sat and took the chair opposite.

'So what do you want?' she demanded almost belligerently, lifting the cup and placing it right way up on the saucer.

'Some information about your friend Sally.'

'If you only want money out of her – '

'It's nothing to do with money. She didn't really order anything from my shop.'

'No?'

'No.'

'So why did you say so in the first place?'

'I didn't want to alarm you by telling you the truth.'

'Which is?' The girl's small, pugnacious face was pale and tense. Her hair, forced back with a comb, flared into a wild frizz behind her ears.

Elizabeth gave the bare facts without any extras. Max was investigating the case and thought Sally might have been worked on by a man they were seeking. 'Anything you can tell us about Sally's social life would be really invaluable,' she said. 'And won't be passed on to the police, I can promise you.'

The girl thought for a minute. Then she said, 'All right. Actually, it's a relief to talk to somebody. It's been so bad at work.'

Elizabeth said, 'I don't even know your name. Mine's Elizabeth. Elizabeth Blair.'

'Gill Carter.' There was an instant in which they shook hands metaphorically and then the girl poured milk into her cup. 'Her social life, you said?'

'Yes. We wondered if she had a boyfriend. Anyone steady. A serious relationship?'

'There was someone, yes.'

'How old was he? Do you know?'

'Older than her. I think. She wouldn't say much about him, though. I got the impression . . .'

'Yes?'

'Well, I sort of thought he might be married, she was so secretive about the whole business. But now and again, she just

151

couldn't resist dropping out a thing or two. Like a child with a naughty secret . . . you know?'

Elizabeth said, 'Do you have any idea what he looked like?'

'Well, he was terribly good-looking, she said.'

'Colour of hair?'

'No idea. Sorry.'

'And how long has she known him?' Elizabeth asked.

'A year. Eighteen months, perhaps. I *think* they met at somebody's birthday party.'

'Birthday party? Whose?'

'She didn't say. Just some friend or other. I told you, she could be pretty secretive when she wanted. All I know is that she was drifting round with this goofy smile on her face all next day. She stayed behind talking to him, apparently, after the party broke up. After the other girls went home.'

Talking to the barman at Wood's Hotel? Would a gauche, overweight girl like Sally be assured enough to sit around on a bar stool and chat up some strange man? She asked, holding her breath in case the answer was in the negative, praying that it wouldn't be, 'So is there anything else you can tell us about him?'

Gill screwed up her little pug's face. 'Sometimes he used to cook a meal for her at her place. Exotic stuff. Something Mexicana, they had once. She didn't like it much, but pretended it was fantastic, she said.'

'How often did she see him? Any particular nights?'

'Wednesday and Sunday, I think. Always Wednesday, because she was useless on Thursday morning. Even more useless than usual and that's saying something. She used to walk round in a lovesick daze . . .'

'So she had it bad?'

'You're telling me! She was . . . well, I suppose you'd say obsessed by him. Especially after he took her off for the weekend back in April.'

'Where did they go?'

'Bournemouth, I think.'

Elizabeth remembered the seaweed. She said, 'This business with the computer. Fiddling the accounts . . .'

Gill looked round cautiously and lowered her voice. 'She wouldn't have done that on her own. Not in a million years.

And if she was doing it, then somebody would have had to put her up to it. I reckon . . .' She looked guarded.

'What do you reckon?' Elizabeth said.

'Well, I reckon this chap had some sort of sexual hold over her. You hear about it on the telly, don't you? She wasn't a bad girl underneath. Honest . . .' She looked at the crumbs of apple cake on her plate. 'Yes, that's how it would have been. Somebody manipulated her into doing it. She'd got funny this last six months. Changed, I mean.'

'What about Larry Aitken? He's the one they've charged.'

'Mr Hollywood?' Gill almost laughed. 'That's what I couldn't understand. How could it have been him? She hated him, just like the rest of us. Waltzing in and out with his airs and graces! I remember her saying one day it was about time somebody took him down a peg or two.'

'So you don't think it was Aitken she was seeing?'

'Don't be daft. *Sally*?'

Elizabeth said, 'But if this boyfriend had a grudge against Larry? How would that fit?'

Gill thought about it. 'Pretty well . . . It makes more sense than the other.'

'You said she'd got funny this last few months. How funny? In what way?'

'Well, she got more . . . secretive about things. She used to stay late at work sometimes, she said it was to catch up. I suppose that's when she was doing it. Fiddling the computer.'

Elizabeth gazed out of the window. 'You probably aren't going to like this question, but – do you think she'd be capable of murder?'

There was a long silence, after which Gill said, with a flushed face, 'Given the state she was in about this bloke – well, I suppose you couldn't rule it out. He could make her do anything, probably. Yes . . . even murder.'

Max was in his office with his feet on the desk when she got back. 'So what's new?' he said.

'What's new?' She sat down on the edge of the window sill. 'Well, I'd say we're on the trail of a man who joined the hotel staff a couple of years back. Possibly a barman in his late thirties

153

or early forties. Brown hair, good-looking, with Oxford connections . . .'

It appeared that Max had his own surprise to spring. He looked odd, she suddenly noticed. Full of suppressed excitement, tense, positively brimming to get whatever it was out into the open.

'So spit it out,' she said.

'Spit what out?'

'Max – I know you, remember?'

In an odd voice, he said, 'All right. It's this. I know somebody at Wood's that exactly fits the bill.'

'You . . . what?'

'It started niggling away at my brain before I fell asleep last night. Something about football . . .'

'*Football?*'

'Yes. Football and Woods . . .'

It didn't sound a likely combination.

'Betsy – I knew there was a connection somewhere, but it took me ages to get it. I lay there for hours and then I dropped off and when I woke again – it was ten past four, I peered at the clock – when I woke, it was all there as clear as could be. I dropped in at Wood's for a drink one night when I was on a case.'

'How long ago?'

'Almost a year. Some time before Christmas. The place was decorated with glass baubles big enough to see yourself in. I didn't go into the main bar because there was a big party in there. You know . . . girls in lilac and pink, crackers, the lot.'

'You shied away from pretty girls?' She didn't believe it.

'I wasn't in the mood that night. I was on a funny case. It was getting me down a bit . . . a messy divorce, everybody accusing everybody else and trying to prise huge sums out of each other. And as I said, Christmas was coming and I felt . . . pretty disillusioned. So when I saw all the jollifications, I turned round to get out of the place – and would have done, except that on my way out, there was this chap in a sort of alcove, crouched over his radio.'

'Chap?'

'Barman, I think. He said he'd ducked out for a minute. They wouldn't let him have the radio behind the bar, apparently. The manager's funny about it. So there he was with his tranny hidden behind the pillar – and he was going mad because Oxford United had just lost a game. A crucial game, he said.'

'What else did he tell you?'

'Nothing much. He went on a bit about the party in the lounge. Chinless wonders, he called them,' Max said. 'Brown hair, the right age, probably the stud type . . . But his name didn't begin with L. It was Jonno. One of the waiters nipped out to tell him his absence had been noticed. "Better get back in there, Jonno," he told him. "Fortescue's on the warpath."'

Jonno. It was the wrong initial, Elizabeth thought. And yet . . . the L on the note *might* have been a curly J, given the slant of the writing. It was definitely worth investigating.

35

Emily Aitken met Max's enquiry with a face like cold marble. Curtly, she said, 'He's still in London.'

There was a pause.

Max said, 'But I need to see him . . .'

'Look – they gave him bail. He can go where he likes,' she said viciously. She was glaring at him as if he was a complete stranger, as if they'd never had that long, flirtatious conversation only a week or two back.

Max shoved his hands into his jacket pockets, tried to sound cool but casual in return. 'Do you know when he'll be back?'

'Sorry.' She didn't look sorry. She just stood there with her pretty nose in the air.

'Then is there some way I can get in touch with him?'

'I can't help you there either. He told me not to give anyone his telephone number.'

'But there are things I have to ask him,' Max said with some desperation. 'I'm working for him, for God's sake . . .'

She looked at him with complete disinterest. 'I shouldn't take that for granted if I were you. Look – I'm on my way out. Could you move your car? It's blocking the drive.'

*

The sense of bewilderment that he felt from Emily's summary treatment of him had changed to depression by the time he got back to Pierrepont Mews. Elizabeth noticed that he looked droopy. 'What's wrong with you?' she said. 'Where's the winning smile today?'

'I've gone off women,' he said.

'Oh, God. Which one is it this time?'

'Emily Aitken. She treated me like dirt.'

She looked at him with a mother's infinite compassion. 'I did try to warn you.'

'Oh, shut up, Betsy. What I need is a coffee.'

Elizabeth thought: What you need is an inoculation against falling for the wrong sort. But then, don't we all? Sometimes you could die when you saw the young look like that. 'Would a splendid lunch cheer you up?' she asked, glancing at her watch. It was almost twelve thirty.

'Not hungry.'

'Well, that's a pity, because I was thinking of taking you for a blow-out.'

The idea did seem to lift the depression. 'Where?' he said.

'How does Wood's Hotel grab you?'

Max decided that perhaps he could locate his appetite after all. 'Give me five minutes to check the answerphone,' he said.

Elizabeth did not walk straight into the dining-room after they had established that a table for two was available, but stopped to read the plaque fixed on the wall inside the lounge door:

John Wood the Elder, the first great architect of Bath, a thrusting and quarrelsome young builder with an obsessive vision of the city as a new Rome, leased land and planned a great square, to be named Queen Square, in honour of George II's Queen Caroline. Building began in 1729 and took seven years. Wood's head was full of plans with which he continuously bombarded both the city authorities and owners of land. The inspiration for his design for The Circus was the Roman Colosseum.

Thrusting and quarrelsome . . . 'You have this mental picture – ' she led the way into the damask-clothed dining-room – 'of the man who built those cool Palladian vistas and it's nowhere near the reality.'

156

'That's life,' Max said gloomily. 'People are never what you expect them to be.'

'But sometimes that's more interesting, Max.'

'You think so?' He waited for her to squeeze into the corner chair.

'I certainly do. Take Emily Aitken – '

'Chance would be a fine thing.'

'A girl who's just a stunning face and figure is pretty damned boring. But a girl like that who exhibits a touch of moodiness . . . well, she's instantly intriguing. Why was she in a mood? you wonder. What had upset her?'

'Her father being arrested on fraud charges, I should think.'

'Which proves that she's got emotions. That she's not just a stuffed dummy. You should feel sorry for her, Max.'

'She made me feel stupid,' Max said. 'Why should I feel sorry for her?'

'There you go then. Problem solved. You don't even like her any more – so why the hell would you want to sleep with her?'

'Who said I wanted to sleep with her?' Max asked. 'A spot of smooching was all I had in mind for a start. I'm pretty hot stuff in the smooching department.'

'Then she doesn't know what she's missing,' Elizabeth told him. 'So – did you get a look at the barman on the way in?' she asked over the vichyssoise.

Max said, 'It wasn't Jonno. He's not on duty today, by the look of it. He might not even still be here. And even if he was our man, he'll probably have cleared out. Sally would have warned him.'

'There's been no mention of him in the papers, so perhaps there's no reason for him to clear out. Anyway, the police think it's Larry that the girl was in league with . . . which was exactly what they were supposed to think. And Sally won't give Fox or Cox away – not if she's in love with him. No, I think there's a pretty good chance he's still here somewhere.'

'If he exists . . .'

'If he exists,' agreed Elizabeth, gazing out of the window at the palace front that formed the north side of the square. The garden in the centre, divided by Wood into symmetrical beds and gravel paths leading to the central obelisk, was now planted with grass and trees. 'Well, let's find out, shall we?' she said, waving a hand in the head waiter's direction.

He arrived with an air of gathering solicitude. 'Is everything as you would wish it to be, madam?'

'Everything is just dandy.' When Elizabeth spoke, her accent was more deliberately Uncle Sam than usual.

Max thought: she's doing it on purpose. I've heard her at it before when she thinks it'll pay dividends.

'It's just that I wondered if you could tell me . . . I'm trying to trace a young man who worked here the last time I was over. He made us feel so gosh-darn welcome. *Nothing* was too much trouble. I guess we just wanted to look him up.'

'We train our staff to give one hundred per cent effort, madam.'

'I guess that's the reason we keep coming back to your great little hotel!' Elizabeth treated him to a bright-eyed smile. 'I recommend it to all my friends, you know.'

He didn't give her a vote of thanks, but said in a warmer voice, 'What would be the young man's name, madam?'

'Our stay just won't be the same if we can't catch up with . . . with . . .' She began to snap her fingers, as if irritated with herself. 'Oh, lord, it's gone! I do believe my brain cells are dying – What was his name, Max?'

Max cleared his throat. 'Box?'

'You'll have to speak up, honey.'

'Box . . . or Cox.' Max found himself trying to reproduce her drawl, though he wasn't sure why.

'Now which is it, Max? He is *such* a ditherer!' she confided to the waiter. Then, 'All I know is that this guy waited bar and it was a positive pleasure to sit and talk to him – and he made the best Rusty Nail in the whole of England!'

There was no one called Box or Cox on the staff, the head waiter told them when he returned, ten minutes later, from making his enquiries.

'No one at all?' Elizabeth said, looking up from her *boeuf en daube*.

'I'm afraid not, madam.'

'But you did have . . . It would have been about two years back.'

158

'We do have quite a high turnover of staff, madam. Not, I hasten to add, because the establishment doesn't suit them . . .'

'Of course not!' Elizabeth looked suitably shocked.

'But by the nature of the business . . . They tend to move around in the course of promotion. I could check the records for you if you were prepared to wait?'

'I'll wait all day,' Elizabeth told him, 'if it means I get to see my favourite bartender.'

'You should have been on stage,' Max said when the waiter had gone.

'You think?'

'Scarlett O'Hara had nothing on that little performance.'

'Good, huh?'

'Ostentatious. Haven't they heard of the word subtle in Yankee-land?'

'My mother told me you get nowhere by hiding your light under a bushel, Max. Anyway, it was meant to be ostentatious. He'll think I'm loaded.'

'And he'll expect a big tip. Oh, well, it's your shout.'

The head flunkey took ten minutes to get back with the bad news. 'No one of those names, madam, has worked here during the last five years, I'm afraid.'

Oh, sugar! Elizabeth thought.

'But I did have a thought . . .'

'You did?'

Pause.

'Yes. We do have a young man by the name of Silcox who works in the bar. A Mr Jonathan Silcox. He was transferred here from our establishment in London . . .'

'That's him!' Elizabeth said, ungrammatically. 'Jonno! That's where I met him. At your establishment in London.'

Max rolled his eyes to the ceiling.

'So is he here today?' Elizabeth asked.

'I'm sorry, madam. I'm afraid he asked for the day off.'

'I don't suppose – ' Elizabeth produced another glamorous, Dallas-type smile – 'you could give me his address? I'm a perfect nuisance, I realize that. But I did so want to reacquaint myself with him before we go on to Stratford tomorrow.'

'It's not normally our policy . . .' he began. But as her smile continued to blaze away at his eyeballs: 'Well, perhaps just this once,' he said lamely. 'If you'd like to pop into the office when you've finished luncheon . . .'

36

'Flat number 3,' Elizabeth said. 'It's probably on the first floor.'

'Looks pretty quiet,' said Max. 'Shouldn't think he's in.'

They were standing on the broad-slabbed pavement opposite number 3, Holbourne Square. Max had made a couple of phone calls before leaving the hotel, then they had walked from Wood's, up Gay Street and into The Circus. Above Margaret Buildings were fine old trees and small, car-encumbered squares. The stone façades had an air of contemplation at this hour of the day, as if they were watching and waiting, but without curiosity.

Number 3 had a dark blue door. There were four bells to the right of it. As Max pressed the one labelled J. C. Silcox, Elizabeth felt for the first time a frisson of – what? Fear, apprehension?

Snail's traces had led them here by a roundabout route, but she was conscious that theory was fast being overtaken by reality.

The door opened suddenly. The man facing them wore jeans and a white shirt. Elizabeth saw that his eyes were greenish and that the dark chestnut hair was flecked, here and there, with silver.

'Sorry to bother you,' Max said, 'but are you Jonathan Silcox?'

'Yes,' he said. No smile.

'I wondered if we might have a word with you. I'm a private investigator,' Max fished out his card.

He stood there staring at it for a moment and then he said, 'What's it about?'

'I'd rather not talk about it here, actually. If we could just come in for five minutes . . .?'

'Suppose you'd better,' he said. No arguments, no fuss.

They followed him up. Sunlight fell through the landing window on to stripped boards and a gum tree. He showed them into a flat that looked neat, quiet, designer-comfortable.

There was a mushroom-coloured sofa with a newspaper open on it, white cushions, a desk with a phone. A single cup and plate – the remains of a sandwich lunch, probably – stood on the glass coffee table.

'Sit down.' He indicated the easy chairs.

'This is Elizabeth Blair,' Max said. 'We're . . . working on a case together.'

Elizabeth took the chair over by the window and said, 'Hi,' but Silcox only threw a glance in her direction. As soon as they were all seated, his casual, authoritative look shifted a little. He regarded them with a sort of taut magnetism.

'You're Jonathan Silcox?' Max began. 'And you work at Wood's Hotel as a barman?'

'Yes.' Silcox's green eyes had dark flecks in them. 'I know you from somewhere,' he said suddenly.

'We have met. We talked about Oxford United one night at the hotel.'

'That's it,' Silcox said. 'I thought you were just another punter.'

'I was . . . then.' Max paused a moment before asking, 'Do you know Larry Aitken, Mr Silcox?'

Silcox shrugged. 'Doesn't everybody?'

'I meant do you know him personally? Apart from his television appearances?'

'Know him personally?'

'Yes. Could you tell us if you've ever met him before? Not here in Bath. Somewhere else.'

'No.'

'Are you sure?'

'Quite sure.' He folded his arms and sat there imperturbably.

Another pause. Max stared at him in the silence of the house. 'It would be better if you didn't mess me about,' he said at last. 'Because I've got certain information about you that proves you did know him.'

'I don't know Larry Aitken,' Silcox said without even the flicker of an eyelid.

Elizabeth felt within herself the stirring of an instinct. She decided that Max was asking the wrong question and shifted in her chair.

'Did you know a man named Roy Hodges?' she asked quietly.

At that point, Silcox turned his head and looked at her. Then smiled. 'Clever lady,' he said. Then, nodding towards Max, 'Are you his minder?'

'Something like that.'

Max attempted to restore his position by clearing his throat. 'So – you know Aitkens as Roy Hodges? Is that right?'

Silcox didn't answer for a moment, gazing out of the window and chewing at his lip.

'All right,' he said finally.

'You knew him?'

'I knew him.'

'And where was that?'

Silcox raised his eyebrows. 'Don't you know?'

'I know,' Max said doggedly. 'I'd just like you to tell me.'

After a moment, Silcox said, 'I knew him in Oxford.'

Odd that he seemed to accept with calmness the fact that someone was on to him. That his face should just wear the faintest of smiles.

Elizabeth thought to herself: Yes . . . a cool customer.

'And how many years ago would that be, roughly?'

'Oh . . . nineteen. Twenty.'

Max nodded. He said, 'Could you tell me about your relationship with a girl called Samantha Tabernay, Mr Silcox?'

'I could. But I don't see why the hell I should.' Now for the first time, there was unpleasantness lurking somewhere behind the smile. A twitch in his jaw that could not fully be controlled.

'It might be better if you did.'

'Better than what?'

'Better than calling in the police.'

It was a quiet, casual reply, but Elizabeth saw Silcox's gaze flicker towards the window. 'Sod off!' he said harshly.

It seemed suddenly colder in the room. Violence had spread from his voice into the atmosphere.

After a moment's silence Elizabeth said, 'It was tragic what happened to Sammy, we know.'

'Don't call her that!' said Silcox savagely.

'I'm sorry. Isn't that what you called her?'

Silcox said violently, 'Exactly! I call her that. *You* don't.'

No, thought Elizabeth. That was a mistake. 'I'm sorry.' She spoke soothingly now, as if to a child. 'But wouldn't you like to tell us about what Ait . . . Hodges did to her?'

162

He turned to stare at her, his eyes heavy with hatred. 'You want to hear, do you? You won't like it.'

'That's all right.'

'We used to be in love. We used to have fun together. We planned to get married. Now she's a paraplegic, half blind, incontinent – and she doesn't know what the hell my name is any more. Is that enough for you or do you want me to tell you how much baby food they spoon into her mouth every day?'

The words fell uselessly between them. Elizabeth said, 'No. No, I don't. Do . . . you still visit her?'

'Of course I do.'

'Often?'

'Every couple of months.'

Max said, 'Tell us about Iain Tabernay. You were friends, weren't you?'

'Iain? He was a good bloke. Hodges killed him too.'

'Did you come to Bath especially to track him down?'

Silcox was still staring at his feet. Then as if shaking himself back into the present, he said, 'No. I came to work here entirely by chance. I didn't have any idea that he lived here in his bloody great manor house. I opened the *Chronicle* one afternoon and there he was plastered all over the front page. He likes the front page. Have you noticed?' A harsh laugh. 'Well, he got more of it than he bargained for this time, didn't he? You've got to laugh.'

'You saw the story about the Eadfrith Gospel?' Elizabeth asked.

'The bloody big spread about this Bible thing they toted round the world . . . yes. And this big picture of *Squire* Hodges' (he said it with a nasty sneer) 'lording it up in his great hall.'

'So you started to send the threatening letters?'

He was silent for a moment, then he said, 'At first I just thought I'd make the bastard sweat a little. I thought, why should he be living up there in the lap of luxury when poor little Sammy's lying in a hospital bed like a lifeless doll?'

'So you sent letters and made the phone calls?' Max said, 'And the dog?'

'The dog? Yes. I put down the poison.' He smiled. 'Hamlet! That was in the paper, too. A dog called Hamlet. I mean, how bloody pretentious can you get?'

163

'I expect the woods were handy,' Elizabeth said.

'What?'

'I said Warren Woods must have been handy. I imagine they gave you cover for watching the house. Watching their movements?'

'I used to take my binoculars up there, yes.' His laugh was unpleasant. 'But the secretary was handy, as you put it, as well.'

'The secretary?'

'The Scottish cow. I used to chat her up at Wood's whenever they had their meetings. All sorts of things she used to let out about where he'd be and when.'

'And the Bath and Wessex plan?' Max sat there and waited.

'The Bath and Wessex thing . . .?' Silcox laughed. This time the sound was full of satisfaction – almost elation – as if he didn't care what he told them from now on. 'That was something else. The big one. The thing that would knock him off his perch once and for all.'

'You planned to frame him. To make it look as if he'd been filtering money from the church fund?'

'It came to me blindingly one night just after I met Sally Stewart.'

'Where did you meet Sally?'

'She came into the hotel bar with her mates one night. Laughing and giggling . . . It was somebody's birthday. And then she kept coming in, night after night, throwing herself all over me. I invented a story about having a wife and three kids, but it didn't put her off.'

Max said, 'So how did you find out that she worked for the Bath and Wessex?'

'She just let it out one night. She got tight and started shooting her mouth off about being in charge of the Roof Fund . . . the committee's financial adviser, she kept telling me. When she'd had a few drinks, she could imagine anything, I thought at first. But then it turned out that that boss of hers *had* put her in charge of the St Swithin's file after all. I couldn't believe my luck. After that, it was easy. She was pretty gullible and after I'd bedded her once or twice, she'd have done anything for me.'

He contemplated the packet of cigarettes that lay on the coffee table and then he went on: 'It was Iain who put me on to the idea of siphoning off sums of money on the computers. One night when I was waiting for Sammy to come downstairs – she always took ages dolling herself up – he started on about how easy it was to fiddle the computers. He was joking. We had a good laugh about it, but he told me all about how it was done. We joked about getting ourselves a Swiss bank account and fiddling ourselves a fortune.'

'But you didn't want a fortune?' Elizabeth said.

'No. All I wanted was revenge. So I got one of my old girlfriends to open a Bath and Wessex account in Sammy's name in Oxford – told her I wanted to put money in it every month in case Sammy ever recovered – and then the coast was clear for little Sally to move sums into it from the St Swithin's fund. A couple of thousand would do it. It's not the exact amount, is it? It's the disgrace of Mr Bloody Philanthropist being caught with his hand in the till. That's what I wanted.'

'And when were you going to have him exposed?'

'In a month or two. When we were ready.'

'And you didn't really care that Sally might be found out? Might lose her job?'

'She hated the job anyway. She thought we were both going to do a disappearing act. I spun her a yarn about taking her abroad to live.' He laughed. 'She was going to leave a note saying that Lover Boy Larry had an affair with her and made her do it. We were going to send it to the *Sun* newspaper. She hated him, too, you see. That helped. She'd had a crush on him for a while . . . went all gooey every time he came into the office. But one day he snubbed her and then she started saying she hated his show-off voice . . . No, it wasn't hard to persuade her to help take him down a peg or two.' He gave a laugh. 'And it worked, didn't it? They've got him on a charge, and he deserves all he gets.'

Elizabeth said. 'You know that Sally's disappeared? That the police are looking for her?'

'Sally's a silly bitch. She deserves it too.'

Max said, 'So tell us about the whisky that killed Dr Wetherell. And Crichton's death. How much did he find out?'

The question seemed to work him up to a new level of contempt. He had no intention, it seemed, of incriminating himself further. His face wore only a faint smile as he said, 'I'm not answering any more questions.'

'You'll have to talk about it sooner or later,' Max told him.

'Nothing to do with me,' Silcox said, with a shifty glance in the direction of the door. 'If you've got any more questions, I want my solicitor.'

Elizabeth, watching him from her seat by the window, felt the tension rise a notch or two.

'Ask Sally,' Silcox said viciously.

'I will . . . when they catch up with her.'

'It's nothing to do with me. Ask *her*!'

'Is that why you seduced her? So that she'd take all the blame?'

Silcox, looking at Max stonily, refused to talk. Silence, he had decided, was his best ally. He couldn't be forced to admit anything against his will.

Max leaned forwards in his chair. Should he put the boot in by taking the conversation back to Sammy? 'Did Crichton confront you with what he'd found out?'

Silence.

'Did he?'

Silcox sat with his feet apart, as if waiting for an attack.

Then suddenly he moved.

Made for the door, fast, before anyone could get to him.

37

Sally Stewart was picked up by the police two days later at her mother's home in Reading.

'They've been charged with fraud,' Max said, when Elizabeth brought two mugs of coffee up to his office. 'Silcox and Sally.'

She said, 'It's lucky you'd alerted your friend, Andy. That Silcox ran straight out into the arms of the law.'

'They're also being charged with the murder of Crichton and Wetherell's manslaughter.'

Elizabeth said, 'You look busy for once. What on earth are you doing?'

'Totting up a great big bill to send Larry . . .' he said cheerfully. 'A bloody great bill! That should keep the bank happy for a while.'

Elizabeth picked up one of the newspapers that lay on the chair. AITKEN INNOCENT! its headline screamed. Her expression changed from one of amused indulgence to thoughtfulness. 'You know, Max,' she said, 'there are some odd things about this case, don't you think?'

'Mmn?' Max considered the figure he'd entered on the computer screen and added an extra 0.

'David Crichton, for instance. He was always up there, wasn't he? At the Manor, I mean. Talking to somebody or other. Emily. Or Julia. Or Larry. Several witnesses have said so. Why was he always there?'

'Friend of the family?' Max suggested.

'I suppose . . .'

But there were other loose ends that she found hard to tuck in place. 'How did Silcox know that Crichton would be up at the Manor at eight o'clock that evening? The evening he was killed?'

Max said, 'Crichton rang Larry from the Bath and Wessex to make the appointment and Sally overheard. She rang Jonno to tell him.'

A little tenuous, but she supposed it would hold water. 'There's another thing,' she said. 'I can't really understand why he was killed so close to the house. Right by the front door. If I were Silcox and I'd been waiting for him, I'd have done the dirty deed over by the Schoolhouse where Crichton left his car.'

'Too near the Lodge windows,' Max said.

'But what about the Manor windows, for heaven's sake? If you or Larry had glanced out at just the wrong time . . .'

'Filthy night,' said Max. 'All the curtains were tight drawn.'

'Yes . . .' Making her voice quietly casual, she said, 'You saw Larry draw the curtains, didn't you?'

'Mmn. Why?'

'Was it a perfectly normal act or did he seem nervous?'

'He was pretty het up about Le Grice pinching the picture. I suppose he did seem a bit twitchy.'

'So what didn't he want to see, I wonder?'

Max stopped tapping pound signs into the computer. 'You

mean you've still got him down as Crichton's murderer? But he was in there talking to me . . .'

'We agreed before that he might have had an accomplice who did it for him.'

'Such as who?'

'Oh, I don't know.' She was annoyingly vague. Unusually vague. 'Just testing a few hypotheses, Max.'

The third thing that was niggling at her was the biggest and the most puzzling. She went on staring at the computer screen without seeing it. 'What exactly was the point', she asked, 'of Silcox killing Crichton?'

'He knew Crichton was going to spill the beans about the fraud to Larry. Cause a big fuss.'

'But wasn't that exactly what Silcox wanted? A big public fuss about Larry defrauding the Roof Fund? Wasn't that what he'd plotted and planned his way towards for months? Crichton was doing Silcox's job for him, wasn't he? Why would he want to stop him?'

'God, Betsy, you're like a dog chewing at an old bone! Perhaps Silcox wanted to expose Larry himself in his own time and his own way. He didn't want Crichton to do the job for him. Or perhaps he thought Larry would manage somehow to shut Crichton up. Buy him off . . . what with him being such an old family friend, as you were just saying.'

'But why kill him? It doesn't add up.'

'Perhaps Silcox changed his mind and panicked at the last minute. He was afraid Sally might point the finger at him if they hauled her in.'

'Then why didn't he kill Sally instead of Crichton? Or simply disappear and leave her and Larry to face the music? Far easier, surely, than bumping off the accountant and digging yourself more deeply into the muck-heap?'

Max said, 'For God's sake – you're never satisfied! You can stop playing Sam Spade now, you know. They've got the killers, haven't they? With my help, of course.'

Playing Sam Spade . . . Was it true? Well, perhaps.

She'd enjoyed herself. Had fun letting rip with the theories, dipping her nose into other people's business. Except for one horrifying night, she'd been shielded from the harsh reality of violent death and its consequences.

But now, sitting here in Max's overheated office, she had for the first time an uneasy feeling. As if something to do with the case required her urgent attention . . .

And yet – it was so irritating – she didn't know what.

38

Max, leaning with one elbow on the bar at the rugby club, said, 'He's a tough bugger, Silcox.'

'Tough as hell.' Andy Cooper pushed his glass towards the bartender and ordered two more pints. He was a tanned young man whose fair hair seemed dried and stiffened as if with too much salt and sun. 'He's still refusing to confess to the murders. Says he's got a waterproof alibi for the night Crichton was killed. He was in bed, upstairs at Wood's, from seven o'clock until eight fifteen-ish with a woman called Kim Pickering. She's a trainee chef at the hotel. Lives in. She's been there three months.'

'Any witnesses?' Max asked.

'You're joking. They don't have see-through mirrors at Wood's, you know. It's not that kind of establishment.'

'Suppose you're right.' Max spread his hands round his new pint. 'And she corroborates the story, I suppose?'

'Yes. But then she would, wouldn't she?' Andy gazed at the portraits of past and present rugger heroes ranged along the wall. 'Given that she's obviously besotted with him . . . And he's no fool. He's not going to confess to murder when he could get off with minor offences.'

'There was nobody downstairs on reception who saw him arrive or leave?'

'The woman on reception thought she might have seen him go out when he went off duty at six, but she couldn't swear to it. It may have been the day before, she says. She can't honestly remember.'

Elizabeth, meanwhile, was unpacking a new batch of quilts that had arrived from the States. As she did so, her mind wandered back over the events of the last few weeks. No one could say it had been a quiet end to her first year in the West Country!

It was a still night and very cold. The radio had forecast a heavy frost. The council workman who had been fixing up Christmas lights had loaded his ladders into his truck and gone home.

She still couldn't quite accept that the Aitken case was over.

And yet she didn't know why.

She told herself again and again that the police were satisfied, that most of the loose ends had been tied and knotted. Yet there was still something simple but elusive drifting around her mind . . . Now almost visible, now gone again, like a small boat lost in a deep mist out at sea.

Every now and then, she would catch sight of it very dimly, at a great distance. But before she could get a bearing, it would have vanished . . . disappeared beyond the horizon of her conscious mind.

The shop was warm-smelling and quiet on this November evening. Five large cardboard boxes filled the limited space between the counter and the door. The nearest one was sealed so tight that it took ages to tear off strip after strip of gummed tape and prise open the top. She lifted out the top layer of tissue – and for a moment it was as if she was back in Turkey Creek. She could smell that very American brand of . . . What was it now? Sugar and corn meal and clean linen and Sunday church clothes . . .

Or was it purely imagination? Funny how the brain could monkey around with your sense perceptions . . . Load up a perfectly ordinary piece of tissue paper with a whole bunch of sights and smells from another time and another place. *Fans going round, whish, whish, whish in Grandmother's house next door to the Episcopalian Church. Aunt Cicely cutting up an old, worn-out homespun shirt. Finished blocks wrapped square in tissue on the table beside her . . . A thimble flashing and clam chowder for supper simmering away in the kitchen.*

Now, lifting out the Courthouse Square quilt that was to replace the Broken Star in the window display, she said aloud, 'Aunt Cec was an awkward old buzzard, but she could fix a mean quilt!'

The Courthouse Square swung slowly open to reveal its full

splendour . . . Real fancy in plaids and stripes with feather quilting thrown in. She thought to herself: I wonder if I should send the dry cleaning bill for the Broken Star to Jonathan Silcox. It'll cost a small fortune to restore it to its original glory.

She hadn't any real qualms about selling it to some unsuspecting customer back home in the States. Quilts and sudden death, she reminded herself, were in no way alien to each other. Why, in the old days, when there was no such luxury as a separate room to shield the dead and dying from the eyes of the rest, many a quilt hung round the sick-bed.

And she remembered reading once the diary of a grieving mother:

February, 1918:

George buried today. Died of meningitis Camp LeRoy, Georgia. Captain sent home the quilt I made him. Sterilized, he said. I meant to lay it on his bed, but cannot bear to look at it . . .

Was there a mother somewhere mourning Crichton, she wondered? Funny, there had been surprisingly little talk in the village of where he came from or where he was to be buried.

She laid the Courthouse Square over a couple of chairs. Started on the next two boxes, which yielded a Tree of Life and an Ocean Wave. Really, Jim Junior had excelled himself this time! She'd ring him and say so in the morning. When she'd first sent him round to scour the county for quilters, he hadn't much cared for the idea. Had mumbled something about it being women's work and he sure felt a fool . . . But lately – well, she rather thought he was getting hooked on the hunt.

Yes, people could surprise you.

Take Brenda Macmillan, for instance. She remembered the morning when Big Mac had turned up at the shop . . .

It was a couple of days after Crichton's body had been found. She had mooched round, frowning, picking up knick-knacks and putting them down again.

'I need a new packet of needles.'

Plainly an excuse: she hadn't even known what size or what they were for.

171

All she had been interested in was the state of Crichton's body.

She had said abruptly, 'Would he have seen his murderer, do you think, Mrs Blair? I mean, were the wounds in the chest or the back?'

'In the chest, most of them,' Elizabeth told her. 'There were some at the back of the forearm and the shoulder, as if he'd tried to turn and run, but for the most part it was a full-frontal attack. I'd say he must have seen the attacker.'

'Even in pitch darkness?'

'Well, of course, that's a point. I can't honestly tell you. All I know is that it was a ferocious attack.' Elizabeth had shuddered. 'I never want to see such a sight again.'

'I imagine . . . well, the murderer must have been blood-stained too?'

'Must have been. That's for certain.'

There had been this rigid, wooden expression on Brenda's face. And a high colour as she said, 'He . . . would have had to ditch what he was wearing somewhere fairly quickly? Whoever it was . . .'

'I should imagine so.'

'In the woods, perhaps. But the police didn't find anything . . . How long does it take blood to dry, do you think?'

'I really haven't the least idea,' Elizabeth had said.

And had wondered for a moment if Big Mac was unhinged, standing there staring at her with eyes like pale marbles . . .

Recalled to the present by the ache in her bent knees, Elizabeth gathered up the strewn paper and the empty boxes. How absurd to keep going back over it all! To have *something* about the case always creaking away in your head like a broken shutter in an October wind . . .

She took the packaging outside for the dustbin people to dispose of, then tackled the last box. Unsealed it where it stood, right there in the middle of the floor. From its depths she drew out a Rebel Patch. Sunflowers leaping clean out of a bone-white background . . .

A Rebel Patch with the deep warm colours of the harvest field.

And suddenly, as she gazed at it, something went click inside her. Went click in a vital part at the back of her brain. She thought of the diary that had fallen out of David Crichton's pocket the night he was murdered.

And she said, 'Oh, boy!'

She'd been going along like a horse in blinders.

She thought to herself: We almost outsmarted ourselves, Max, and that's a fact . . .

39

At home the following morning, she rang Caroline. 'Listen, something's come up. Could you possibly manage on your own for an hour or two?'

Caroline said, 'Oh, right. Er . . . the tea caddy's almost empty. Do you want me to bring some in?'

'Fine. Take the money from petty cash.'

'Er . . . Earl Grey or English Breakfast?' Caroline said.

Elizabeth imagined her standing there in her tiny flat in her silk dressing-gown, eyes wide, interrogatory, intent. 'You're the expert, Caroline. You choose.'

'Oh, right,' said Caroline. 'I could bring some of each . . .'

Elizabeth put down the receiver and went to boil herself an egg. The kitchen was in a mess, but the clearing-up process could wait a few hours. Sometimes she liked to be a plain slob for the day.

And there were certain things she had to check on.

A half-hour later, she was taking a stroll in the lane behind Dottie's cottage. It was a fine day. On her right, the stream trickled in little bursts inside the wood. In the distance she could just see the Church Farm barns, red pantiles against the deep grey of the sky.

The Manor wall twisted down over the hill, in and out of the trees.

She surprised herself by climbing quite athletically over it at a point where successive generations of cows had scratched their backs and crumbled the stonework.

The sound of the river was more distant on the Manor side of the wall. She made for the low stone barn that backed on to

Dottie's orchard, waited briefly in the shelter of the trees to make sure no one was around, then made for the side window set into the thickness of the freckled stone wall.

Her feet seemed to whisper through the long grass. She didn't want to be there longer than she could help . . .

She peered just once through the window – then disappeared round the side of the barn.

At two o'clock, she drove to Sydney Hill, parked the Citroën and sat gazing at a house that neither she nor Max had thought to investigate until this moment. A fine house in a fine street . . . Long Windows, black ironwork balconies on the first floor and arched doorways with bootscrapers in the shape of thin, Egyptian cats . . .

Houses designed for what Jane Austen called 'the elegant stupidity of private parties'. Houses taken in Bath's heyday by parsons, generals and admirals living out their last years in modesty and gentility. Houses now, for the main part, divided into flats.

Elizabeth locked the Citroën and crossed to the steps of number 16. She scanned the neat row of bells. It was the middle one that she was interested in, but she pressed the bell to the ground-floor flat and stood there waiting for someone to come to the door.

Music was playing somewhere at the back of the place. Something exotic and South American. Rather relaxing . . .

The music stopped.

She waited on the doorstep. Admired, through the window, the tall Adam mantelpiece with its octagonal mirror. The French clock, the jug of dried larkspur, the pine table and the loaded bookshelf . . .

A curtain was dragged back from the window. A face looked out. Then disappeared again.

There was, supposed Elizabeth, a possibility that her search would be in vain – but she did not for one single second believe it.

The church clock struck the half-hour at the bottom of the hill. The latch turned, and the door opened.

A woman stood there.

Elizabeth said, 'I wonder if you could help me?'

*

174

When she got back to the cottage, she rang Max, but he was out. She left a message on his answerphone, then dialled Aitken's number. It seemed a long time before anyone answered.

40

The idea had come to her, quite suddenly, as if out of a dream. But since then, as the bits fell into place, it had settled into a concrete reality.

She had confided in no one, had not even spoken about it to Max as yet.

'Listen,' she had said to his answerphone machine when the pips had stopped, 'something quite amazing just occurred to me. We were wrong. Silcox didn't kill Crichton, but I know who did. Ring me when you get back from wherever the hell you are. By the way, I read in the *Independent* that most private detectives work nine to five, six days a week. So how come you never found out, Max? Ring me, you hear?'

She hadn't told anyone, but then she didn't need to. For the whole thing was cut and pieced now, inside her head. Scraps that had been lying round in a mess for weeks had suddenly given a shake – and worked themselves into a pattern.

She had checked meticulously to see what fitted where and what didn't. Had examined shapes and angles and tones in a good light to make sure they were right. And now, standing in the Manor porch at seven in the evening, she knew that there could be no mistake.

Some folks weren't going to like it, but she had this particular design fixed neat and perfect in the frame . . .

The light was on in the porch, but the garden was dark all around. There was no moon. The wind lifted the branches in the unseen woods and threshed backwards again towards the darkened windows of the Lodge.

The place felt raw and unwelcoming. She was tempted for one moment to turn tail and run – but fought the impulse. For she had rung the beautiful, listless Emily and insisted on a meeting.

'What's it about?' Emily had asked.

'I can't tell you over the phone.'

Silence. Elizabeth imagined the girl examining her nails in a bored sort of way and wondering whether to humour this weird Yank or tell her to take a running jump.

The athletics were out, it seemed. Emily said, 'Does it have to be tonight?'

'I'd rather it was.'

Silence again. Then the girl said, 'I'm not in the mood for visitors.' There was more than a hint of arrogance in her voice. 'But I suppose you'd better come at about seven.'

Now, looking out into the dark recesses of the garden, Elizabeth said aloud, 'Spoiled brat! Doesn't give a damn for anything or anybody.' She'd got Max all wound up . . . But then, Max was a mite too soft for his own good under that pretty exterior. Also too nice.

'Spoiled brat!' she said again. 'What she needs is cutting down to size.'

The door suddenly opened. Emily Aitken stood there. For one long moment they looked at each other. The girl wore a pair of old jeans and a grey sweatshirt. Her hair fell loose and uncombed over her shoulders and she wore no make-up. Perhaps it was that which made her face look more acutely angled, thinner.

Elizabeth thought: She's not beautiful at all. At least, not tonight.

Emily said, 'You'd better come in.' Her eyes rested broodingly on the Citroën parked by the orangery.

Elizabeth thought: As I expected – you can't bear to look at it! She said calmly, 'I'm sorry I had to bring the car up here again. I know it's a nasty reminder.'

'Not really.' The blue-green gaze was still uptilted, but something had jerked briefly into the girl's eyes and gone again and Elizabeth was in no doubt that the weapon had struck home.

Emily led the way through the hall and into the drawing-room. Elizabeth had expected to see Larry, but before the

176

thought had even had time to register, Emily said, 'There's no one else here.' She looked, on the whole, pale but quite calm.

'Just you and me . . .'

'Yes.'

Slowly, Elizabeth walked past the girl and over to the fireplace. So how did you fix that? she wondered. With care and cunning, no doubt, as is your wont. The radiators were on full blast, but a fire still burned in the grate. The room was overpoweringly hot.

'So what did you want to see me about?' Emily said.

'Don't you know?'

'I haven't the faintest idea.'

'You're quite sure?'

'Absolutely,' Emily drawled, but moved restlessly over to the window.

Well, it wasn't unexpected. Elizabeth paused, considering, then said, 'I thought you might like to tell me about your relationship with David Crichton.'

'My what?'

Elizabeth said, 'I hope you won't waste time bothering to deny it. I have evidence, you see.'

'What evidence?'

Now that's more like it, Elizabeth thought. A genuine reaction for once! Fear and surprise, all in one little involuntary question.

'I had a chat with the person who lived . . . still lives . . . in the flat underneath his.'

Emily lifted her chin a fraction, but said nothing.

'When exactly did you start your affair with David Crichton? You did have an affair with him, didn't you?'

Emily worked her lips and tried to swallow. 'Yes,' she said at last, almost in a whisper. 'Yes. I had an affair with him. But I don't see what this has to do with you. Why are you here?'

Elizabeth said, 'I'm assisting Max Shepard. You kept the affair very quiet for a long time. You didn't tell your parents.'

'No.' Again the muted whisper.

'Why didn't you tell them? Wouldn't your father have approved?'

'He . . . he was always so fussy about who I went out with.' No emotion now. No agony. Yet Emily's fingers were twisting in her lap.

177

'And Crichton wasn't good enough for his daughter?'

'I . . . probably not.' Emily's eyes darted now from the window to the door. 'I thought it easier for David if we kept it quiet for a while. That's all.'

Elizabeth digested this piece of information. 'So when did it start? While your parents were away in Australia?'

'How did you know?'

'I have a daughter . . .' Elizabeth said.

Emily reached over to the box on the table. She took out a cigarette. Lit it with shaking fingers, then said, 'All right. I'll tell you. They were away in Sydney and David came up to the house one night with . . . oh, I forget, some papers or other for Brenda Macmillan – and I offered him a drink. I was at a loose end. We talked for ages and in the end, he took me out for a meal. We were both starving, you see, and neither of us had got anything else planned.'

'Your mother seemed to like David Crichton,' Elizabeth said. 'Surely you could have told her?'

There seemed to be a long pause. Emily glanced at her, then down again. 'When did you talk to Mother?'

'When I came up here one day. She asked me to bring some patchwork kits. We had a long chat.'

Her face bore an odd mixture of agitation and watchfulness. 'So what else did she tell you?'

'Oh . . . that she doesn't go much on being an actor's wife. How about the actor's daughter? How was it for you, having a famous father?'

'Sometimes it was OK.' With a flash of aggression she said, 'She had her garden and her gallery! She wasn't that lonely.'

'But you were?'

'I used to get fed up. Yes. I hate village life. It's boring. I wanted to go to London to live with friends, but she wouldn't let me.'

'So you had an affair with David Crichton to spite her?'

'No. She liked David. You just said so. What would have been the point?'

An answer as smart as paint. Elizabeth counted to ten, then stopped pussyfooting and went for the jugular.

'So what happened when David discovered the fraud in the Roof Fund accounts?'

178

Emily went very white. 'He . . . didn't believe it at first. He just didn't believe that Daddy could be filching money away to an account in Oxford. I didn't believe it either. But it was so difficult to get it straight in your head. All the evidence was against him. David said he had to challenge him about it.'

'And you didn't want him to?'

'Of course I didn't want him to. I was scared as hell about what would happen. I . . . we had the most terrible row about it.'

'You and David?'

'Me and David. But he was so damned stubborn! He wouldn't change his mind, no matter what I said to him.'

'And so . . .?'

Smoke curled from her cigarette. 'How did you know about David and me?' she asked.

'From your nickname.'

'My nickname?' She looked startled.

'What does your father call you? What has he always called you since you were little?'

'Rebel.'

'Rebel . . .' Elizabeth said. 'Big M . . . Miss Macmillan mentioned it by chance one day when we were talking. David Crichton called you Rebel too, didn't he?'

'When he was teasing, yes.' She sounded hollow now. Her voice was that of a child, utterly broken.

'It was in his diary, you see.'

Silence.

Elizabeth crossed to the sofa and looked down at the girl. It's no good feeling sorry for her, she thought. The truth has to come out. 'So what did you do when David refused to ignore the evidence of fraud?'

'I . . . threatened him.'

'And?'

'And he refused to give in. I thought he was in love with me, but I couldn't make him change his mind.'

'He wouldn't hush it up?'

'No. And so . . .'

'And so?'

Emily gave a funny laugh. 'I yelled at him that I'd kill him if he went to Daddy with his stupid suspicions.'

Another long silence that went on and on. Then Emily let out a shuddering breath. She cried out, 'It's all my fault! If I hadn't fallen in love with him . . . he'd still be alive.'

'Dr Wetherell, too?'

'Dr Wetherell, too.'

She looked wildly at Elizabeth. At the drinks table. At the telephone extension on the bureau.

Great, racking sobs shook her slender frame.

'I killed them,' she whispered. 'They both wanted to drag Daddy through the mud and I killed them. You'd better call the police.'

Elizabeth gazed at Emily's tear-stained face, let it imprint itself for ever.

Somewhere behind them, a door opened.

Julia stood there. She had entered so silently that no one heard her. She looked pale and frail. 'What is it?' she said. 'What on earth is going on?'

Emily tried to answer her, but the words wouldn't come.

She made, instead, a frantic dash for the hall.

A minute later, the front door slammed. For the first time, Elizabeth wished she had brought Max along for the ride.

41

Julia stared at her across the length of the room.

Elizabeth, remembering how they had last sat together in the garden, thought to herself: We talked like friends. But now the space between us is loaded with tension. How will she react if I simply spring the truth on her?

But perhaps it wouldn't be necessary. Perhaps she would have guessed. She wasn't stupid . . .

Yes, perhaps she knows.

'Why are you here?' Julia said tautly. 'What's happened? What is it?'

Elizabeth didn't answer. The fire leapt and threw flickers on the wall. The cat turned over in the chair and went back to sleep.

Julia took a step nearer and held on to the chair back. 'Emily – she told you . . .?'

Elizabeth said, 'Yes. She told me.'

'Oh, God! What will she do? Shouldn't we . . .?'

Elizabeth shook her head.

'I must ring Larry.'

'Not . . . just yet.' Elizabeth held Julia's desperate gaze. She said, 'Better to talk first.'

'You think so?'

'I think so.'

And this, at last, was the moment which had been hovering round her consciousness since the morning. The moment she had dreaded.

She kept her voice perfectly steady as she said, 'How long did your affair with David Crichton last, Mrs Aitken?'

Julia's sharp intake of breath was her only sign of alarm. She swallowed, then sat down as if her legs had gone. 'All right,' she said after a silence. 'All right. So you know.'

She sat there with her hands clasped about her knees and her face like parchment. It was as though, bracing herself against the back of the sofa, she was almost relieved. With a note of resignation she said, 'It was bound to come out in the end.'

Elizabeth's voice was quiet. 'So Emily knew that he'd had an affair with you before he . . . took up with her?'

'Not until after he . . . after his death. No.'

'You told her?'

'I . . . Yes. *Then* I had to.'

'How did she react?'

'How do you think?'

Silence for a moment and then Elizabeth said, 'Do you want to tell me about it?'

'If you want to hear.'

'It would fill in a few gaps.'

Julia sat in silence for a moment. Then she said, 'David . . . used to come up here a lot. He helped run the ghost walks and he was a wonderful help to me when I started the gallery. He went over the books with me. Nothing was too much trouble. We became great friends. That was how it started. Perhaps it would have been better if it had stayed that way . . .'

'But it went further?'

181

Julia looked at her blankly. 'Yes. The affair started in June. I'd had a row with Larry. We don't often row, but when we do, it gets nasty. You've never felt the lash of his tongue, have you?'

Elizabeth's face gave the answer.

'No, well, he's vicious.' Julia spoke a little unsteadily, as if she was only half awake. 'He'd be vicious . . . and then quite suddenly he'd be nice again. His conscience would get the better of him and he'd try to make amends. He can be loving, you know. When he chooses. Just like he can lose his temper and go mad. There are bright and dark threads to his nature. I discovered that very early in our marriage. Anyway . . . we had this row. He'd been away for weeks on tour and when he came home, he seemed – I don't know – tense still. And he made some patronizing remark about the gallery. Spiteful! Disparaging. "For God's sake, shut up about your bloody gallery," he said. "You wouldn't have it without my money to pay for it. You'd be bankrupt within a year."'

'And that wasn't true?'

'No. It wasn't! And I wasn't going to let him get away with it. The gallery's been running itself for ages. So I tore upstairs and I grabbed the audit sheets that David had done for me and I waved them in front of his face and told him to read them. But he didn't want to know. He was thinking about something else. Some woman probably. Oh, I know what goes on behind the scenes. I'm not a fool. Anyway, I threw a vase at his head and stormed out of the house . . .'

Elizabeth thought: Perhaps you should have done it years ago. She said, 'Where did you go?'

'That night I slept down at the studio. He didn't even come looking for me. He just went off, the next morning, on some shoot or other in London. He managed to put himself out enough to leave a note. *See you Wednesday. For God's sake, cheer up. I've had enough of your moods. You don't need the gallery, so why make a bloody fuss about it?*'

Elizabeth waited.

Julia glanced at her. 'Well, who was he to say what I needed and what I didn't? How could he know?' Her voice was hard and bitter. 'He made me so angry. So frustrated. By the time David came up – he wanted to give Larry a bit of a lecture about overestimating his expense sheets – I was a nervous wreck. I burst into tears as soon as I saw him and sobbed out the whole story. That was when we finished up in bed together. Well, not in bed, exactly. On the couch in the studio, to be more precise. He was so very sweet . . . very gentle. He kept holding me and smoothing my hair and telling me I mustn't mind. You see, he knew just how . . . swamped by it all I was sometimes.'

Elizabeth listened in silence. It was much as she had expected.

'He used to make me laugh and then I'd feel better. He had this wicked sense of humour, you know. I think he probably felt sorry for me. And I'm sure he regretted the affair almost as soon as it had started.' A new expression crossed Julia's face. 'But he came back for more, so I couldn't have been quite so useless in bed, could I? I was good at something.' Bitterly she said, 'It didn't last long, of course. A matter of weeks. Perhaps six at the most.'

Julia said, 'I suspected he was seeing someone else – another woman – because after we got back from Sydney, I rang his flat and the cleaner told me he'd gone off in his car with a young lady. And he stopped coming to the house . . . well, except for business and committee meetings, things he couldn't avoid. I had it at the back of my mind that he'd found someone else. Someone younger. Well, it's natural, I told myself. He's only thirty, after all. What do you expect, Julia? That he'd want to stay with some middle-aged freak for the rest of his life? You should think yourself lucky that you had him for a few weeks. Or at all.' Her face was suddenly pasty. 'But somehow it felt different when the suspicion became fact. I rang his office one morning – the day Hamlet was poisoned – to confirm a date they'd given me to come to the gallery to do an audit. And the girl on the switchboard said she'd have to change it. Mr Crichton couldn't come in mid-November any more because he'd booked a holiday in the Seychelles with his girlfriend . . .'

'And you couldn't bear the thought . . .' Elizabeth said quietly.

'It almost drove me mad. Jealousy's a dreadful thing . . . It eats into your brain, destroys your judgement entirely.'

Elizabeth said, 'Was it you who drugged the whisky?'

Julia nodded. There was a faint smile on her lips now. 'I wanted to get back at David somehow . . . To show him that he couldn't keep coming up here and acting as if we were strangers

'. . . as if we'd never been anything to each other. He might at least have had the manners to know that he couldn't do that.'

'So you used Larry's pills?'

'Yes. I saw them lying on the bureau the afternoon of the sub-committee meeting. And I thought, David's the only one who drinks whisky when they meet here. I'd forgotten about Bob Forbes, but as it happened, it didn't matter. I'll teach him a lesson! And I picked up the pills and I shook some of them into the decanter and swirled it round a bit and after a while . . . they were all dissolved. It was almost as if someone else was doing it, you know. Really a most peculiar feeling. I could feel myself unravelling . . . And then when they all arrived, I went and worked in the garden, within sight of the drawing-room. I was curious to see how it would affect him. I didn't want it to happen too soon, whatever it was. I half hoped that he'd get into his car after the meeting and pass out on the way back down to Bath and have a crash and kill himself. But at the same time . . . I didn't.' Her eyes seemed to be getting odder by the minute.

Elizabeth thought, she's half-mad. The weight of all that guilt has slowly been tipping her over the edge.

The patchwork kit lay half-done on the stool.

Julia said, 'I was very sad about Charles Wetherell. I liked him, you see. He wasn't a bad old sort. But I couldn't tell anyone what I'd done, could I?'

There was a silence while Elizabeth marshalled her thoughts. Then she said, 'But when you drugged the whisky – you didn't know that it was your own daughter that Crichton had been seeing?'

'No.'

'So when exactly did you find out?'

The room was entirely silent for a moment. Then Julia spoke. 'It was the afternoon of David's . . . death. I was upstairs changing for supper. And the telephone extension in the bedroom sort of tinged . . . and I picked it up. I'm not sure why. Some kind of sixth sense, I suppose. Emily had refused to tell me where she was going that evening, you see. She'd tried to fob me off with some story – so I picked up the extension. And *he* was talking to my daughter! Making arrangements to see her that evening at his flat. He couldn't be there until nine thirty, but she was to let herself in – she had a key, you see – and wait. And he'd *make it up to her* when he arrived . . . And suddenly . . . it was perfectly obvious where Emily had been spending her nights! She'd been spending them with *him*. Sleeping with David . . .' Julia's head tipped forward. 'Do you imagine he told her he'd slept with her mother? I can't make up my mind about that, but I think he must have done, because Emily changed so much, you see, over these last few months. Towards me. Not towards Larry. I felt – I can't tell you how I felt when I put down the receiver. As if . . . I were . . . dangling out of time. Do you know how that feels? No – you wouldn't.'

Elizabeth said, 'Perhaps I do, Mrs Aitken.'

'No. You don't!' Her voice now was dangerously quiet, almost a whisper. 'Men scoop you up, don't they? They scoop you up out of one safe little place and when *they* decide, they dump you somewhere else where you're frightened and it hurts. Larry. My father, David . . . They set up this blaze in you and then they extinguish you. And they think you'll just smile and say, "Thanks for the trip. I had a lovely time. Thank you for having me."'

'Some men are pigs,' Elizabeth said. 'But then, so are some women . . . I don't think you can define it by gender. There are just givers and takers.' She looked at Julia's ravaged face. 'So how did your husband react when he found out about it all? He did find out, didn't he?'

'Yes . . .' Julia said in a painful whisper.

'Did he . . . get violent?'

'He was violently sick. Then he started to sweat . . . and shake. I don't honestly think it was me that he was agonizing about . . . but his precious little girl. David had sullied her, he said. That was what was eating at him.'

Elizabeth stood there waiting. Her nerve ends tightened. At last she said, 'But he didn't find out until *after* Crichton's death?'

'You know that, too? How do you know so much?'

'Intuition, I guess.' Okay, Elizabeth, she thought. This is it. This is the big one. Very quietly she said, 'So . . . tell me how you killed Crichton, Mrs Aitken.'

Julia held Elizabeth's long, unflinching gaze. Then she said, 'It was surprisingly easy. I fetched a knife from the kitchen and I hid it in the pocket of my painting smock. I knew he was coming up to the house at eight, so I pretended to be going off down to the studio and I hid in the shrubbery until David came walking up the drive in the dark – and then I killed him. When the porch light went on, it startled me. I had to bundle him . . . the body . . . into the car and slam the lid on it.'

'Then you went back to the studio?'

'Yes. I stripped off the smock – so much blood, it was awful – and I shoved it up into the wood stove and burned it and I sat there shaking until I was in a fit state to come back to the house an hour later. If they asked why I hadn't been to my class, I was going to say I had a phone call about the sale of a picture and went to the gallery instead.'

Silence. She stood there gazing at Elizabeth and then she walked robot-like to the bureau. When she turned, there was a gun in her hand.

Elizabeth thought, I always saw her as pretty and frail. I was wrong. Underneath, there's the toughness of fine-beaten steel.

And I'm going to have to talk my way out of this, God knows how . . .

She said, 'Mrs Aitken . . .'

Julia said, 'Save your breath, Mrs Blair. I'm terribly afraid that I shall have to ask you to come for a little walk with me.'

42

Outside, the night swallowed up all sound except for their feet crunching on the gravel and Elizabeth's heart pounding. Most of the windows of the big house were dark.

'I'm sorry that it's come to this,' Julia's voice said behind her. 'But you must see there's no other way. I can't let you go to the police with what you know.'

'They'll find out anyway.' Elizabeth's brain raced ahead, trying to think how to stall Julia. 'Emily will tell them.'

'I don't think so,' Julia said. 'I can handle Emily. Keep walking, Mrs Blair. Straight ahead. That's right.'

Play along until you can get your bearings, Elizabeth told herself. Until there's a chance to cut and run.

But you couldn't see a hand in front of your face . . . And the gardens seemed to offer no cover on either side. How good a shot is she? Elizabeth wondered, and heard an owl hoot in the pitch black of the woods.

The gun dug persistently into the small of her back. Julia held the torch in her left hand, swinging it a little from side to side as they walked.

Suddenly Elizabeth stiffened. What was that? That movement over there under the trees? She felt her eyes tense with concentration . . . A greyish shape . . . too big for a dog. Crouching perhaps.

Could it be Emily?

No – just the wind in a low branch.

The beam moved on.

Not Emily at all. Which way had the girl gone when she left the house? There was no way of telling.

Would anyone hear if she yelled? Probably not.

'Where are we going?' she asked steadily. 'To your studio?'

'Past it, I think.' Julia's voice was cool now, and equally calm. Frighteningly impassive. 'There's an old boiler room at the back where we keep scraps for the horses . . .'

Dottie's mice, Elizabeth thought.

Cautiously they moved on over the uneven ground, the gun pressing now against a spot between her shoulder blades. A twig snapped underfoot, and the gun twitched and prodded with a convulsive movement – but still they moved on.

No sound now except the soughing of the branches above their heads. The path had narrowed . . . seemed more cramped. Barely wide enough for a couple of wheelbarrows side by side.

Elizabeth's eyes were growing accustomed to the darkness. There was dark undergrowth on the right stretching downwards . . .

'Keep walking! Don't slow down.' Julia shook the torch beam to reinforce the order. Then prodded again with the gun.

But Elizabeth's quick brain was working. How to do it – distract her – walk at a snail's pace – invent some excuse –

Julia's voice was dangerous, menacing. 'Faster, I said!'

Elizabeth said, 'I've got something in my shoe.'

She bent, as if to remove the something. And then she sprang. Launched herself head-first at the undergrowth . . .

187

She heard the splat of the gun.

Heard, at the same time, a shout.

'Elizabeth!'

Max's voice? How could it be?

Her rolling body landed, eventually, in earth and wet leaves, then hit something immensely solid that knocked all the breath out of her.

A long time later, a torch shone on her face.

'Elizabeth?' Max was standing looking down at her with a peculiar expression in his eyes. 'What the hell were you trying to do, coming up here on your own?'

'Julia . . .' she said. 'Where is she?'

'It's all right. I've sorted her out. Locked her in the studio.'

'She's got a gun.'

'No, she hasn't. Not now.'

Relief possessed her – enormous, exquisite relief.

'Thank God,' she said. Then, 'Max – be a good boy and get me out of here.'

Two days later, Max came to call on her at the cottage. Bruises in unmentionable places had kept her away from Martha Washington. Her emotions had taken a slight battering, too.

'I felt just awful when the police came to fetch her,' she told Max.

'It was her or you, Betsy.'

'I know that.' She put water in the kettle and found the Earl Grey. 'But it doesn't help any.' She remembered the look Julia had thrown her as she climbed into the Panda car. Dull, resigned . . . yet unbearable just for one moment.

She said, 'How did you know where I was? What brought you up there?'

'You weren't at the cottage, so I went next door to ask your Miss Marchant. She'd seen you go up the path towards the Manor.'

Elizabeth thought: Thank the Lord for Nosy Parkers!

Max said, 'So what put you on to Emily's part in all this?'

'It was the Rebel Patch.'

'Rebel Patch?'

'It's the name of a quilt design,' she said absently. 'I was sitting there unpacking the Rebel Patch and it suddenly struck me. The REB in David Crichton's diary . . .'

'I'm still not with you.'

'Well . . . I was up there at the Manor that day waiting for Julia to find her purse to pay me for the cushion kit. Not that she was really interested in the patchwork, you understand. She'd got me up there to try and suss out how the land lay . . . to find out whether you and I were on to her or not. And possibly to throw me off the track by making me feel sorry for her.' She remembered all that stuff Julia had fed her about Larry's vicious temper, hints about violence. 'And she was flattering me a little by treating me as a family friend. I realize that now. I've got to say this for her – her reactions were damned quick. When I asked about Crichton, she really did make it sound as if he were just a very nice young man who had helped her with her business affairs. Clever . . .'

'Or desperate,' Max said.

'Yes . . . well . . . She'd gone to find her purse and I was standing in the hall and Brenda Macmillan started rabbiting on about how Emily played them off against each other. Larry and Julia . . . She'd spend all her allowance and then sneak into Larry's study while Julia's back was turned to borrow huge sums from her father.'

'*She twists him round her little finger,*' Brenda had said. '*He can't refuse her anything!*'

Elizabeth said, 'And then she told me Larry's nickname for Emily. Rebel, he calls her . . . Only I didn't think any more about it until I took out the Rebel Patch. It suddenly struck me: it wasn't Rebecca Forbes that Crichton had been seeing – it was *Emily*. No wonder Crichton tried to keep the relationship quiet. He knew there'd be trouble if Julia found out.'

Max said, 'You took a risk going up to confront them about it.'

'I didn't think so at the time. I'd checked around a bit, you see. I was pretty sure of my facts.'

'Checked around?'

'Yes. I took a look round Julia's studio. It wasn't locked, fortunately. And there was a portrait of Crichton tucked away in the corner that very much revealed her feelings about him. I also called on his neighbours.'

'The neighbours?'

'The woman who lived in the flat below Crichton on Sydney Hill. I showed her Emily's photograph. And Julia's. And she told me that Julia had visited him in the evenings several times a week during June and July.' She shook her head. 'Poor Julia . . . She's obviously been falling apart for weeks.'

'Several shades of potty,' was Max's opinion.

'It's understandable though. Don't you think?' What else could you feel but compassion for a lost soul? Then she found a wry smile. 'Dottie says she doesn't know what all the fuss is about. Crimes of passion happen all the time. They're by far the most interesting . . .'

'She's probably right.'

'Mmn,' said Elizabeth. 'I saw Rebecca Forbes in the village yesterday. There was this look of semi-triumph on her face. Wasn't it positively dreadful about *poor* Julia? she asked. But her eyes told a different story. They were sanctimonious . . .'

'You think she'll be round at the Manor doing a spot of consolation?'

'I figure she'll try. But she'll have to get a move on. Her husband has decided on a career move, she tells me. He's accepted a post in Carlisle. They're moving next month.'

Not that it would do Rebecca much good to visit Aitken, she told herself, if Larry's present state was anything to go by. She remembered how he had looked when she called round to see him. What did you say to a man whose wife had just been charged with murder?

'I'm . . . so sorry, Mr Aitken.'

She had found him sitting half-way up the staircase, a lonely figure, his chin thickly dusted with stubble. For perhaps the first and only time in his life, he'd had nothing to say.

But more touching than any words had been the haunted look in his blue eyes as they stared blankly at Julia's awful mauve and pink canvas on the wall behind him. Bewilderment and real agony on a face that until now seemed to have specialized in registering counterfeit emotions.

Broken Star, she had thought. How terribly appropriate. The old order had somehow been triumphant . . . Wetherell would have been pleased.

Or would he? She honestly didn't know.

'Your daughter,' she had said. 'How is she?'

Aitken's head had turned for the first time. He stared at her blankly. 'Emily? She's . . . gone to London. Gone to stay with friends.'

Dead eyes, dead voice. Nothing, no one to console him.

But then Brenda Macmillan's voice had cut in from behind, had whispered hoarsely in her ear. 'I've been trying to protect him from the callers. You can see how he is. Devastated. Poor lamb . . .'

Back in the present, Max said, 'I bumped into Le Grice in town yesterday.'

'And?'

'And Aitken isn't pressing charges about *The Brown Boy*. He's said they can keep it. Big of him, I suppose.'

Elizabeth said, 'He's got worse things to worry about than one little painting.'

'Yeah. The papers are having a field day. Think he'll survive?'

'Probably. He's tough, old Larry . . .' She looked at him for a moment, then said, 'I know I shouldn't say it, but . . . on the whole . . . I enjoyed this case, Max. I had a good time. How about you?'

'Not bad. Not bad at all.' He sat there grinning at her. Then he said, 'I should take you on as a sleeping partner.'

'You're the one who does all the sleeping. And you couldn't afford me.'

'You Yanks and your damned dough . . .'

But it was said affectionately. The kettle had boiled and Elizabeth went to fill the pot, to find cups, to clink spoons and spread a cloth. She carried the loaded tray into the sitting-room.

'Muffins?' he said.

'*Blueberry* muffins,' she told him. 'A special old recipe passed down through the family. My ma-in-law used to make them so light, they lifted themselves off the plate.'

Max thought the morning was looking up. 'I'm in for a treat, then?' he said.

'I wouldn't be too sure about that. Mine are always as hard as rocks.'

But, she thought, if anyone could eat them, it would be Max.

'Help yourself,' she said cheerfully. 'Tuck right in.'

Max gazed at her and she said, 'You got me out of a fix the other night and I always like to pay my debts.'

It was odd that he suddenly remembered an urgent phone call. Mumbled that he really ought to be getting back to the office.

Elizabeth said don't worry about it, she'd brown-bag them so that he could have muffins for lunch instead.

As she told him on the doorstep, it gave you a real good feeling to take care of your friends.

Wasn't it, after all, the least you could do?